Praise for *USA TODAY* bestselling author Margot Hunt

"Will please fans of psychological thrillers, especially those featuring unhinged, vengeance-seeking women."
—*Booklist* on *For Better and Worse*

"A twisty tale for fans of domestic thrillers."
—*Kirkus Reviews* on *For Better and Worse*

"Roller-coaster action."
—*Publishers Weekly* on *For Better and Worse*

"Margot Hunt's cleverly constructed thriller kept me guessing till the very end."
—Peter Swanson, author of *The Kind Worth Killing* and *Her Every Fear*

"[*Best Friends Forever*] constantly pushes forward, asking readers to question every conclusion and warning them to never completely trust anyone... The characters are well-drawn, speaking easily for themselves and standing out as unique people who feel real."
—*Kirkus Reviews*

"Friends or husbands? Who do women tell more truth? Give more allegiance? Margot Hunt shocks and astounds as she explores these tugs of loyalty in *Best Friends Forever*, a psychological thriller that kept me off balance even after turning the last page."
—Randy Susan Meyers, bestselling author of *The Widow of Wall Street*

"*Best Friends Forever* is a clever thriller that asks how far we'll go to protect our friends. Margot Hunt will keep you guessing until the final, satisfying twist."
—Alafair Burke, *New York Times* bestselling author of *The Ex*

Also by *USA TODAY* Bestselling Author Margot Hunt

For Better and Worse
Best Friends Forever

the
last
affair

USA TODAY BESTSELLING AUTHOR

MARGOT HUNT

mira

mira

Recycling programs
for this product may
not exist in your area.

ISBN-13: 978-0-7783-0922-2

The Last Affair

Copyright © 2019 by Whitney Gaskell

All rights reserved. Except for use in any review, the reproduction or utilization
of this work in whole or in part in any form by any electronic, mechanical or other
means, now known or hereafter invented, including xerography, photocopying and
recording, or in any information storage or retrieval system, is forbidden without the
written permission of the publisher, MIRA Books, 22 Adelaide St. West, 40th Floor,
Toronto, Ontario M5H 4E3, Canada.

This is a work of fiction. Names, characters, places and incidents are either the product
of the author's imagination or are used fictitiously, and any resemblance to actual
persons, living or dead, business establishments, events or locales is entirely coincidental.

® and TM are trademarks of Harlequin Enterprises Limited or its corporate affiliates.
Trademarks indicated with ® are registered in the United States Patent and Trademark
Office, the Canadian Intellectual Property Office and in other countries.

For questions and comments about the quality of this book, please contact us at
CustomerService@Harlequin.com.

www.BookClubbish.com

Printed in U.S.A.

For Sam, with all of my love.

the last affair

prologue

Other than the woman's blood-covered body splayed facedown in the grass, it could have been any typical upscale Floridian backyard.

There was the ubiquitous pool with a water fountain feature, a patio furnished with both a dining set and outdoor sectional couch, and an enormous gas grill capable of cooking hamburgers by the dozen. A large pergola with a tropical vine trained over it covered part of the patio. The dining area was shaded by a black-and-white-striped awning. It was the very picture of suburban domestic bliss. It could have been the set for a commercial advertising anything from laundry detergent to allergy medicine.

Again, except for the dead body.

The area had already been taped off. The first officers on the scene appeared with an ambulance in response to a frantic 911 call placed by the woman's daughter. The paramedics had assessed the situation, and quickly determined that the woman was dead. The fact that the back of her head had been bashed in with what looked like a paving stone, conveniently dropped next to her prone body, made it immediately clear that it had not been a natural death. The responding officers called the sheriff, who responded by sending in a full investigative team. The medical examiner was now doing a preliminary examination of the body, while police officers combed the area for additional evidence. Two detectives, Mike Monroe and Gavin Reddick—separated by twenty years and sixty pounds—were overseeing the operation, standing at the edge of the patio under the shade of the pergola. It was the third week in April, but this was South Florida and the temperature had already climbed into the low nineties.

"The paving stone came from the stack out in the front yard. They were delivered last week by the company who's installing the driveway," Detective Reddick said. He was the younger of the two men and had a wiry frame and angular face.

"Weapon of convenience. Suggests it wasn't premeditated," Detective Monroe said. He had a ruddy complexion and a full head of thick dark hair, swept back off his face. A strand never moved out of place, even in a strong wind.

"Plus he dropped the weapon, rather than taking it with him. Probably panicked."

"Could be a she," Monroe said mildly.

Reddick shrugged. "Blunt force trauma to the back of the head? You know the stats. Overwhelming likelihood that it's a man, and probably someone the victim was intimately involved with. Husband, maybe a boyfriend."

"The husband was with the daughter when she called it in."

"Doesn't mean he didn't do it, and then had her place the call."

"No, it doesn't."

The family had been sequestered indoors, both to keep them

out of the way, and so that the officers waiting in the house with them could observe anything they did or said. Other than the husband, there was a daughter in her early twenties and a teenage son. The daughter was reportedly distraught, while the husband and son had both been eerily quiet. It was possible they were in shock.

"Do we have an ID on the victim?" Reddick asked.

"It's her house," Monroe grunted.

"Yeah, but I like doing things the official way, you know? I's dotted, t's crossed, all of that. Building a case, basic detective work."

Despite the chilling scene in front of them—the woman's body still sprawled on the grass, the back of her head a pulpy, bloody mess—the corner of Monroe's mouth quirked up in a half smile. "Sure, kid, tell me all about basic detective work. I've only been doing this for, what…thirty-two years now? The husband ID'd her. Victim is Gwen Landon, age forty-nine. Married, mother of two. Husband said she hasn't had any recent conflict with anyone."

"Other than the person who caved in the back of her head with a paving stone," Reddick pointed out.

"Wouldn't be the first time a husband didn't know his wife as well as he thought he did."

"Possible. But there's another possibility, too."

"What's that?"

Reddick turned to look at his partner. His eyes were small and dark, and he had a habit of squinting when he concentrated intently on something.

"The husband is a liar," Reddick said.

six months earlier

chapter one

---

nora

When Nora's life began to unravel, first slowly, and then with terrifying speed, it occurred to her that there were two very different ways of looking at the world. One was that everything is connected in some way, a row of dominoes set up to fall in a preordained order. The other was that life is nothing but a series of random events, influenced by things like free will and tragedy, but not set on a predetermined path. A man, distracted by his mobile phone, is about to step off a curb and into the path of an oncoming delivery van. Before that happens, a stranger grabs his arm and pulls him safely back onto the sidewalk. The first philosophy would point out it wasn't his day to die. The second would say he just got lucky.

Nora wasn't sure which philosophy scared her more.

The thing was, she almost didn't go to the National Conference of Culinary Bloggers. It was being held in Orlando, a two-hour drive from Shoreham, the small seaside Floridian town where Nora lived with her family. The distance, and the fact that the conference was being held over two days, meant she'd have to stay overnight. And while, like most mothers, Nora usually welcomed the small luxury of a night alone in a hotel—room service, solitude, the ability to control the television remote—the conference was scheduled in the middle of a school week in mid-October. The invitation to attend had arrived in July, and Nora was leery of committing to be away from home so far in advance. Who knew what dramas would be unfolding in her household by then?

Nora didn't worry about Dylan, seventeen, and who would be starting his senior year of high school. He was one of the lucky ones, the sort of kid whose life had always rolled along easily. He was tall and almost unbearably handsome, did well in school, excelled in sports. The only times he ever caused trouble were typical teenage antics—a broken curfew, the occasional whiff of beer on his breath after a party. But Matt, her middle child, was going to be a freshman, and he was as unlike his older brother as two boys could be. Matt was shy, sensitive, and happier sitting alone in his room drawing or playing around on his computer than socializing with other kids his age. High school could potentially be a difficult adjustment for him. And then there was Nora's youngest, Katie, who was thirteen and about to start the eighth grade. She was going through a stage—at least Nora hoped it was a stage—where she thought she knew everything about everything, and had no patience for anyone who didn't recognize and acknowledge her obvious superiority. Nora kept reading articles about teenage girls who suffered from low self-esteem, but quite to the contrary, Katie seemed to have been zapped with a megadose of self-confidence. Frankly, there were days she terrified both Nora and her husband, Carter.

But Nora did end up attending the conference.

It started when she received an email inviting her to be on a

panel discussing food photography, which was especially grat-
ifying, as that was an aspect of her blog, *Scones and Jam*, that
Nora was particularly proud of. Over the years since she'd first
started the blog, she'd become known for setting up visually
arresting photographs of the recipes she featured. She'd arrange
the food next to a lacy vintage towel, for example, or in front
of a short vase of pink peonies. And then her publisher's publicist had called to tell Nora they'd reserved time for her in their
booth on both days of the conference so that she could sign
copies of her recently published cookbook.

"I know it's bad timing, falling in the middle of a school
week, but I should probably go," Nora had told Carter that July
evening after he got home from the office.

He'd shed his jacket and loosened his red-and-blue-striped
tie, but he looked remarkably fresh faced and crisp for such a
hot day. And so unlike he'd been in the past, when workdays
were almost always followed by an extended stint at one of the
bars he used to frequent during his drinking days. Carter was
in sales at a commercial real estate firm. He viewed this as a
"real job," unlike hers, which he jokingly referred to as a "fun
job," even as her earnings continued to creep closer to his in
amount every year.

"Don't worry about it. I can hold down the fort for a few
days," Carter had replied before returning his attention back to
obsessively scrolling on his phone. From his intense concentra-
tion, Nora suspected he was on a sports gambling app, despite
his promise that he wasn't going to gamble anymore.

But, then, Carter had never been good about keeping his
promises. Or controlling his impulses.

Nora felt an almost irresistible urge to snap her fingers in front
of his face to get his attention, but managed to restrain herself.

"It's a lot to keep track of," she'd said instead. "Three kids in
two different schools, with different drop-off and pickup times.

Dylan will have soccer practice, although he can get there on his own, but you'll need to take Katie to volleyball."

"Got it," Carter had said, not looking up. "Drop-offs. Pick-ups. Soccer. Volleyball. Check."

Nora wasn't convinced, but that evening, she fired off an email to her publicist, confirming she'd attend the conference.

She had no idea then how much that one decision, the simple act of RSVP'ing "yes" to a conference—predetermined or random, whichever it was—would become one of the biggest regrets of her life.

The National Conference of Culinary Bloggers was held in a conference room at a large corporate hotel in downtown Orlando. The first day passed by in a blur of panels, signing cookbooks and meeting dozens upon dozens of people in her industry. Every time Nora turned around, there was another person who wanted her attention. Some were colleagues of sorts, fellow bloggers whom she'd gotten to know over the years from attending similar events. Others were just starting out and seeking her advice on how to turn their fledging blogs into a success.

Consistency and quality, Nora always said, while silently adding, *and a hefty dose of good luck*.

The market for culinary blogs was already crowded, and getting more so every year. Everyone wanted a publishing contract for a cookbook, or even more ambitiously, a cooking television show preferably combined with a line of cookware or knives to be sold at a big box store. Even writers who'd only blogged for a month or two were agitating for more fame, more attention, more money. Nora understood their ambition, but not their assumption that the path to success would be so easily obtained. By the time she was finally able to escape from the crowded conference room, Nora was exhausted from talking to people.

She rode the elevator down to the hotel lobby, where she'd

remembered seeing a bar earlier that day when she checked in. Nora drank only occasionally, largely because Carter was a recovering alcoholic, and so they didn't keep alcohol in the house. But she'd always loved hotel bars. There was something so deliciously decadent about having a cocktail in one, especially when she was out of town by herself. The hotel bar was perfect for her current mood, with its soothing low lighting and a long concrete poured counter with a row of metal stools lined up in front of it.

Nora perched on one of the stools. She was surprised the bar was so empty, considering how large the convention upstairs was, but she was glad for a quiet place to unwind.

"What can I get you?" the bartender asked.

When she did drink, Nora usually stuck with a glass of white wine. But she was craving something different that evening. "A Manhattan," she said spontaneously.

"With a cherry?"

"Do you have to ask?" Nora laughed. The bartender did not. "Yes, please."

The bartender—young, muscular and looking mildly bored— set about making the drink, which included vigorously shaking it until the metal flask was dripping with condensation. He poured the contents into a chilled coupe glass, added a toothpick speared with three sour cherries and placed it in front of Nora on top of a cocktail napkin. She took a sip. It was perfection.

Her phone beeped. Nora checked it, and saw a text had come in from Katie: Where r my volleyball shorts.

She texted back: Check the dryer.

Did...duh

Nora shook her head. When she returned home, she was going to have a serious talk with Katie about her attitude.

Ask your dad, Nora typed. She set down her phone and

picked up the Manhattan, but before she could take another sip, the phone had beeped again. This time it was Dylan: What's 4 dinner?

"Unbelievable," Nora said out loud. She quickly typed out another text: I left a lasagna in the fridge.

Where r u? Dylan responded.

I'm in Orlando. Remember?

Right 4 got. don't feel like lasagna. Can I order pizza?

Another ding. This time it was Matt: I want pizza too.

Ask dad, Nora typed again. This time, she turned the ringer off before setting her phone facedown, so it would stop beeping at her. She knew it was unlikely that Carter would be any help with either locating the missing volleyball shorts or changing up the dinner plans she'd left in place, and her children would continue to text her endlessly. She was determined to enjoy her Manhattan in peace.

"Nora?" a voice said behind her.

Nora stifled a sigh, anticipating she'd have to endure yet another conversation with a conference attendee. The day had been successful, or at least she thought it had been, but all she wanted now was to be left alone. It was one of the things about working from home. She usually spent hours of time on her own, and wasn't used to having to always be on, interacting with people for hours on end. But when she turned around, the man standing behind her was not someone she was expecting to see.

"Dr. Landon," she said, surprised. "What are you doing here?"

Josh Landon was an orthodontist who also lived in Shoreham. He'd straightened the teeth of all three of Nora's children, and his younger son, Simon, was in the same freshman class as Matt.

"Please, call me Josh."

Nora smiled. "Okay. What are you doing here, Josh?"

"Attending a conference," he said. "The American Association of Orthodontists. Very exciting stuff."

"Me, too," Nora said. "The conference part, I mean."

"Do you mind if I join you?" Josh asked, gesturing at the empty bar stool next to her.

"Of course not."

Josh flagged down the bartender and ordered a draft beer. The bartender deftly drew one from the tap, and set it in front of Josh.

"I'm guessing you're attending the foodie convention," Josh said. He paused and took a sip of his beer. "Unless you're secretly an orthodontist in your spare time."

Nora smiled. "Is that a thing? Secret orthodontists?"

"Yes. They're like superheroes, but solely focused on the teeth."

Josh grinned at Nora, and she felt a slight *whoosh* go through her.

What the hell is that? she wondered.

She realized it was something completely unexpected, and something she hadn't experienced in a long time…a frisson of attraction. She found the sensation both unsettling and exciting. She'd never really considered Josh in terms of how attractive he was. He'd always just been Dr. Landon, the pleasant and slightly goofy doctor who had joked around with her kids while checking on the progress of their teeth straightening and bite corrections. But now, sitting with him in this unfamiliar bar, it occurred to Nora that he was actually a very good-looking man. He was slightly older than her—probably in his early fifties—but now she noticed that he had a slim, muscular build and a nice face: high cheekbones, a well-defined jaw, kind brown eyes that crinkled pleasantly when he smiled.

Dr. Landon was kind of hot.

Good God, Nora thought.

Josh glanced around.

"This place isn't exactly hopping. You'd think that everyone who goes to these things would be desperate for a drink afterward. I had to attend a three-hour panel discussion on anterior open bites. I'm now considering drowning myself in vodka."

"That sounds almost as bad as the presentation I had to go to on the best fonts to make your website pop."

"Brutal," Josh agreed.

"You have no idea. I would have bailed on that one, but I knew one of the presenters."

"So how're the kids? Teeth still straight?"

"They're all doing great. How's your family?"

Nora had met Josh's wife, Gwen, a few times at school functions, but didn't know her very well. Gwen had always been outgoing and charming, Nora supposed, but she'd also always seemed slightly aloof, the sort of woman who had her barriers set high. She knew that in addition to their son, Simon, the Landons also had an older daughter in college.

"Everyone's fine," Josh said. He shrugged. "Although I feel like I barely see them. Abby's at FSU, and Simon spends all of his time locked in his bedroom playing computer games. I kind of miss the old days when the kids were little."

"Hmm." Nora stirred her Manhattan with the cherry-stacked toothpick. "I'm not sure I agree with you there. Life with teenagers keeps you busy, but at least there aren't any diapers involved."

Josh laughed. "True enough. I think I'm just going through a restless period right now."

Nora had the feeling the conversation had just taken an unexpected turn. It was one thing to chat about work, or their kids, but the word *restless* seemed to swerve toward a more intimate place. And yet, she was intrigued. Dr. Landon—Josh—had always seemed to be about the most grounded, least restless person she knew. His life seemed perfect, right down to the family photo that hung in his interior office, which was visible from the waiting room. Everyone was dressed in white, standing on the beach, their arms around one another, all beaming. Nora had stared at that picture on her many visits to his practice while she sat waiting for one or another of her children to have their bands changed and wondered what it would be like to have that sort of a family. One where your spouse was an actual partner, and not a constant source of worry.

"Restless. How so?"

"I don't know. Everyone's fine, work is fine. I really don't have anything to complain about." He shrugged. "Maybe I'm having a midlife crisis."

"Have you bought an overpriced sports car yet?"

"No, but that's mostly because Simon's only a year away from driving, which is a truly terrifying thought."

"Trust me, I know. When Dylan first got his license, I don't think I slept for a year."

"I just think back to how I was at that age..." Josh began to say.

"And wonder how we survived it?" Nora quipped.

"Exactly. The dumb shit I used to do."

Nora leaned forward slightly. "Oh yeah? Like what?"

"I'll tell you what," Josh said. "I hate eating alone. Have dinner with me, and I'll regale you with stories of my misspent youth."

"Deal," she said. He raised his beer in a toast, and Nora gently clinked her coupe glass against it.

Nora first started to sense the looming danger over dinner. Josh's eyes would linger on her own for a few beats too long, and she'd feel that same swooping sensation in her stomach. At first she wondered if she was imagining it. Was she so desperate for a ripple of excitement in her otherwise boring life that she was inventing an attraction between the two of them that didn't really exist? But, no, she didn't think so. Even though Josh didn't touch her or make a single inappropriate comment, there was an energy between them. It shimmered there, almost like a separate entity, a third party sitting at the table with them.

Nora knew she should pull back. She tried to remind herself that she was married—not happily, of course, she and Carter hadn't been happy in years. But still. And Josh was married, too. Then there were the kids to think of, her three and Josh's two. This was not a path they had any business starting down.

"When did your restlessness start?" Nora asked.

Josh tilted his head to the side as he thought about this. "I think it was after Abby went to college. It was like this huge buildup, getting her through the high school years, and the college entrance exams, and the applications and the school visits. Then suddenly…she was just gone. Even though Simon's still home now, he'll be gone in a few years, too. And then what?"

"Retirement. Weddings. Grandkids."

Josh put a hand over his heart with mock horror. "Grandkids? Oh, my God. I'm far too young for any of that. I think of myself as still being in my thirties."

Nora smiled. "I know. It's crazy how fast it's all passing by. Doesn't it feel like time sped up once the kids came along?"

"Absolutely. Then they go away, and you're left looking around and wondering what it was all about."

"Having kids?"

"No, having kids is great." Josh buttered a piece of warm focaccia bread. "I highly recommend it. It's just the perennial question. What do you do once they've grown, and suddenly, you find yourself living with someone who, over the years, has become a stranger?"

Nora stilled, knowing he was talking about his wife, Gwen. She didn't want to discuss Gwen, or Carter. She wanted to pretend, just for a short while—even if it was only this moment, and never extended past it—that neither of their spouses existed. That she and Josh were both unattached, unencumbered.

Besides, whatever sad tales Josh had about his marriage to Gwen, Nora was fairly sure she could match them with her own. Carter's drinking years had left behind a lot of scar tissue.

"How is everything?" Their waiter appeared beside the table, eyeing their mostly untouched entrées. They'd been so caught up in conversation, they'd barely noticed the food in front of them.

"Everything's fine," Nora assured him. "The snapper is delicious."

"Do you want another drink?" Josh asked. "Or how about a glass of wine?"

Nora knew that she should say no. That she should thank him graciously for the company and the lovely dinner, and then stand up and head straight to her hotel room. Alone. They were both married, both parents, both lived in the same small community. Walking away was the only rational decision.

"Actually, I'd love another Manhattan," Nora said.

The time passed without either of them noticing. It was as though they were encased in a bubble that contained just the two of them. And, despite the bubble, and the alcohol that was starting to blur the edges, Nora was at the same time hyperaware of every detail. The slight cross-hatching of lines that appeared next to Josh's eyes when he smiled. The dark hair on the tops of his wrists. The glint of the golden wedding band on his left hand. And all the while, she sat there reveling in his attention, intoxicated by it. When the waiter finally brought the check, Josh looked at it, startled.

Nora glanced around, and realized they were the last ones left in the restaurant. "We closed the place down."

Josh followed her gaze. "Did we really?" He took out his wallet and pulled out a credit card. Nora reached for her bag, but he waved her away. "No, of course not. This is on me."

"Thank you, that's very kind."

Josh paid, and they both stood. Nora was slightly unsteady on her feet, but she thought that had more to do with nerves than alcohol.

"Are you staying here at the hotel?" Josh asked.

"Yes."

"I am, too."

Josh held out a hand for Nora to go first, and after a slight hesitation, she turned and walked ahead of him out of the restaurant, through the hotel lobby with its thick green-and-cream patterned carpet and enormous crystal chandeliers, and toward the bank of elevators that ferried guests up to the tower of rooms. The lobby was eerily quiet, especially compared to the last time Nora had passed through, when it had been mobbed with people attending the conventions, along with tourists in town vacationing at the amusement parks. Now there was hardly anyone around, other than a few employees speaking in hushed voices to one another behind the check-in desk.

When they reached the elevators, Josh pressed the up button. They stood side by side in silence, listening to the elevators hum into motion. A pair of gold doors swished open in front of them with a ding. Nora stepped onto the elevator, and Josh followed her.

"Which floor?" he asked.

"Nine."

"I'm on twelve." He pushed the button for the ninth floor. "I'll walk you to your room."

The elevator doors shut, and they were alone. Truly alone for the first time. Nora turned toward Josh, just as he moved toward her. Suddenly, they were kissing, his tongue sliding into her mouth, one hand gently cupping the back of her neck. She leaned into him, resting her hands on his waist. And then the doors were opening again with another ding. They broke apart.

"That's one fast elevator," Josh said. Nora laughed and felt herself flush.

And just like that, the decision had been made. Nora wasn't sure which of them had made it, or at what moment it had happened, but as she and Josh padded down the hallway toward Nora's room, their fingers lightly entwined, she knew for certain that they were going to sleep together.

chapter two

---

gwen

Gwen Landon ran down the road, feeling her lungs burning with the exertion and reveling in the discomfort. There was something primal about gasping for your next breath while pushing your body to move forward past its limits. Gwen not only endured the pain, but also welcomed it. It was the only time she truly felt alive.

The houses she ran by were decorated for Halloween, and ambitiously so. Skeletons propped up against gravestones, witches on broomsticks suspended from tree branches, artful arrangements of pumpkins.

Why does Halloween prompt competitive decorating? Gwen wondered. When she'd been a kid, no one had bothered to do more than put out a badly carved jack-o'-lantern or two. Everyone's need to look perfect on their various online social platforms had become a ridiculous by-product of modern life.

She turned the corner onto her street and increased her speed. It was her habit to end every run with a full-out sprint. Gwen was so focused on finishing strong—leaning forward, lengthening her stride, pumping her arms—that she didn't notice the dark gray SUV parked in her gravel driveway until she'd reached her house. Gwen stopped and braced her hands against her knees, waiting for her breath to return and her heartbeat to steady.

"Hi, Gwen!" a voice called out. "My goodness, you run fast!"

Gwen looked up and saw Tara Edwards standing on the Landons' front porch, holding a plastic container. Tara had long brown hair, and very round brown eyes that made her look perpetually surprised. She was wearing a loose tank top over yoga pants, as though she were on her way to work out. Gwen glanced at her phone. It wasn't even nine in the morning. Who dropped by unannounced this early? Gwen adjusted her expression to what she thought of as her public face. Broad smile, eyes crinkled with practiced warmth at the unexpected visit. Gwen was good at faking the social niceties. She'd spent years perfecting the skill.

"Hey, Tara," she said. "What a lovely surprise!"

"I had the twins in to see Josh last week, and he mentioned how much he loved the brownies I brought to the Powells' barbecue last month, so I promised I'd make some for him." Tara smiled widely and held up the container. "I'm on my way to hot yoga, so I thought I'd drop them off while I was passing by."

Gwen, still smiling, walked up the steps to the porch. She'd never cared much for Tara, even though the woman was almost maniacally friendly. Or maybe that was the turnoff—the way Tara so desperately wanted to be friends. Her neediness was off-putting. And of *course* she was going to hot yoga. It had become the de rigueur activity for Shoreham mothers, as ubiquitous as insisting on soy milk for lattes while having earnest discussions about the importance of conscious parenting. Frankly, it all bored Gwen to death.

"That's so nice of you." Gwen accepted the container. "I'm sure Josh will love them. He's always had a sweet tooth, even though he's an orthodontist and should really know better."

Tara laughed loudly and reached out to squeeze Gwen's arm. "You're hilarious!"

Gwen knew she should probably invite Tara inside for a cup of coffee, but decided against it. She didn't want to spend the rest of her morning playing hostess, and besides, she didn't have any soy milk to offer up with the coffee. Still, Tara didn't look like she was in any hurry to leave.

"Everyone always loves my brownies. I get asked for the recipe all the time, but I'll never tell!" Tara prattled on. "I always say, I'm taking that secret to my grave!"

"Well, thank you again," Gwen said. "You're such a sweetheart to think of us."

"You'll make sure to let Josh know that these are from me, right? I was hoping to catch him before he left for work."

"Josh's at a conference in Orlando," Gwen said. "He'll be home this evening. But, of course I'll let him know you dropped them off."

"A conference." Tara looked disappointed.

"Yes. Anyway, I should probably go hop in the shower," Gwen said. She was hot and sticky post run, and desperately wanted to peel off her sweat-soaked clothing.

"Oh…okay. I'll guess I'll get going."

"Thanks again. Enjoy yoga."

Tara leaned forward and gave Gwen an awkward hug, which Gwen found strange and slightly gross, considering how sweaty she was. Maybe hot yoga had made Tara impervious to other people's perspiration. "It was great seeing you! Say hi to your family from me."

"You do the same," Gwen replied.

Tara pivoted, and headed down the steps toward her SUV. Gwen waited while Tara got into her vehicle, started it up and reversed out of the driveway, spraying gravel as she left.

We really need to get the driveway paved, Gwen thought. It had been on their to-do list ever since they first moved into the Hibiscus Drive house over two decades earlier, when Gwen was pregnant with Abby. She wondered absently how much it would cost. Then she looked down at the plastic container in her hands and wondered what Tara's real motive had been in dropping off the brownies. *She probably has a crush on Josh*, she decided.

It wouldn't be the first time. Josh had always been good-looking, and rather annoyingly, had gotten more handsome as he aged. He also had an easygoing manner, which had turned out to be a benefit in his chosen profession. He joked with the kids as he adjusted their bites, and charmed the moms who accompanied them. Over the years, there had been several women who had made it clear they were attracted to him, flirting with him at cocktail parties or planting themselves next to him in the bleachers at school sporting events. However, this was the first time one of them had shown up at the house bearing baked goods. Gwen didn't think Josh had ever cheated on her, but then again, who knew? They'd been married for twenty-four years. Anything was possible. She wondered, almost idly, how much it would bother her if she found out he had been unfaithful.

It would, she decided. Josh was lucky to be married to her. Everyone said so. She remembered once reading an article where a therapist espoused the view that in every marriage, one of the partners was the pursuer and the other was the catch. It made complete sense to Gwen. She had no doubt whatsoever that she'd been, and continued to be, the catch in their relationship.

Gwen went inside and deposited the brownies on the kitchen counter. Josh would be lucky to get one. Once Simon returned

home from school with the usual friends in tow, they'd probably devour them.

Oh, well, she thought. *Not my problem.*

She showered, got dressed and then went into the home
office—a small space located just off the front foyer—where she
turned on her laptop. Once she had the internet browser up,
she ran a search for Repaving Driveway Cost, but after click-
ing through a few websites, quickly became bored with the
subject. Instead, she opened up her bookmarked file—what
she thought of as her secret file, although that was silly. It was
hardly anything salacious. The file contained websites of travel
destinations—Morocco, Croatia, Argentina, the Galapagos
Islands and dozens of other places. Gwen found it a furtive pleasure to scour the internet for travel articles to add to the list,
imagining herself in each new location, the way some people
might fantasize about changing careers or buying a new house.

Gwen had a secret.

It had started when Abby first went off to college two years
earlier. Gwen had braced herself for how hard the transition
would be. She and Josh wouldn't be empty nesters, not with
Simon still at home, but still…after eighteen years of her life
revolving around motherhood, she had expected to feel her
daughter's absence keenly. This belief was only strengthened
from conversations with friends who had older children who'd
already left for college, and who had confessed to being deeply
depressed in the weeks and months following their children's
departures. Some had even gone into therapy to cope with the
life change.

But the only emotion Gwen had felt after dropping Abby off
at her freshman dorm had been a surprising surge of pleasure
at the freedom. Or, maybe more specifically, the taste of what
freedom from the daily grind of familial obligation would one
day feel like.

It wasn't that she didn't love Abby, but the truth was, Gwen was tired of being a dutiful mother, wife, housekeeper. She'd worked as a paralegal before they had Abby, but she'd hated it and had been happy to leave it behind to become a stay-at-home mom. She'd quickly realized that she'd traded in a paying mind-numbing job for an equally boring nonpaid one.

Other women would talk about how they couldn't bear to take a weekend trip away from their baby, or how they'd sat weeping in the parking lot on the first day of nursery school drop-off. Gwen had never felt like that. She'd tried telling herself she wasn't a bad person. After all, she'd never resented her children. It was more like she viewed caring for them as her responsibility, her job, and a choice she'd willingly made. But the truth was, motherhood had never completed her, or fulfilled her on a fundamental level.

Mothers, however, were not supposed to admit to such things. So Gwen kept her growing restlessness to herself, and put in her time car-pooling, and volunteering at her children's schools, and attending what felt like a thousand different dance recitals, school concerts and sporting events, and always, always putting on a good public face as she did so. But Simon would be off to college in less than four years. And Gwen found herself craving adventure, independence, a different future than the one that had been set into place on the day she'd accepted Josh's marriage proposal almost twenty-five years earlier. She'd thought at the time she was making the right choice, a good choice. But lately—no, longer, for at least the past three years—Gwen couldn't shake the feeling that she'd made a poor deal. And worse, that she was running out of time to change that.

Gwen knew that no one would understand, and especially not Josh. It was why she was keeping it a secret. For now. Once Simon was safely off to college, well…then. That's when she'd make a change. For now, she would price driveway pavers, and compare them to the cost of a trip to Montenegro. By herself.

Gwen spent the rest of the day repotting several orchids and hanging them outside, walking their black Labrador, Izzy, and making a trip to the grocery store. When she'd finished those chores, she started to chop onions and peppers for the pot of chili she'd planned for dinner that night. Simon was home from school and in his room, playing computer games with his friends, but she had no idea what time to expect Josh back from his trip to Orlando. It had been a hot, sticky day, so chili wouldn't have been her first choice, but she figured the stew could simmer for as long as needed, and everyone could just eat when they were ready.

The front door swung open and slammed shut, startling Gwen. The knife she was using to cut the onions slipped, cutting into her finger. A sharp, bloody line appeared.

"Shit," Gwen said out loud. She grabbed a paper towel and wrapped it around her finger. The blood instantly soaked through the towel. "Josh, is that you?"

"No."

Gwen looked up from her bloody finger, puzzled by the voice she was hearing.

"Abby?"

Her daughter appeared in the doorway to the kitchen. Abby, who was supposed to be at college on the other side of the state. Gwen stared at her daughter, taking in Abby's pale skin, disheveled hair and the fact that she was wearing an oversize T-shirt over plaid flannel pajama bottoms.

"What are you doing home?" Gwen asked. "And why are you in pajamas?"

"I dropped out of school," Abby said. "I don't want to talk about it."

chapter three

abby

Abby knew there would be questions. Lots and lots of questions. Never ending questions. Her mother started in right away.

What do you mean you dropped out of school?

Did you officially withdraw, or are you taking a semester off?

Why didn't you call us before driving all the way back home?

What happened?

"I don't want to talk about it," Abby said again. She shouldered the duffel bag she'd brought home, and took it to her bedroom, shutting the door behind her. She'd packed only some of her clothes and toiletries, leaving behind the vast majority of her belongings in the off-campus apartment she shared with two other juniors. She'd left a note on the counter in their diminutive kitchen saying that she was going home for a few days without going into further detail.

She had no intention of ever returning.

Being home was both a relief and a fresh new source of stress. Her parents were never going to stop questioning her until she offered up some sort of explanation for why she'd left school. But now, standing in her childhood room, with its comforting familiarity—the posters she'd tacked to the walls during her teen years, the quilt on her four-poster that had been a fourteenth birthday gift from her grandmother, the sound of Simon chattering in the next room with his friends—she felt calmer than she had in days.

Abby heard the front door open and then bang shut.

"Why is Abby's car here?" her dad called out.

Abby swiftly went to her bedroom door and cracked it open, so she could eavesdrop more easily on her parents' conversation. They lived in a one-story ranch-style house, which made it easier to hear, especially when her parents raised their voices. Actually, Gwen was usually the one who became louder when she was angry, while her dad's voice was usually softer, more placatory. Abby sat cross-legged on the floor by the door, listening intently.

"Because Abby drove it home."

"She's home?" her dad asked, sounding puzzled. She could hear his footsteps echo against the hardwood floors as he walked from the foyer toward the kitchen. "Is everything okay?"

"No, everything is definitely not okay. Apparently, she's dropped out of school."

"What?"

"You now know as much as I do. She's in her room, refusing to discuss any of it with me." There was a bang, which sounded like a pot being tossed into the sink. Gwen had always had a habit of angry cleaning. Abby could picture her scrubbing at the already perfectly clean counters.

"Please calm down," her dad said.

"She's dropped out of school, Josh. Why would I be calm about that?"

"I just think we need to take a deep breath and talk to Abby."

"You don't think I've tried talking to her? She won't tell me anything. It's like she's just shut down. Do you know, she showed up here in her pajamas? She drove across the entire state of Florida wearing pajamas. Do you think it's possible she's on drugs?"

"Of course not. This is Abby we're talking about. She's the most straitlaced responsible kid I've ever met. Let's just give her some space and time, and I'm sure she'll tell us what's going on eventually," her dad said in the sort of soothing voice Abby knew drove her mother crazy.

Predictably, Gwen became even more agitated. "*Time?* We have to call FSU and at least make sure she hasn't done anything irrevocable, like withdrawing from school. I'm not going to let her ruin her life."

Abby rolled her eyes at her mother's tone. It was just so typical for her to respond with anger, rather than worry or concern.

It was an open secret in the Landon household that Abby had always been closer to her father. When she was younger, it had been treated as a joke, part of their family lore. Abby would always want her dad to read her bedtime stories, and he was the one she always turned to when she had a scraped knee or needed help with a school project. When she was in fifth grade, she—or, more accurately, *they*—had won her school's science fair with her project on the effect of soda on tooth enamel. But in truth, it was more than just preferring her dad, who was laid-back and easy to be around. Abby had always found it hard to feel close to her mother.

"What's gotten into you?" Gwen was still addressing Josh. "You're acting weird."

"I'm just tired. I've been at a conference for two days, and then drove home in heavy traffic."

For the first time, Abby felt a pinch of guilt. Her father did sound weary. She knew that appearing at the house without notice was going to cause drama, but she hadn't really thought through the repercussions. All she'd been able to think about was getting as far away from Tallahassee as possible.

"Still, you seem… I don't know. Odd."

"I wasn't expecting to walk into a family drama. Give me a minute to adjust."

"We don't have a minute. We need to deal with this *now*."

Abby closed her door, not wanting to hear any more. She got up and went to stand in front of the full-length cheval mirror in the corner of her bedroom, examining her reflection. She took in the lank dark hair, the sallow complexion, the too large nose, the too small breasts. And even though she was thin—even thinner than usual since she hadn't been able to keep any food down for the past few weeks—she was so freakishly tall, she always felt like she took up too much space in the world.

"God, you're hideous," she said out loud to herself.

Why couldn't she look more like Lana, her ex–best friend and now ex-roommate? Lana was practically perfect—tiny, blonde, with a little pert nose and the sort of perfect curving body that looked amazing in a bikini. Even her few flaws—the eyes that were set a tad too far apart, the slightly crooked front tooth—were somehow adorable.

Colin had clearly thought so.

The thought of Colin caused a searing grief to rip through Abby. She climbed into her bed and curled up in a ball. The pain was so overwhelming, so raw, it was almost like it was a living, breathing creature that had invaded her body. *Colin.* Colin, with the blue-gray eyes that changed shades depending on what color he was wearing. Who always smelled like soap, and mint, and the slightly spicy body spray his mother always bought him for Christmas. Who every time he kissed her, made

Abby feel like she was falling toward something both incredibly exciting and sweetly safe.

They'd started dating the previous February, when Abby was a sophomore at FSU and Colin was a junior. They'd met at a mixer her sorority had hosted, and had become a couple almost overnight. Colin had wanted to spend every free minute he had with her. That summer—just a few months ago!—he'd accompanied her family on their yearly vacation to Amelia Island. One night, they'd walked down to the beach and climbed up onto one of the lifeguard stands. With the full moon shining down on the ocean, the dark water lapping gently up on the shore, Colin had wrapped his arms around her. He'd kissed her, and then murmured in her ear, "I love you."

"I love you, too," Abby had breathed back.

It had been the most exquisitely perfect moment of her life.

But then school started, and suddenly everything changed. Colin had changed. The warmth and intimacy between them seemed to drain away. He'd been distant and slightly embarrassed when he'd told her that he wanted to break up.

"Break up?" Abby had repeated stupidly. "You mean take some time off?"

"No," Colin had said, his voice oddly stiff. "I mean for good. I need to focus on school and studying for the MCATs. I don't have time for anything else in my life right now."

The humiliation was almost more than she could bear. She'd cried. She'd tried to talk him out of it. She'd begged him to give her another chance.

Abby now curled into an even tighter ball, wrapping her arms around her legs, wishing there was some way, any way to dull the overwhelming horror of it all.

And the worst part was that it wasn't even true. Colin hadn't broken up with her because he needed to focus on schoolwork or applying to medical school.

He'd dumped her for Lana.

Lana, her best friend, roommate, confidant. Ever since she and Abby first met freshman year, they'd been so close, they swore they were more like sisters than friends.

And now she knew that Lana and Colin had been sneaking around behind her back for months. She found out the truth only when their third roommate—Zara, who was so blunt and sharp-tongued, Abby had always been a little intimidated by her—had cornered her in the kitchen, where Abby was making a cup of herbal tea, tears dripping down her face.

"You know they're fucking, right?" Zara had said, her tone almost accusatory.

Abby had glanced up, confused.

Zara spent her younger years training as a ballerina, and although she no longer danced, she retained the sinewy grace her training had instilled in her. She wore her thick dark hair twisted up in a bun, heavy black eyeliner that flicked up at the ends in little wings, and bloodred lipstick, and somehow managed to pull it all off without looking clownish.

"Who?"

Zara looked at her with a pitying expression. "Colin and Lana. I caught them coming out of her bedroom a few weeks ago, when you were at class. I already suspected something was going on, but that pretty much confirmed it. He had his hand on her ass."

Abby didn't remember much of what happened after that. She'd turned and walked woodenly to her room, where she'd sat cross-legged on her bed, a pillow clutched in front of her. She wasn't sure how long she stayed there, or even what she'd thought about as she waited. It was like her mind had switched off and her body had powered down. Lana had returned home at some point—Abby could hear Zara and her conversing in their small living room—and then a few moments later there was a soft knock on her door. Abby ignored it, but the door swung open anyway.

Lana stood there, her eyes shining with tears, her lips curving down in an adorable pout. "I wanted to tell you. I promise you I did. I just wasn't sure how to."

"How long?" Abby had asked. Her throat felt scratchy and dry, and the words came out in a croak.

Lana stared at her.

"How long has it been going on?" Abby had repeated.

"Two and a half months," Lana had whispered. "Since school started."

Now, lying on the bed in her childhood bedroom, Abby pushed the conversation out of her thoughts. Her parents were talking again. She crawled out of her bed, and over to her door, cracking it open again.

"We have to deal with this," her mother was saying. "She's going to ruin her future."

"Can it wait until tomorrow? I'm exhausted. I really need to eat something, and shower."

There was a long silence before Gwen finally responded in the irritable tone of voice she used only with her family. "Fine. We'll talk about it tomorrow."

chapter four

nora

Nora wasn't sure how she managed to drive home from Orlando without crashing into something. She clutched the steering wheel so tightly that an hour into her journey, her hands started to cramp up.

What did I do? she wondered over and over. *What have I done?*

Nora had always been a good person. She worked hard. She took excellent care of her children. She'd stuck by Carter during the bad years, when he was drunk more often than sober. She volunteered reading books to disadvantaged preschool children once a week. She suspected that most years, she overpaid their taxes.

And now, suddenly, without even having meant to, without any premeditated intent, she'd become an adulteress.

How had it happened? She replayed the events from the previous night in her mind, trying to figure out how she'd gone from sitting by herself in the hotel bar, enjoying a cocktail at the end of a long day, to tangled up in bed with Josh.

That's when she nearly sideswiped a Hyundai passing her on the left.

Stay calm, she told herself. *Keep it together. Getting into a car accident on the turnpike is not going to change what happened.* No, for that, she'd need a time machine. And, apparently, a better developed code of morals.

But the flashbacks kept hitting her, the entire night playing on an endless loop in her mind. Josh's tongue flicking against hers when he kissed her. The moment when he slipped her dress off over her head. The touch of his fingers against her skin. The almost electric sensation she'd felt when he slid into her. It had caused Nora to gasp.

She hadn't had sex in over three years.

Was that it? Was what happened the previous night just a reaction to the celibate existence she thought she'd come to terms with? And, if so, what did that make her? Just another horny housewife, a horrifying stereotype? Nora thumped her hands against the steering wheel. No, that couldn't be it. That wasn't who she was.

Josh had spent the night in her room. They'd been up most of the night, and when they did catch a few hours of sleep, they'd curled up together, his arms wrapped around her. In a way, that was even more intimate than the sex. She couldn't remember the last time she'd fallen asleep with someone touching her, much less holding her through the night. Even when their relationship had still been intimate, Carter had never been a snuggler.

There had been an awkward moment that morning, when Josh came out of the bathroom. Nora was still lying in bed, and when she saw him—a man, who despite their recent intimacy, she barely knew—she'd felt the first real reverberations of panic. But then Josh had slid back into bed next to her, kissed her deeply and pulled her gently against him, so that her head was resting on the flat of his chest.

"I didn't expect this to happen, but I'm really happy it did," he'd murmured into her hair.

"You don't think this makes us bad people?"

Josh sighed and pulled her in closer. "I think life is difficult and complicated. How bad can it be to find a small sliver of happiness in the middle of it?"

He'd left shortly after, saying he needed to go to his room to shower and change his clothes. Once he was gone, kissing her one last time before departing, Nora had felt equally relieved and bereft.

I miss him already, she realized. *What is wrong with me?*

The second day of Nora's culinary conference somehow passed by, although it seemed like it would never end. Nora didn't have any panel duties, thank God—she doubted she'd have the wherewithal to pull that off—but she did spend a few hours signing cookbooks and chatting with readers. Afterward, she couldn't remember anything she said, just that she forced herself to smile until her face hurt, and she tried to follow along with the conversations to the best of her ability.

Now, driving home, the exit for Shoreham just ahead, Nora switched on her turn signal and felt a sense of impending doom. The ride south—which she normally found long and boring—had passed by in a flash. She didn't want to go home. She could only imagine the chaos that had erupted in her absence—last-minute school projects, missing homework assignments, an empty refrigerator. As soon as she walked in the door, there would be a cacophony of demands on her to solve problems and smooth out petty disputes. She glanced at her reflection in the rearview mirror and was startled at how strained she looked. Or was that what guilt looked like?

She couldn't go home until she composed herself.

Nora activated the voice control in her car. "Call Maddie."

The phone rang, and a minute later, Maddie Archer answered. "Hey, girl. I thought you were in Orlando?"

"I'm just getting back in town. I know this is last minute, but would you mind if I stopped by for a few minutes?"

"Sure. Is everything okay?"

"Yes. No. I don't know. I think I just need to see a friendly face."

"Come over. It's Allen's week to have the boys, so I'm all on my own."

"I'll be there in fifteen minutes."

Nora pulled off the turnpike and drove to the apartment complex where Maddie had lived for the past ten months since getting divorced. It was a pretty development, with two-story buildings, thick clumps of palm trees and ponds with water fountains spraying up in the middle. Nora parked her car in front of Maddie's building and walked up to her second-story condo. Maddie answered the door with a wide smile. She was tall and gorgeous, with dark skin and curly hair that fell down around her shoulders.

"This is a nice surprise." Maddie hugged her, and Nora breathed in her friend's familiar citrusy fragrance. "I thought I was doomed to a night alone with Netflix and microwave popcorn."

"I can't stay for long," Nora apologized. "But I wasn't ready to go home yet."

Maddie tipped her head and gazed appraisingly at her friend. "You sounded weird on the phone. Come in, I'll get you a glass of wine. You look like you could use one."

Nora followed Maddie into her condo, which was small but open and bright. She and Allen had sold their house when they divorced, and Maddie had moved into the compact three-bedroom condo. She had custody of her sons, Leo, twelve, and James, ten, every other week. Allen, meanwhile, had moved into a large house on the water with the partner in his cardiologist practice he'd left Maddie for.

"What's going on?" Maddie asked as she poured sauvignon blanc into two wineglasses in the small galley kitchen.

"Nothing." Nora shook her head. "I think I'm just tired from the conference. It was a long few days. How are you?"

"Well, Halloween is almost here, which is basically the kickoff to the whole post-divorce holiday nightmare." Maddie clinked her glass against Nora's. "But at least I'm not bitter. Let's go sit in the living room."

They curled up on Maddie's gray velvet love seat and sipped their wine. Nora thought her friend looked down, but that wasn't surprising after what she'd been through over the past year. Allen's abrupt announcement that their marriage was over had flattened Maddie. The subsequent blows that he was leaving her for someone else, and that from now on she'd only get to live with her sons part-time, had nearly destroyed her.

"You and the boys are still planning to come to our house for Thanksgiving, right?" Nora asked.

"Yes, of course. And thank you for the invitation. It will give them a chance to see what a perfect family holiday looks like now that we'll never have another one ever again."

"What happened to *not* being bitter? And you know there's no such thing as a perfect family."

"I don't know. With your perfect children, and perfect meals, and perfect pictures of your children eating your perfect meals, you do a pretty good imitation of one."

Nora flinched, and Maddie reached out and put her hand on Nora's arm. "Oh, I'm sorry. That was a stupid thing to say."

Maddie knew more than anyone what Nora had gone through when Carter was still drinking. She was one of the few people Nora had trusted, and even then…Maddie didn't know about everything that had happened. Nora couldn't bring herself to share the darkest moments, not even with her best friend.

She'd certainly never told Maddie that there was a time when she hoped every single day that Carter would die, because that would be the easiest way to rid him from her life.

"I know being married to Carter hasn't always been easy," Maddie said. "But you know how much I admire you for how you stuck by him. How you kept your family together. Not many women would have done that. You're one of the few honestly decent people I know. Trust me. You wouldn't believe how many so-called friends have ghosted me since Allen left me for The Whore. You're one of the few who stuck around." She squeezed Nora's arm. "You're a treasure."

Nora realized then that she couldn't tell Maddie about what had happened with Josh. Of course she couldn't, even though she desperately wanted to talk about him, to sort out the intensity of the feelings she'd been experiencing over the past twenty-four hours. But…no. It would be cruel to ask that of Maddie, after she'd been cheated on by a husband she adored and thought she'd be married to forever. In fact, who would understand? Nora had done something terrible. If anyone in their small town found out what she'd done, she'd be branded a pariah.

"No, it's fine. It's just… I don't want you to think that everyone else's life is perfect," Nora said. "No one has a perfect marriage, or perfect children. Everyone struggles with something, even if you don't see it. Some people are just really good at hiding it."

Maddie took a large gulp of her wine. "I do know that on some level. But there are days when my life feels so much less perfect than everyone else's."

Nora nodded. "Trust me. There are days I feel like that, too."

"I find that hard to believe."

"Why?"

"Because you make your own piecrust from scratch? And wrote a cookbook? And your Christmas decorations are always on point. I don't know how I'll even manage to put up a tree this year." Tears shimmered in Maddie's eyes.

"You will," Nora said. "I'll come help. I make great bows, you know."

"Of course you do, you bitch."

Nora laughed, and sipped her own wine. "You'll get through the holidays. It will be tough, but you're tougher."

"We shall see," Maddie said. "Will you really help me with the tree?"

"Of course."

"We have a totally dorky tradition. We drink eggnog, even though it's vile, and watch *It's a Wonderful Life* while we trim the tree. I thought about trying to do something different this year, but I don't want the boys to feel like this divorce is going to make them miss out on all of our traditions."

"I'll bring the eggnog, and we'll totally geek out to Jimmy Stewart."

"Thanks." Maddie smiled wanly, and then looked closely at Nora. "Are you sure you're okay? You seem a little distracted."

Another flashback of the night before skittered through Nora's thoughts. *Josh above her…his hand stroking down the curve of her waist…the expression on his face when he first pushed into her.* She blinked and shook her head, trying to banish the memory.

"Nora?" Maddie frowned. "Seriously, what's going on?"

"Nothing," Nora said quickly. "I'm sorry. I'm just a little distracted. But otherwise fine. It was actually nice to be on my own for a few days."

"I bet. Although, I have the opposite problem. I'm on my own too often."

"Is the custody schedule getting any easier?"

"It isn't called custody anymore. It's 'child sharing.' Isn't that cute? I think it's supposed to make it sound normal and natural, even though the whole thing is hideous. We're all adjusting to it, I suppose. But it's never easy."

Nora reached out and took Maddie's hand. She wanted to tell her friend that her new freedom seemed glorious to her, especially through the prism of Nora's unhappy marriage. That although, yes, of course she could see that being apart from her children for a week at a time every other week would be a difficult adjustment...but at the same time, living with a man you no longer loved was maybe even harder. And that after last night, after having sex for the first time in *years*, and enjoying every exciting second of it, something had awoken inside her that she didn't know still existed. It both terrified and thrilled her.

"It will get easier," Nora said instead. "I promise it will."

"Hello? I'm home," Nora called out as she walked in her front door, rolling her small suitcase behind her. She left the suitcase at the bottom of the stairs and headed toward the kitchen to see if her family was there. They weren't, but the kitchen looked like a crime scene. Tomato sauce—or at least, that's what Nora hoped it was—was splattered over the marble countertops and white glossy cabinets. Huge streaks of it, as though someone had taken a spoon and flicked the sauce around with abandon. The sink was piled with dishes, and there were empty pizza boxes—open, and crusted with yet more sauce and dried-out cheese—spread out on nearly every surface.

Nora took a few steps into the kitchen and tripped over something lying on the ground. She looked down and saw that it was Katie's neon pink backpack, abandoned in the middle of the floor. She could feel her temper rising.

"Hello?" she said again, this time louder. "Where is everyone?"

"Hey, Mom," Dylan said, wandering into the kitchen. He was still wearing his muddy soccer clothes, although at least he'd switched out his cleats for slides. At six foot four, he towered over her, which was still surprising. *When did the little boy who used to fit comfortably in my lap turn into this man?* she wondered.

"Please tell me you weren't sitting on any of the furniture wearing that," Nora said.

"Just the couch and the white armchair," Dylan said. "I rolled all over them. Best way to get the mud off my uniform." He slung an arm around his mother's shoulders. "I kid, I kid."

"Ha ha," Nora said. She kissed her son on the cheek, and then gave him a gentle shove away. "You're going to get me muddy. Go shower and change. Where is everyone?"

Dylan shrugged. "No idea."

"I'm here. What's for dinner?" Matt sauntered into the kitchen. He hadn't yet gone through as drastic a growth spurt as his brother, and he looked pale, which concerned Nora. He spent too much time indoors, and too much time alone. It had been so different when Nora herself was young, and all the neighborhood mothers would shoo their kids out of the house during daylight hours. That childhood rite seemed to have disappeared, which made Nora sad. Although she supposed that at fifteen, Matt was too old to be shooed anywhere anyway.

"What about... 'Hi, Mom. How are you? I missed you while you were gone,'" Nora said.

"Right, all of that," her younger son replied. "What's for dinner?"

"I have no idea. I just walked in the door. I would have suggested pizza, however—" Nora gestured at the stack of pizza boxes on the counter "—it looks like you did that last night."

Matt headed to the pizza boxes and opened each one. "Shoot, it's all gone."

"Please tell me you wouldn't eat pizza that had been sitting out on the counter for twenty-four hours."

"I wouldn't?" Matt asked.

"I did," Dylan said. "Had the last slice an hour ago."

"Go shower!"

"Okay, okay." Dylan left, heading in the general direction of the stairs, although past experience told Nora the chances that he'd actually head straight to the shower were slim.

"Where are your father and sister?" Nora asked Matt, just as the back door that led from the kitchen out to the garage swung open.

"Right here," Carter said, heading inside, followed by Katie. He pecked Nora's cheek in greeting, a gesture so bland that it yet again vividly reminded her of the way Josh had kissed her the night before. Shame flooded over her. She turned away from her husband, worried that he'd read the guilt on her face, and smiled brightly at her daughter. Katie was coltish and leggy, and was wearing her nearly white-blond hair in a long braid down her back.

"I needed poster board," Katie said, lifting up the giant sheet she was carrying in front of her.

"What for?" *Please not a last-minute school project. Please not tonight*, she thought wearily. All she wanted to do was find something she could throw on the table for her family to eat, and retreat to a bubble bath.

"My country project for social studies. I'm doing Ireland," Katie set the poster board on the table.

"When is it due?"

"Tomorrow," Katie said carelessly. "But don't worry. I already have almost everything I need. I just need to type it up, print it all out and glue it on. And look." She pulled a few bottles out of a shopping bag. "Dad got me glitter!"

Nora looked around at her kitchen, already a disaster site, and decided it might be wiser to put off the thorough cleaning it needed until after Katie had finished with her glitter. She couldn't leave the tomato sauce, however.

"How was your trip?" Carter went to the refrigerator and took out a can of seltzer, his drink of choice these days.

"Fine." Nora got out spray cleanser and paper towels, and began wiping down the counters and cupboards.

"You seem a little tense," Carter remarked.

"That's probably because it looks like someone had a food fight in here. What happened?"

"We had a food fight," Matt deadpanned. "It was epic. I nailed Dylan with a meatball."

Carter looked around as if just noticing the mess for the first time, which was probably accurate.

"You kids did make a mess," he said.

"I'll clean it up," Matt offered, reaching for the cleanser. "You don't have to do it, Mom."

"I'd help." Katie set the bottles of green and gold glitter next to the poster board on the kitchen table. "But Ireland awaits."

Nora smiled at her middle child and gave him a quick hug. "It's okay, I'll do it. What should we do about dinner?"

"Chinese takeout?" Matt suggested.

"Awesome," Katie agreed.

"Call it in and I'll pick it up." Carter smiled at Nora. "You okay? You look tired."

Another wave of guilt washed over her. She turned her attention back to scrubbing the counter. "I am. Just a long couple of days. I'll be fine."

Later that night, Nora lay in bed, unable to sleep despite her exhaustion. Her brain whirred with memories and worries and shame. Next to her, Carter slept soundly, snoring loudly. Nora nudged him gently, which prompted her husband to roll onto his back and snore even louder. Nora looked at the glowing numbers on her clock. It was just after one in the morning.

Nora slid out of bed and padded out of the bedroom and down the stairs. She'd make a cup of chamomile tea, she decided. That might settle her down enough to sleep. She put the kettle on the stovetop, and while she waited for it to boil, she picked her phone up off the charger. She always left her phone downstairs, after reading articles about how keeping it on your bedside table could interfere with your sleep.

There was a notification that she'd received a text from a number she didn't recognize. Nora clicked on it.

I can't stop thinking about last night. I can't stop thinking about you. XX, J

chapter five

gwen

Since returning from school, Abby had categorically refused to discuss why she'd left. Gwen repeatedly tried talking to her about it, but Abby just stared at her, waiting silently until Gwen ran out of words.

"It's your turn," Gwen finally told Josh.

"Why do you think she'll talk to me?"

"Because you've always been her favorite."

"That's not true," Josh protested, although they both knew she was right. Abby had always been daddy's girl.

Well, fine, Gwen thought. *Then let Daddy handle it.*

Josh gamely went to Abby's room, and after knocking on her door, went inside to talk to her. Gwen resisted the temptation to listen in and waited for him in the living room. It wasn't long before Josh returned.

He shook her head. "She won't tell me anything. Do you think it's possible she's depressed?"

"Well, since she refuses to leave the house, barely eats and hasn't changed out of those flannel pajama pants since she got home, I would say yes, there's a pretty good chance she's depressed."

"Why are you snapping at me?"

"Because you don't seem to be taking this seriously."

Josh raised his hands and let them fall back down to his sides. "Of course I'm taking it seriously. Why would you think that I'm not? I'm just as concerned as you are."

Gwen shook her head mutely. She wasn't sure why she was so annoyed at him. Abby's situation wasn't his fault, any more than it was hers. They'd given Abby every opportunity in life. *Is that the problem?* Gwen wondered. Had they made life too easy for her? Had they failed to teach her that even kids who came from privileged backgrounds had to work hard to be successful, to fight hard to secure their place in the world?

"I'll see if Dr. Thomas can fit her in tomorrow," Gwen finally said.

Gwen sat in the waiting room at the office of their family doctor, Belinda Thomas. At first, Abby had flatly refused to go to the appointment her mother scheduled for her. But after Gwen spent the better part of an hour lecturing Abby that she was on the brink of ruining her life, and the very least she could do was agree to meet with a doctor who could possibly help prevent that, Abby had finally given in and agreed to go to the appointment. Gwen knew Abby was motivated entirely by wanting to shut her up, but she was fine with that.

Once they reached Dr. Thomas's office, however, Abby wouldn't let Gwen accompany her into the exam room. Even more annoyingly, her attempts to charm the receptionist into allowing her to go back with Abby had been flatly refused.

Gwen had no choice but to go along with it. Abby was technically an adult, no matter how ridiculous the idea seemed, especially considering her recent behavior.

As she waited, Gwen wondered when Josh had started affecting her like this. Was it normal to be constantly irritated with your spouse? Actually, it was more than just an irritation. Gwen realized that on some level, she was sick to death of him. Josh was almost always pleasant, a good provider, a loving father. And yet…the thought of having to look at his face every day for the rest of her life made Gwen feel like ripping the skin off her body.

When had that started to happen? She supposed it was right around the same time she started to fantasize about traveling the world. Alone.

The door from the back office swung open, and Abby slouched out into the waiting room.

"Let's go," she said.

"What did Dr. Thomas say?"

"I don't want to talk about it here."

Gwen glanced around. The waiting room was empty, other than the staff manning the check-in window. But she nodded, and silently followed Abby out of the office.

"They called in a prescription for me," Abby said once they were in the car.

"For what?"

"An antidepressant."

"We'll stop at the pharmacy on the way home. Did Dr. Thomas say anything else? How long you should take it for, or what the underlying cause might be?"

Abby was quiet for so long, Gwen assumed that this was yet another question that would go unanswered. But then her daughter surprised her by speaking.

"Colin and I broke up."

"I'm sorry to hear that."

"I loved him. He didn't love me back."

Gwen glanced over at her daughter. There were tears streaming down Abby's cheeks. Gwen turned back to face the road, tightening her grip on the steering wheel, and tried to check her growing irritation.

"Breaking up with a boy isn't a reason to drop out of school."

"I knew you wouldn't understand."

"Understand what? You haven't told me anything."

Abby hesitated. "Colin dumped me to go out with Lana."

"Oh." Gwen exhaled, and tapped her fingers on the steering wheel. Abby's sudden departure from college was making more sense. However, that didn't mean it wasn't an idiotic choice. "Well, we'll find you a different apartment. Maybe you could move into the dorms—"

"I'm not going back there," Abby said flatly. "And you can't make me."

Gwen again had to hold back her words. *Yes, I can make you,* she wanted to say. *No, you're not going to spend the rest of the year, much less your life, camped out in your bedroom. Dropping out of school has consequences, like finding a job and learning to support yourself. And how could any child of mine be so weak they'd let a breakup derail their life?* Gwen couldn't imagine ever letting anyone affect her that way.

But it had only been a few days. Maybe Abby just needed a little more time to realize how ridiculous she was being.

Gwen drove to the pharmacy to pick up Abby's prescription, then they headed back home. Abby spent the rest of the ride silent and staring out her window, hunched away from her mother.

As soon as Gwen turned onto their street, she saw that their dog, Izzy, had gotten out. The Labrador was cavorting in the middle of the road—running in circles, sniffing a neighbor's shrubbery, picking up a stick and tossing it about. Izzy looked like she was having the time of her life.

"Why's Izzy out?" Abby asked.

"I don't know."

Gwen tried to remember if she'd latched the gate before they left for the doctor's office. Izzy had always been an escape artist. Back when she was still a puppy, they'd installed an invisible fence, but Izzy had barreled through it so many times, they'd given up and installed a tall wooden fence with a dog-proof latch. Even then, Izzy still managed to make the occasional escape. Gwen had gotten into the habit of double-checking that the latch was secure whenever she left the house. But now she couldn't remember if she'd checked it that day. She'd been preoccupied with taking Abby to her doctor's appointment, and also with the fact that she'd checked Simon's grades online that morning, and discovered he was failing algebra.

Is parenting supposed to get harder as your kids get older? she wondered. *Why do they need such constant maintenance?*

When Gwen was growing up, no one worried about her grades or emotional well-being. Hell, by the time she was Simon's age, her father had permanently disappeared out of her life, and her mother was coping—or, not coping, to be more precise—by downing half a bottle of vodka every day.

"Help me catch her," Gwen said as she pulled into the driveway and parked the car.

They both hopped out of the vehicle and attempted to trap the dog in a pincer movement.

"Come here, Izzy," Abby said, clapping her hands. It was the most animated Gwen had seen her since her sudden return home.

"Come on, girl," Gwen called out. "I have a cookie!"

But even with the offer of that beloved treat, Izzy didn't allow herself to be cornered for another ten minutes. Every time one of them got close to her, she'd wheel around and take off, looking back over her shoulder to see if they were giving chase. She clearly found it to be the most entertaining game she'd ever played. Finally, Abby found one of Izzy's tennis balls, and threw it through the open gate into the backyard. Izzy chased happily after it.

"Good thinking," Gwen said, quickly closing the gate and trapping their quarry. She looked at the lock and jiggled it. It seemed securely shut. "I wonder how she managed to get out?"

"Maybe someone let her out."

"Why would anyone do that?"

"People do all sorts of terrible things."

Gwen again had to suppress her frustration at her daughter's moodiness. Maybe most mothers, good mothers, would only have empathy and endless amounts of patience for a child going through the trauma of a breakup. But dropping out of college, and disrupting her entire life, over some boy who was never going to be anything but a footnote in Abby's life? It was crazy. Gwen wished she could somehow inject the perspective of her forty-nine years into her daughter.

"That's true, if a little dark," Gwen said. "But I doubt anyone would let Izzy loose on purpose. She's a menace. And she's lucky she didn't get hit by a car."

Abby shrugged, her brief burst of energy already spent. She turned and walked into the house.

Later that night, while Abby was taking a shower, Gwen found Josh in the living room, sprawled on the couch, Izzy stretched out beside him. The dog's tail thumped at Gwen's approach. There was a football game on the television, but Josh wasn't paying attention to it. Instead, he was holding his phone in both hands, staring down at it as though it held all the answers to his life.

"What are you doing?"

Josh looked up, startled. "I was just checking something. It's nothing." He set down the phone, screen side down, on the table next to him.

Gwen perched on the ottoman across from him and leaned forward.

"Abby broke up with her boyfriend. Or, more to the point, he broke up with her. That's why she came home."

"That's a relief."

"What?"

"I mean, I know having your heart broken isn't fun, but I was worried it was something more serious. Like, clinical depression or something like that."

"I took her to see Dr. Thomas today, and she put Abby on an antidepressant."

"Why?"

"What do you mean *why*? She's depressed. The doctor thinks she needs to be on one."

"She's sad about a boy. Does she really need to be medicated for that? Those drugs can have side effects."

"I know," Gwen said. The sound of the shower running stopped, and she raised her fingers to her lips.

Josh leaned forward and lowered his voice. "Did you talk to the doctor about possible side effects? Or whether this drug is the best one for Abby to be on?"

"No, I didn't."

"Why not?"

Gwen could feel her temper, already frayed from the day's events, begin to rise at this implied criticism. "Because Abby is technically an adult, and she wouldn't let me go into the doctor's office with her. I wasn't part of the conversation."

"I don't know. I don't like the idea of taking psychotropic drugs because of a breakup."

"What exactly was I supposed to do? She's an adult."

"Adults don't drop out of school because they break up with someone."

"Trust me, we are in total agreement on that point."

"Stop talking about me," Abby said.

Gwen and Josh both looked up, startled. Their daughter was standing there, hair dripping wet and dressed in the same pajamas she'd driven home in. Abby crossed her arms over her chest and glared at her mother.

"I can't believe you told him."

"I didn't know I wasn't supposed to." Gwen wondered why it was that everyone was blaming her for a situation that she had not caused, had no control over and was doing her best to sort out.

Jesus, she thought. *It's not like I particularly feel like dealing with any of this.*

"I'm sorry about what happened with Colin, Abs," Josh said. "I thought he seemed like a nice kid."

"Mom couldn't stand him."

"Wait, what?" Gwen asked. "I never said that."

The truth was, Gwen hadn't liked Colin, but she thought she'd successfully hidden that fact from Abby. She'd found him a little too smug, too entitled. When they'd brought him along on their annual family trip to Amelia Island the previous summer, he'd been polite. But, Gwen had gotten the definite sense that he wasn't grateful for the invitation. Instead, he acted like he considered his presence there as a special treat for the people who were providing him with a free vacation. More significant, Gwen could immediately tell that Abby adored Colin far more than he did her, which was never a good position to be in. She had tried to instill in her daughter the importance of maintaining the upper hand in relationships, but clearly that lesson hadn't sunk in.

"You know it's true," Abby said, practically spitting the words out. "I could tell."

"Please stop being so dramatic," Gwen said.

Abby rolled her eyes. "I'm going to bed, so feel free to go back to talking about me behind my back."

"Abby, you're being overly sensitive," Gwen began, but her daughter had already spun around and marched furiously away, toward her room. A minute later, the door slammed. Gwen raised a finger. "That is completely unacceptable behavior."

"Don't let her get to you," Josh said. "She's just upset. She's going through a lot."

Gwen just shook her head. She'd had enough of her family for the evening.

"I'm going to bed, too. Oh… I forgot to tell you. Tara Edwards stopped by the other day. She brought you brownies."

Josh looked puzzled. "What? Why would she do that?"

"She said you raved about them, and so she baked you a special batch. But I think Simon and his friends ate them all."

"That sounds like Simon. I don't remember discussing brownies with her, though."

Gwen studied him, wondering if Josh was feigning surprise. And then wondered when she'd stopped being able to read her husband. There had been a time when she'd always known what he was thinking, which had never been that hard with Josh. He was the least secretive person she'd ever met. But there was something different about him, something that Gwen could sense, even if she couldn't quite put her finger on it.

She didn't like it one bit.

chapter six

abby

Ten days after her abrupt return home, and six days after she'd started taking the antidepressants Dr. Thomas had prescribed her, Abby began to wonder if she was losing her mind.

For one thing, she couldn't sleep. At night, she lay in bed, trying not to think about Colin, and especially trying not to think about Colin and Lana together, and of course, failing miserably. It was all she could think about. She couldn't stop examining every memory she had of the two of them through the prism of their betrayal. Like the time Colin and Lana had stayed up late studying together for a sociology exam, and she had heard them laughing over something. Abby had actually felt a bubble of happiness rise up inside her that her boyfriend and best friend got along so well. Now she wondered if they'd been laughing at how foolish she was. This was the point where she'd usually pull the blankets up over her head, as though she could somehow smother away the pain and mortification at how oblivious she'd been. Even worse were the interactions she could only imagine, like Colin tucking a strand of Lana's blond hair behind her ear before leaning forward to press his lips against hers.

That image alone could keep Abby up half the night.

Then, during the day, she felt listless and spacey, like the world was always just slightly out of focus. She didn't know if it was the medicine, or the lack of sleep, or a combination of the two. Whatever it was, Abby kept finding herself sitting and staring into space while the days expanded, stretching out longer than she thought possible.

Her mother kept trying to engage her in various activities.

"Let's go get a pedicure together," she'd suggest. Or, "Would you like to bake banana bread with me?"

Abby would just stare at her, wondering what planet this woman had beamed down from. They'd never had a pedicure-and-bread-baking sort of relationship before, so why exactly would they start that now? Anyway, Abby could tell that her mother didn't really want to do any of these proposed activities any more than she herself did. Gwen was just going through the motions of Let's-Pretend-I'm-A-Good-Mother. It was an act Abby had caught on to years ago. Her mother had always been far more interested in how people saw her—a devoted wife, or an invested mother—than being those things. Abby had even found herself imitating her mother in this respect. It had always been important to her that her teachers and friends' parents thought of her as the nice girl, the good student, the one who would never get into trouble. However, this flurry of suggestions that they spend time together was something entirely new, and Abby wasn't quite sure where it was coming from.

Anyway, Abby had better things to do. Well, one thing to do. These days, her only activity of choice was stalking Colin and Lana on social media. Neither had bothered to unfollow her on any of the platforms they used, and Lana was addicted to posting pictures of herself. Now her various feeds were filled with photos of her and Colin. Abby pulled up Lana's Instagram on her laptop, and of course, there were two new pictures.

I have the best boyfriend! He brought me a mocha latte today, just because he was thinking of me. #love #coffeetime #bestboyfriend #happy. Lana posted this next to a photo of herself smiling coyly while holding up a paper coffee cup. Her long blond hair was shiny and curled at the ends, and her lips were a glossy pink. She looked like a model.

Colin never spontaneously brought me coffee, Abby thought sadly. It had been the other way around, with her stopping by the apartment he shared with three friends, bearing little gifts for him. Like the oatmeal chocolate chip cookies he loved, or a mug with a picture of a unicorn farting out a rainbow, which Colin had laughed at when he saw it at a campus gift shop.

The second photo was captioned, *Romantic walks are the best walks! #love #photooftheday #happy #falldays #romance #instagood.* This one showed a picture of two hands, their fingers entwined.

"I hate you both," Abby said out loud. Even as she spoke the words, she knew it wasn't true. She *did* hate Lana, hated her with a ferocity Abby hadn't known she was capable of. It was just so unfair that Lana had been born into this charmed life where she was beautiful, and adored, and nothing bad ever happened to her. Every time Abby heard a story on the news of someone dying in a car crash, or being attacked in some terribly violent way, her first thought was, *Why couldn't that have happened to Lana?* She knew such thoughts were like a poison slowly spreading through her, infecting the core of who she was. And yet, she couldn't seem to stop.

But Colin. Try as she might, Abby couldn't bring herself to hate him. She knew that this, too, was wrong. He had betrayed her just as deeply and terribly as Lana had. But if Colin appeared at her door, contrite and full of regret—another fantasy she indulged in far too often—Abby knew she'd take him back. She wouldn't even hesitate. That's how weak she was. Of course Colin would prefer Lana, who was gorgeous and self-confident. Abby was so pathetic she'd even tearfully begged Colin not to break up with her. He'd just stared at her in horror, as if he couldn't possibly imagine what he'd ever seen in her.

It had been the lowest moment of her life.

There was a knock on her door.

"What?"

"It's me." It was her brother, Simon, his voice muffled through the door.

"I'm busy. What do you want?"

"Um, to talk to you? Obviously?"

"Fine, whatever."

Simon opened the door and hovered in the doorway to her room, looking awkward. Abby realized he had grown taller since she'd left for college that summer, and was surprised she hadn't noticed before. His legs were long and lanky, and he looked skinnier than ever. He was going to be a handsome guy, she realized, especially once his frame filled out. And if he ever bothered to brush his hair or wear something other than T-shirts with video game characters on them.

"What's up?"

"Mom wants to know if you want to—"

Before he could finish, Abby raised a hand and shook her head. "No."

One corner of Simon's mouth quirked up in a half smile. "You don't even know what I was going to say."

"It doesn't matter. I'm not going to want to do it."

Simon hesitated. "Are you okay?"

Abby shrugged. She was anything but okay, but, still, she was touched by her brother's concern. Despite their six-year age difference, they'd always been close. Or maybe they were close because of the age difference, which probably dampened any sibling rivalry that would have occurred if they'd been born closer together. But Abby had been so focused on her misery, she'd barely spoken to Simon since her return home.

"Do me a favor," she said. "Don't grow up to be a dick."

"I'll do my best."

"I'm serious."

"So am I. Who wants to be a dick?"

Abby laughed darkly. "You'd be surprised by how many dicks there are out in the world, happily going through life, not caring who they hurt along the way. Narcissists. Sociopaths. Sadists. They're everywhere."

Simon shifted uncomfortably. "*Oh*-kay, then. Good talk. I'm going back to my room."

"Shut my door," Abby ordered.

She focused her attention back on her laptop and continued scrolling through Lana's pictures. There was one that she couldn't stop herself from returning to again and again. It was a close-up of Colin's face, taken while he was lying in Lana's bed. Abby recognized the butterfly-printed sheets. He was smiling in that way that still made her pulse hum. *My boyfriend is so hot*, Lana had written, followed by a series of heart emoticons. *#love #handsome #happy #mancrushmonday #picoftheday*.

There was another sharp rap on her bedroom door. Abby sighed. Why wouldn't her family leave her alone?

"What?"

The door cracked open again. This time, it was her mother, wearing a faux expression of concern that made Abby's skin itch.

"Whatever it is, *no*. Just no. I don't want to go the mall or pop popcorn and watch a movie or bake anything."

Gwen crossed her arms. "Fine. I'll make a deal with you, then. I'll stop pushing you to get out of your room and out of those pajamas on one condition."

"What's that?"

"You leave the house once a day and go for a walk."

"What?"

"I read an article about it. Walking is a mood elevator. There's an argument that going for a brisk walk every day can be as effective as antidepressants."

"I'm already taking an antidepressant."

"I know, but getting some exercise and fresh air could help. At least, it wouldn't hurt. It's not healthy for you to be cooped up in here by yourself all the time."

Abby didn't see how going for a walk was going to solve anything. It wouldn't cause Colin and Lana to break up, which was the only possible thing that would make Abby feel better.

"If I do that, you'll really stop trying to get me to bake shit?"

Gwen nodded. "You know, I don't actually enjoy baking myself."

"I know, that's why it's so weird that you keep trying to get me to do it."

"I'm just trying to help you fix this...well, whatever this is that you're going through."

Abby felt a sudden rush of fury flare up, piercing through the numb sadness that had become her default emotion. She didn't know why her mother affected her this way, but she also wasn't particularly in the mood for self-reflection.

"I don't need your help," Abby snarled. "Just leave me alone."

Gwen folded her arms, her expression now cool. "I told you my price for leaving you alone. One walk, every day, for at least an hour. Starting today."

"Fine." Abby stood and shoved her feet into her running shoes. "If that's what it will take to get you to stop harassing me, *fine*. I'll go walk."

"You're wearing pajamas," Gwen pointed out. "Why don't you put on some running shorts instead? Or any other clothing meant to be worn outside the home?"

"Dictating my wardrobe was not part of the deal."

Abby brushed by her mother as she walked out of her room and out the front door. Once outside, she stopped for a minute, blinking into the unbearably bright sunshine. Abby quickly realized that it was actually too hot outside to be wearing brushed flannel pajama pants. Her mother was right; she should have changed into running shorts. But she was hardly going to go back inside and admit that. So...now what?

"I guess now I go for a fucking walk," Abby said out loud. She folded her arms over her chest and set off down the road.

chapter seven

nora

Nora didn't text Josh back.

It was the right thing to do, she reasoned. The only rational choice. If she texted him, and he replied, it would just continue. This was how affairs happened, Nora realized. It wasn't something she'd ever put much thought into before, although now she was forced to examine it. They started as flirtations that spiraled out of control. After all, who would just shrug and think, *Hell, I should start an illicit relationship with a married man that could possibly lead to the downfall of not one, but two families.* Certainly not someone like Nora. And, she suspected, not someone like Josh, either.

But she didn't delete his text.

At first, she'd wondered how he'd gotten her cell phone number, but then remembered that it would have been included in the paperwork she'd filled out when her children became patients at his practice. She felt almost absurdly flattered that he'd sought it out.

You can't respond, she told herself over and over again. *You absolutely cannot.*

And yet, she looked at the text every day, multiple times a day. And every day she didn't answer, she'd feel an odd mixture of pride and deflation. Glad that she was doing the right thing, and yet depressed that the single most exciting thing that had happened to her in years was over, never to be repeated.

Then four days later, Josh texted her again. Her phone dinged the alert just as Nora was whisking eggs for the quiche lorraine recipe she was featuring on her blog the next day.

I need to see you. Can you meet me?

When Nora read the text, she felt the same swooping rush of excitement, although this was quickly followed by a sickly panic. What if Josh needed to see her because someone had found out about their night together? They'd both been attending professional conferences, so it wasn't implausible that someone who knew one or the other of them had seen them together in the bar or restaurant or—and this thought caused her anxiety to spike even higher—entering the elevator together. Did Josh want to warn her that this wrecking ball they'd set in motion was about to swing toward her and destroy her life?

"Oh, my God," Nora said out loud, her hand fluttering up to her throat.

"What?" Katie asked.

Nora started. She'd thought she was alone.

"God, Mom, why are you so jumpy? I'm your daughter, not a serial killer."

"Yes, thank you for pointing that out."

"Did you get bad news?"

"What? Why do you think that?"

"You were looking at your phone, and said, 'Oh, my God!'"
Here Katie did a remarkably good imitation of Nora's voice. "I
used my powers of deduction."

"No. I mean, yes, I was reading a sad news story. About a
house fire."

"Here? In Shoreham?"

Nora blinked. She was, she realized, a terrible liar. "No.
Um… Dayton, Ohio."

"*Right.*" Katie went to the refrigerator, opened it and stared
inside. All of her children did this, and it normally drove Nora
crazy, since she was sure it was contributing to their already as-
tronomical power bill. But she was so freaked out over the possible implication of Josh's text, she didn't chastise Katie, even
as her daughter slowly took out each yogurt cup one by one,
studying each flavor in turn.

"We're out of peach yogurt," Katie complained. "It's all blueberry or, yuck, cherry. Why would you even buy cherry yogurt? It's gross."

"Matt likes it," Nora said, amazed at how normal her voice
sounded. "And the reason we're out of peach is that you eat
three containers a day."

"I do," Katie agreed. "But that just means you should buy
more at a time."

"Then you'd eat six containers a day."

"Entirely possible. Is there anything else to eat? I'm starving."

"String cheese, crackers, protein bars." Nora listed the snacks
off robotically. She desperately needed to be alone so that she
could figure out what to do, how to respond to this text. "Oh,
there's a container of those peanut butter–filled pretzels you
like."

Katie brightened. "Awesome. Is it okay if I take them to my
room?"

"Sure, go ahead."

Katie tipped her head and looked at her intently. Nora could feel her breath catch in her chest. Was her daughter sensing her emotional turmoil? Had she already realized that her mother couldn't be this upset by a fictional house fire in another part of the country, and was going to start asking more probing questions about what Nora had really being reading on her phone?

"Did you know you're getting lines by the side of your mouth that look just like Gran's?"

"What?"

"Right here." Katie pointed to the side of her own mouth. "Are they genetic? I hope I don't get them, too."

"Katie, as much as I would love to discuss my wrinkles with you at length, I have to finish making this quiche."

Katie shrugged. "Just thought you should know, in case you wanted to get some new moisturizer or something. Or one of those chemical peels. That might work, too." This advice dispatched, Katie spun around and skipped out of the kitchen.

Nora looked back down at her phone, and reread Josh's text.

I need to see you. Can you meet me?

Nora took a deep breath. She didn't have a choice. She had to know if they'd been caught.

Yes, she typed, and then hit the send button.

They made a plan to meet at the beach. It was the only place Nora could think of. The only people who went to the beach in the middle of a weekday were tourists and surfers, so it was unlikely they'd run into anyone there who knew them. Still, Nora was shaking as she drove east toward the ocean late the following morning, terrified both at the prospect of seeing Josh again and at the risk of getting caught.

"What am I doing?" she murmured to herself. "This is insane."

Nora could feel her heart skitter in her chest, and the uptick of her pulse reminded her of the panic attacks she used to get when she was a teenager. They had been terrifying, that overwhelming feeling that death was imminent, looming in front of her. She hadn't had an attack in years, and gulped in breaths of air, trying to stave it off as she turned into the beach parking lot. The sky was gray with clouds, rain occasionally spitting down. The weather must have kept the tourists away, because there was only one other car parked there, a silver Mercedes sedan. Nora pulled in next to it and looked over.

There he was. *Josh.* Nora inhaled sharply as their eyes met.

Josh got out of his car and tried to open the passenger-side door on Nora's SUV. It was locked. She fumbled for the button to unlock it. He opened the door, slid inside, and before she could say anything, he was kissing her. His hand cupped the back of her neck and pulled her toward him. They leaned over the center console, and Nora lost herself in the moment, in the taste and touch of him.

Finally, they broke apart. Josh leaned back slightly, his eyes intent on hers.

"I had to see you again," he said. "I can't stop thinking about you. About that night."

Nora nodded. "Me, too."

"I'm glad you texted me back. I wasn't sure you would."

"I wasn't sure I would, either," Nora admitted. "This is crazy, right? I mean...we can't do this. Can we?"

Josh shook his head slowly, and Nora felt a rush of disappointment. *Do I want him to talk me into having an affair?* she wondered. *Is that the real reason I agreed to meet him?*

"I don't know. I just know that the idea of not seeing you again wasn't an option."

Nora hated herself for how happy these words made her feel. But then Josh took her hand in his, and she looked down at their intertwined fingers, marveling at how right it felt.

"I do not have a happy marriage," she said quietly.

"I know."

"How do you know?"

"Well, I think if either of us had happy marriages, we wouldn't be here right now. But I also know your husband."

"You do?" This surprised Nora. She had always been the one to take the children to their orthodontist appointments with Josh, and she couldn't remember them ever meeting at a party. The only time she ever ran into the Landons was at school events, and Carter rarely accompanied her to those.

"Just from the gym. But honestly? I've never cared for him. Even before you and I…well. He's always struck me as being a little arrogant."

Nora considered this. It was hard to disagree. Carter *could* be arrogant. It wasn't his worst trait, not by a long shot, but there was certainly a side to her husband where he always believed he was the smartest man in the room. She'd seen him corner people at parties, talking at them in his loud, blustery way, while they anxiously looked around for an escape route. It was moments like those—and the other times, the bad times—when Nora wondered what she had ever seen in Carter. When they'd met, she'd found his confidence attractive. Had she been so in love, she'd blinded herself to the man he really was? It wasn't a thought she liked to dwell on.

"But I'm hardly a disinterested party," Josh continued. "I probably wouldn't like him if he was the greatest guy in the world."

He was stroking her inner wrist with his thumb as he spoke, and Nora was surprised at how erotic she found the sensation. What was it about this man that every time he touched her it caused every nerve in her body to vibrate?

"He's not. But… I don't know, it feels weird to talk about this."

"Our marriages?"

"Yes. Doesn't it just compound our disloyalty?"

"Possibly, but I think it's something we probably need to talk about. Isn't it?"

These are questions with no good answers, Nora thought. Of course, they shouldn't discuss it. Just like they shouldn't continue down this path. Yet here they were, sitting in her car on a gloomy rain-speckled day, holding hands, and Nora felt more alive than she had in years.

"What went wrong in your marriage?" she asked.

Josh considered this.

"I think it took a long time for me to see my wife for who she truly is," he said. "When we first met, when we were first dating, I was a little starstruck. Gwen can be so charming, so quick-witted. She's one of those people who walks into a room and everyone is drawn to her."

"I can see that," Nora said. "I don't know her very well, but she's always seemed very charismatic." *Almost scarily so,* Nora added silently. Gwen was the sort of woman who sucked all the oxygen out of the room.

"Yes. That's just it. She's charismatic. But that's something she puts on in public. It's not the person we live with at home. That Gwen, the private one, can be very cold. And very calculating."

"What do you mean? She's not affectionate?"

Josh laughed without humor. "No. Gwen has never been affectionate. Not with me, not even with the kids when they were younger. Our daughter, Abby, showed up last week and announced she'd dropped out of college—"

"Oh, no!"

"Tell me about it. It's been stressful couple of weeks. And it's not like Gwen is ignoring the situation. She took Abby to the doctor to deal with her depression, and I know she's made an effort to get Abby out doing things. But…sometimes it just seems like…"

Josh stopped and ran a hand through his hair.

"Like what?"

"Like she's just going through the motions. Like she knows what an engaged mother should look like and is doing her best to imitate one." He squeezed Nora's hand. "I know. That sounds terrible, and I can't even exactly explain it. Gwen's not engaged on some fundamental level—with anyone. I don't think she's capable of it."

"You must have had a connection at some point. In the beginning, at least."

Josh shrugged helplessly. "That's just it. I don't think there actually ever was one. I think I saw what she wanted me to see, not what was actually there. By the time I'd started to figure that there were serious issues, we were already married, and we'd had Abby and Simon. Besides, I was working a lot of hours establishing my practice, so I had an outlet. It's just recently, as the kids have gotten older, that I've realized how stuck I am. And at that point, I thought it was too late."

"Unfortunately, I know exactly what you mean."

"You do?"

"Yes. Well, maybe not the playacting part. I don't think Carter does that. But, we make these huge decisions when we're in our twenties—who we're going to marry, what we're going to be, how we're going to spend the rest of our lives. And yet...we have no real perspective. The twenty-five-year-old me had no clue what the forty-five-year-old me would end up wanting and needing in life. Much less that the man I had chosen to spend my life with would never be the partner I needed him to be."

"Yes, that's exactly it. Then you take stock of your life, and think, how could I have made such an enormous mistake? But then I met you." Josh squeezed Nora's hand. "And it occurred to me that my life isn't over. I don't have to stay on this path, with this woman."

"So, what are you saying? That we just abandon our families? Run away together?"

"I don't know. I didn't exactly plan any of this." Josh leaned forward and kissed Nora again, this time his lips brushing lightly against hers. "But I know I want to see you again. Can we do that?"

Nora stared into his kind brown eyes, which were intent on hers. She thought of all the reasons why she should say no—all of the people they would hurt if they were found out, the damage they would do their relationships with their children, the horror of being the topic of a small-town scandal. Then Nora looked down at their hands still linked together, and knew that she wasn't ready to let go of him. Not yet. Maybe not ever.

"Yes," she said.

chapter eight

gwen

After Gwen dropped off Simon at his math tutor—who, so far, had not proved to be much help in improving Simon's abysmal algebra grade—she headed to the grocery store to shop for Thanksgiving dinner. It was the very last thing she wanted to do.

Of all the holidays, Thanksgiving ranked almost lowest on her list, just above St. Patrick's Day and the Fourth of July. It meant at least two days of cooking and cleaning, only to have to force-feed everyone roast turkey and assorted heavy side dishes on a hot November Florida day. Even worse was the part where they had to pretend to be a happy family, when nothing could be further from the truth. Abby was still home, and still spending most of her time moping in her room. Josh was distant and distracted. Simon, at least, rarely required emotional tending, although Gwen knew she probably let him get away with spending too much time playing video games.

Limiting screen time was one of the main jobs of the modern mother, and yet another parenting issue Gwen had little patience for. She even hated the term "screen time," and the way the other mothers loved to discuss earnestly and at length what the appropriate limits were on it. Gwen would nod along and pretend to agree with what was being said, while never offering her real opinion, which was that it felt like an imposition that she was supposed to spend huge swathes of her time policing her son.

When she'd been fifteen, her parents were already divorced, her father had disappeared from their lives, and her mother rarely paid any attention to what Gwen was doing. She didn't monitor her homework, who her friends were or even knew where the hell she was most of the time. Gwen had been a good student, was never in trouble, so her mother mostly left her alone. She had no idea that Gwen was hanging out with not the best crowd by that point. Her friends back then were kids who dabbled in drugs and drinking, and various other destructive behaviors.

These days, among the helicoptering Shoreham mothers brigade, that sort of benign neglect would be considered practically illegal. But there was a side to Gwen that had always liked flirting with the edges of danger, just so long as she didn't get caught. And she never did.

Gwen wheeled a grocery cart into the store, and an unbidden thought came to her.

I should never have had children.

It wasn't the first time she'd thought this, and she usually tried to suppress it. But she knew it was true. She was missing something, some necessary maternal gene.

The grocery store was busy, unsurprisingly, everyone swarming in to buy last-minute turkeys and sweet potatoes and large bags of green beans. Gwen consulted her handwritten list, crossing off each item as she tossed it in her cart. She was making a homemade pumpkin pie at Simon's request, but had already decided she was taking some shortcuts, like frozen dinner rolls and canned cranberry sauce. Gwen rolled her cart—which, of course, had one rickety wheel—around, sidestepping shoppers dithering over which kind of salt made the best brine, or picking through the varieties of box stuffing.

"Gwen!" a voice rang out.

She had to stop herself from shuddering. The last thing Gwen wanted was to run into someone she knew, which of course meant that it was inevitable that she would do so. She looked up to see who was flagging her down. It was Tara Edwards, she of the brownies and manic smile.

"Happy holidays!" Tara cried. She leaned forward to hug Gwen, who had to stop herself from stepping back from the embrace. "Are you here shopping for Thanksgiving, too?"

Well, duh, Gwen thought. *This woman isn't just annoying, she's an idiot.*

Gwen forced herself to smile warmly. "I obviously put it off too late. This place is a madhouse."

"I know, I thought the same thing, but you can't buy your produce too far ahead of time. Then again, they're out of leeks, so I don't know what I'm going to do. I always make a leek gratin that the twins love and have to have every year. I guess I'll have to drive around to see if any other stores have them in stock."

Gwen tried to think of any reason that would induce her to spend the Tuesday before Thanksgiving grocery store–hopping in search of an elusive vegetable, and couldn't of a single one. *Is this the missing maternal gene popping up again?* she wondered. *Isn't it enough that I'm going to spend tomorrow making a homemade pie, when frankly, I'd rather curl up with a good book and a cup of tea?* She glanced in Tara's cart and spotted bags of cranberries, envelopes of yeast and both sweet and Yukon Gold potatoes. Clearly, Tara wasn't into shortcuts.

"It sounds delicious. Good luck finding them."

"Did Josh like the brownies?"

"To be honest, I don't know if he ever got to try one. I think Simon and his friends gobbled them all up."

Gwen sensed that this response would needle Tara, but she couldn't help herself. And, she was right. Tara looked stricken.

"He didn't get any? Oh, no! Well, I guess I'll have to make him another batch. Maybe I should drop them off at his office instead?"

"I'm sure he'd appreciate that, although, I think his staff is just as bad as Simon when it comes to eating treats that are brought in."

"Oh." Tara frowned as she puzzled out a solution to what she clearly saw as an enormous problem. "I guess I'll wrap them for him, so no one else gets to them first."

"That's a great idea." Gwen could feel herself itching to get away. Stupid people had always gotten on her nerves. "I really should get going. I still have shopping to do."

"Yes, of course. Me, too. It was great seeing you again! Maybe we can all get together one night and go out for dinner? As couples, I mean."

Gwen tried to picture Tara's husband. She knew she must have met him at some point, at some event, but try as she might, she couldn't picture his face. He clearly hadn't made an impression.

"What a wonderful idea. We'll have to set that up," Gwen lied smoothly. There wasn't a chance in hell she would willingly spend an entire evening with this woman, who was needier than a puppy and possibly had a crush on her husband. "Have a great holiday and give my best to your family."

Later that evening, after dinner—a tuna noodle casserole that Abby and Josh picked at, and Simon devoured three helpings of—Gwen stood in her kitchen, dreading the cooking she was going to have to tackle over the next two days. Josh wandered in and retrieved a bottle of beer from the refrigerator.

"What are you doing?" he asked.

"Nothing. Just thinking."

"About what?"

About how much I don't feel like going through the motions of a family holiday. About how everything just feels off this year. About how much I fucking hate turkey, Gwen thought.

"Nothing important. I ran into Tara Edwards today."

Josh frowned. "The name sounds familiar. I know I should know it."

"Her twin sons are patients of yours. And she brought you brownies last month."

"Oh, right, I remember now. You told me about the brownies. I never did get to try one."

"She was quite upset about that."

"She was? Why didn't you just lie and tell her I loved them?"

"I don't know," Gwen mused. "Maybe I didn't want to encourage her to keep showing up at our door with baked goods."

Josh twisted the top off his beer. "She seems harmless enough. Maybe a little…"

"Moronic? Is that the word you were looking for?"

He shrugged. "I was going to say a little overeager. She probably doesn't have many friends."

"She asked us to have dinner with her and her husband. Under no circumstances will that happen."

"Okay. It certainly wouldn't be my top pick for an evening out."

"Does she have a crush on you?" Gwen wasn't sure why asked. If Josh was having a flirtation with Tara Edwards, he'd hardly admit it to her. Maybe she just wanted to poke at it and see how he'd react.

"What?" Josh looked genuinely startled. "Why would you say that?"

"Why would she say what?" Abby asked, wandering into the kitchen, Izzy lumbering behind her. Abby walked to the refrigerator, opened it and stared inside. She was still wearing the same flannel pajama bottoms she'd returned home in. The dog sat at Abby's heel and looked hopeful that a treat might appear.

"Nothing," Josh said. "Just a weird idea your mother had."

"Shocking," Abby said.

"Are you hungry?" Gwen asked.

"No," Abby said, closing the refrigerator door. "I was just looking to see if there was anything other than tuna casserole."

"What's wrong with tuna casserole?"

"Um, it's disgusting?"

"Well, feel free to take over cooking dinner whenever you'd like. I'd be more than happy to share the chore. In fact, I could use some help with Thanksgiving dinner, so let me know if you feel like making a pie tomorrow."

"What happened to our deal?" Abby asked.

"What deal?" Josh asked.

"Nothing," Gwen said.

"Mom promised she'd stop asking me to bake things or do crafts or go places if I went for a walk every day. And I've been walking. Every. Single. Day."

"Good!" Josh smiled. "Walking is a great mood stabilizer."

"Are you saying I'm unstable?" Abby asked, her tone spiky.

Josh looked surprised, and Gwen felt a stab of vindictive pleasure. Usually, Abby reserved her vitriol for Gwen. She was more than happy for her husband to be on the receiving end of it for once.

"Of course not, Abs. I just want you to feel better."

"And if I don't ever feel better? Then what?"

Josh sighed and took a long drink from his beer. "I know it might not feel like it now, but you will eventually get past this.

There's that saying about time being the great healer. There's a lot of truth to that. Life is long. The pain will lessen, a little bit at a time, and then one day you'll be surprised to realize it's not there anymore."

"Thanks for the pep talk." Abby's voice was heavy with sarcasm. She turned and stalked out of the room, the dog still trailing after her.

Josh looked at Gwen, shaking his head. "What did I say?"

"Welcome to my world," Gwen replied.

"She doesn't seem like she's getting any better. She's been taking those antidepressants for what, three weeks now?"

"I don't think they're supposed to be a cure-all."

"They don't seem to be a cure-anything."

Yet again, Gwen could feel her temper rising, pushing up inside her, hot and angry. She slapped her hand on the granite counter, trying to ignore how much the gesture stung. "You know what? I'm doing the best I can with her, and, as always, it's never good enough. And over the next two days, I have to stand in this kitchen and cook ridiculous amounts of food that no one will appreciate. So forgive me if I'm not in the mood for a parenting lecture at the moment."

"I'm not lecturing you." Josh stared at her with that familiar expression—part hurt, part confused—that just irritated Gwen further. "If you don't want to cook, don't cook. We'll go out. I'll make reservations somewhere."

"Right. And what am I supposed to do with the twelve-pound turkey and ten tons of vegetables I bought today?" Gwen snapped. "Offering to make reservations a week ago would have been great. Today? Not so much."

"I'm just trying to help."

"Do me a favor. Stop helping."

chapter nine

abby

Abby would never admit it to her mother, but she had started looking forward to her daily walk. It wasn't that she enjoyed it exactly. In her current frame of mind, she wouldn't enjoy anything, except maybe hearing that Lana had been run over by a bus or been savaged by a pack of wild dogs. But it was good to get out of the house for a while. Abby still thought about Colin and Lana as she walked, but when she was outdoors the despair didn't weigh on her in the same way. She didn't break down in tears or feel like curling into a ball in the middle of her bed.

Instead, she thought about ways to get even.

She'd heard the saying about living well being the best revenge. Jesus, her mother had even dropped that into a conversation a few days earlier as though it were an original thought instead of total bullshit. The best revenge was getting actual revenge. So Abby spent her time walking thinking about what that would look like. What did Lana deserve for what she'd done? Death? Possibly too drastic, and Abby certainly didn't want to end up in jail. Physical disfigurement? Fun to fantasize about, but Abby doubted she'd have the stomach to pull it off. Ritual humiliation? Now that was an idea. Seeing Lana exposed to the world for the treacherous bitch that she was, was such a delicious thought, Abby almost smiled.

Today, she was striding down the street, heading toward the beach, Izzy trotting by her side. It felt almost pleasant to have the sunshine warming her face, the light salt-tinged breeze ruffling through her hair. She had on her earbuds, listening to music, although less for entertainment and more as a buffer against having to interact with any neighbors who might be outside, watering their potted plants or retrieving groceries from the car. They'd lived on this street all of her life, and she knew almost everyone. The last thing she wanted was to have one of them wave her down and ask how college was going or what her plans were for after graduation. They'd certainly never believe what that nice Abby Landon, the girl they'd called on dozens of times to babysit their children or take care of their pets while they went on vacation, was actually thinking about.

Revenge, she thought, the word rippling pleasantly through her thoughts. *What would the perfect revenge be for a venomous little pit viper like Lana?*

The first step was figuring out what would most humiliate Lana. She was shameless, both in her lack of morality and her constant need for attention. Every picture she posted on social media was just begging for people to make comments like, *You're so beautiful!* and *The prettiest girl on campus!* It was nauseating. Actually...maybe that was the best way to hurt her, Abby thought. Somehow find a way to get people to stop showering Lana with compliments. But how exactly was she supposed to go about making that happen?

She supposed she could start a rumor about Lana, something

dark and shameful. Something along the lines of accusing Lana of having cheated her way into school or that she had an STD and was knowingly passing it on to her sexual partners. Abby mused on this for a moment, imagining that story spreading around campus and Lana having to face the people whispering about her, casting her horrified looks. It was a tempting thought. Abby even knew how she could pull it off. All she'd have to do was mention it to someone like Lindsay Royce or Jadyn Williams, neither of whom had ever been able to keep a secret.

There was an obvious flaw with this plan. If she did tell Lindsay or Jadyn, they might—and probably even would—also tell everyone that Abby was the one who was behind the gossip. The story might spin out of her control, to one about how Abby she was so pathetic that she'd first dropped out of school, then stooped to making up ugly rumors about Lana.

Which would have the unfortunate fact of being true.

Abby and Izzy turned onto the road that led to the beach. It was a longer walk than she'd undertaken in the past few weeks, but her revenge fantasies were giving her an unexpected burst of energy. Suddenly she wanted to see the broad expanse of the blue-green ocean, to feel the waves lap over her feet while she stared into the abyss of rolling water where it met the cloud-thick sky. Besides, the longer she stayed away, the less likely her mother would try to rope her into participating in the Thanksgiving prep work. Gwen had stayed true to her word and had mostly stopped trying to force Abby into spending time together. However, Abby knew how much her mother hated Thanksgiving. When faced with a turkey to stuff, and all the side dishes to make, she might forget her pledge to leave Abby alone.

What kind of a person hates Thanksgiving, anyway? Abby wondered. *What is* wrong *with my mother?* Weren't moms supposed to get off on holiday, forced-family-togetherness shit?

Abby reached an intersection and hit the button to trigger

the walk light. She waited a minute for the walk signal to light up, then stepped into the road. Almost as soon as she did, an old woodie SUV with surfboards sticking out the back window careened wildly around the corner. Abby just managed to jump back on the curb in time to avoid being hit, pulling Izzy back with her. She stared after the woodie, which accelerated down the road, its tires squealing as it went.

"Asshole!" Abby's pulse was pounding, and she pressed a hand against her chest. She had been within a moment, an inch even, of being splattered on the road.

How would Colin feel if he learned I died? she wondered, then instantly hated herself for that being her first thought. He probably wouldn't care. Even worse, he and Lana would pretend-console each other about her tragic and untimely death. Maybe she'd even make Lana's Instagram feed. She could just see it, a picture of Lana lip-glossed and shiny-haired making her sad face. *#tragedy #embracelife #seizetheday #nofilters.*

Abby looked around to make sure that there weren't any more out-of-control cars in the vicinity. She was depressed, she knew. But she wasn't ready to die.

She and Izzy walked for another ten minutes, Abby still mulling over possible revenge strategies and rejecting them all—her best schemes were too risky or too extreme—until they reached the entrance to the beach parking lot. She turned into it, moving from the concrete sidewalk to the blacktop edged in sand and sea grass beyond. The boardwalk, which stretched over the dunes through a thicket of sea grape bushes growing on either side, was just ahead of her. Abby paused while Izzy relieved herself. She glanced around at the cars in the parking lot. She wanted to see if the woodie that had nearly run her over was there. Surfers did come to this beach, although she rarely saw the waves high enough to attract the more serious ones.

She did not see the woodie that nearly hit her.

She did, however, see a car that looked surprisingly like her father's.

Abby stared at it. Why would her father be at the beach on a workday? Even though it was the day before Thanksgiving, he'd gone into the office as usual. There were always a few kids who had broken brackets that needed replacing ahead of the four-day holiday weekend. Abby took a few steps closer, wondering if it was just a car that looked like her dad's. He wasn't the only person in town who drove a silver Mercedes sedan. But then she saw the Florida State University sticker on the back window. Her father had bought it at the university store the day they dropped her off freshman year.

Abby moved even closer, close enough to see that, yes, it was her father sitting in the driver's seat. Even though he was turned away from her, she recognized the back of his head, and the blue-and-white-striped shirt he'd left the house wearing that morning. She was about to walk over, and ask him what he was doing there, but she stopped suddenly.

He wasn't alone.

There was someone sitting in the passenger's seat next to him.

It was a woman with shoulder-length, wavy blond hair. Abby couldn't see the woman's face, but it definitely wasn't her mother, who had short dark hair.

Then, with dawning horror, Abby realized that her father and the blonde were *kissing*.

Abby pivoted and hurried away toward the boardwalk, pulling Izzy along after her. As soon as she reached it, she started to run, her feet thumping loudly on the wooden boards until she got to the beach. She kicked off her sneakers, peeled off her socks and unhooked the dog's leash. Izzy was overjoyed. She loved to play on the beach and headed straight to the water, romping in circles on the wet sand. Abby followed her, striding down to the coastline until she was knee-deep in the cold seawater. Abby wrapped her arms around herself, staring out at the horizon, a sharp line that divided the water from the sky, her heart pounding in her chest.

Her father was having an affair?

No, she thought. That wasn't possible. But if he wasn't…what was he doing kissing a woman in a beach parking lot?

Abby stood frozen, not sure what she should do. Should she go back out there and confront him? She pictured herself doing just that—rapping her fist against the car window, the two of them startling apart, her asking him what the hell he was doing. But, for some reason, she couldn't seem to move. She realized why. If she did confront him, it would make it real, and she wasn't ready for any of this to be real. After everything that she'd been through over the past few weeks, she couldn't handle her family spiraling into a crisis. Not now.

But…who was the blonde? Was her father in love with her? How long had this affair—just thinking the word caused her stomach to curdle—been going on? Had he done this before? And did her mother know about it?

No, she was pretty sure Gwen didn't know. Abby had long suspected that her parents were not happily married. She'd seen other couples, parents of her friends, who were affectionate with one another, who kissed hello and goodbye, who would rest their hands on each other's back or leg while sitting on the couch watching television. She couldn't remember the last time she'd seen her parents touch, much less kiss. But Gwen had never been particularly affectionate with anyone. The only time she was when she was in public, when people were watching. Then she might rest a hand on Josh's back or curl her arm through his. Abby had always found this pretense a little creepy.

But if they were that unhappily married, why hadn't they gotten a divorce? Surely that would be the more honorable thing for her father to do before he started making out with random women in parking lots.

Abby took a few steps back, away from the water's edge, to

sit on a dry ledge of sand as she watched Izzy still playing happily in the shallows. The dog had found a nice patch of seaweed and began to roll herself in it.

She realized that she was trapped there for the moment. If she walked off the beach, she'd risk running into her father and the woman, and she had already decided she wasn't ready to deal with that. Abby wasn't ready to deal with any of it. She wished there was some way she could unknow it all, but of course that was impossible.

Think, she told herself. *What do I do?*

Suddenly she knew exactly what she had to do. She needed to find out who this woman was. That was definitely the first step. Once she found out the woman's identity…well, she'd figure out what to do with the information when she had it. Maybe then she'd feel up to confronting her father at that point.

Her father. What was he thinking? She thought she knew him, thought she knew his character. He'd always been decent and kind. He would never do anything to hurt his family… except that was exactly what he was doing. Was Abby destined to be wrong about everyone, to never truly know anyone? Would she just go through life being blindsided by the people she loved?

Abby sat for a long time, working out a plan on how she'd discover the woman's identity. It shouldn't be that hard. She'd just follow her father, like a detective, until the next time he met up with her. Then she'd figure out who the woman was.

She finally stood and brushed the sand from her bottom and legs. Abby whistled for Izzy, who for once obediently came as soon as she was called, her tongue lolling out of her mouth. Abby hooked the leash back on her collar, and then they retraced their steps back up the beach. She thrust her still sandy feet into her socks and sneakers and headed down the boardwalk. When she reached the parking lot, her father's car was gone and she let out a breath she hadn't realized she'd been holding.

It only occurred to her later, while she was walking home, that it had been the longest stretch of time in weeks where she hadn't thought once of Colin and Lana.

One betrayal had chased the other right out of her mind.

chapter ten

nora

"Everything looks fantastic," Maddie said, admiring the Thanksgiving spread covering the large island in the middle of the Hollidays' kitchen. "Are you photographing it before we eat?"

"No," Nora said. "I took photographs of the apple-cranberry pie yesterday, to post either closer to Christmas or maybe even next Thanksgiving. But my holiday blogging has been a little lame this year. I just reposted an article I wrote on the pros and cons of turkey brine, then another for a recipe of sweet potato soufflé that I made a few years ago."

"That's not like you."

"I know. I haven't been on my game the past few weeks."

Nora stared down at the meal that she had cooked for her family and guests only to realize that she had more or less done it all on autopilot. She'd managed to roast a turkey, make two kinds of stuffing, five side dishes and three different desserts without even thinking about it. She supposed it wasn't that crazy—cooking was her job, or, at least, a large part of it. But these days, there was only one thing occupying her thoughts, and it pushed everything else to the edges.

Josh.

She thought about him constantly. His smile, his touch, his scent. She rewound and replayed every conversation they had, every moment they spent together. He was there when she was basting the turkey, when she was dropping Katie off at volleyball, and every single night when she was in bed trying to fall asleep, and, more often than not, failing to do so.

Nora and Josh had managed to meet up the day before, and like the few other times they'd seen one another since Orlando, they hadn't been able to stop touching one another. They were like a pair of teenagers making out in a car. Yesterday, Josh had suggested that the next time, they should meet at a hotel. The idea filled Nora with both incandescent joy and absolute terror. If they kept going down this crazy path—and even in her current state of all-consuming infatuation, she knew *this* was crazy—something bad was eventually going to happen. They would get caught. People would be hurt.

"Why not?" Maddie asked, reaching for a carrot stick from the crudités platter and dipping it in blue-cheese-and-shallot dip.

"What?" Nora asked. That was another problem. She had been finding it almost impossible to follow conversations lately.

"You just said you've been off your game." Maddie frowned. "You've definitely seemed distracted lately."

"I am. I think it's just the holidays. They always throw me into a tizzy."

"Oh, please. You always have your holiday shopping done by August."

"No, I don't." Nora laughed as she poured herself a glass of the wine Maddie had brought as her contribution to the feast.

Maddie had asked ahead if that was okay—Carter and alcohol would probably always be a fraught combination—but Nora had readily agreed. It was a holiday, after all, and maybe the alcohol would help her get through it. "What are the kids doing?"

"Playing video games in the den. Leo and James are in awe of Katie's skill at gunning down bad guys."

"I bet. I never promised she was a good influence."

"She's great with them. They hero-worship her. All of your kids, actually."

"Is Matt in there, too?"

"Yes, but he's just mostly watching. Where's Dylan?"

"At his girlfriend's house. He promised he'd be back in time for dinner, but who knows with Dylan. Staying on schedule has never been his strong suit."

Carter walked in. He was freshly out of the shower and looking handsome in a navy blue polo shirt and khakis. *But why does he always look so smug?* Nora wondered. *After all of the ways he's screwed up his life, how can he still feel so superior to everyone else?* She stared at him, suddenly resenting his presence in her kitchen. In her life, for that matter.

This is not good, she thought.

"Maddie! I thought I heard your voice." Carter kissed Maddie on the cheek. "When did you get here?"

"Hi, Carter. Just a few minutes ago."

"And the kids are with you today?"

"Yes, I told you they were coming," Nora said. She'd seen the shadow cross over her friend's face, and was suddenly furious with Carter for reminding Maddie that her life had so completely changed over the past year that it was no longer a given that her children would be with her on a holiday. Then she remembered her own treachery, and the guilt of that doused her anger. "They're all in the den. Will you go see if the boys want something to drink, and make sure Katie's letting them take a turn at whatever hideous video game she's playing?"

"Sure thing." Carter glanced at the glass of wine in Nora's hand, but didn't comment on it.

Good, she thought. *Don't you dare.*

Once he'd ambled out of the kitchen, calling out to the kids with offers of soda or juice, Maddie turned to Nora.

"The wine," she said, her voice low. "You're sure it's okay?"

Nora shrugged, then nodded. "It's not like he's never been around alcohol since he's been sober."

"I don't want to cause any problems."

"You're not. Carter's always been the cause of his own problems." Nora was unable to keep the bitterness out of her voice. But even as she spoke, she realized that even that was no longer true. There was a time when it had been—Carter had been the fuckup, and she'd been the one who'd taken him back, who'd agreed to keep the marriage together. Nora the saint. But Nora had blown up her saint status the moment she stepped on that elevator in Orlando with Josh. Then again, maybe it never had been true. She'd never really forgiven Carter. Her resentment from those years, from the things he'd done, had caused her feelings for him to ice over. She'd stayed in the marriage, true…but if she was being honest, she knew she'd left it emotionally years ago.

"He looks good, though. Healthy. He's lost weight, hasn't he?"

"Yes. He's been going to the gym a lot lately." Nora turned to look at the dishes lining the counter. The turkey was almost done. Once it was out of the oven, the various side dishes would all go in, for varying times. She had a feeling she was forgetting something, and wondered what it was. Whatever it was, it probably didn't matter. There was more than enough food. Her phone, sitting on the counter on the other side of the kitchen, suddenly chirped, signaling the arrival of a text.

"Do you want me to get it for you?" Maddie asked, starting toward it. "It's probably Dylan."

"No!" Nora realized that she'd raised her voice. "I'm sorry. I'll check it in a minute."

Maddie stared worriedly at her. "What's going on? You've been acting weird for weeks, and don't tell me it's the holidays. That's bullshit, and you know it."

Nora gnawed at her lip. It was so tempting, so incredibly tempting, to confess, to be able to talk about Josh with anyone. But she couldn't, she knew that. Maybe she could tell a half-truth.

"To be honest," Nora said, her voice lowered, "things haven't been great between Carter and me. For a while now."

"I know. I've always hoped that things would improve between you two, especially now that Carter's sober."

"I hoped so, too. But…" Nora stopped, and glanced around to make sure that neither her husband nor one of the kids had wandered in. "He's been gambling."

"Are you serious?"

"Yes. I think it's even worse than I know. I noticed some unusual withdrawals he made on one of our accounts. When I asked him about them, he got defensive. He said that the money was for lunches, Christmas presents, things like that."

"And you don't believe him."

"The only person Carter buys a Christmas present for is me. And he never does that until Christmas Eve day. I handle everything else—gifts for his mom, his sister, her kids. It was thousands of dollars, Maddie."

"Jesus." Maddie shook her head and took a sip of her wine. "People can become financially ruined by that."

"Tell me about it. If it is as bad as I think it may be, hasn't he just traded in one addiction for another? I don't know how much longer I can live with that."

"You're thinking about leaving?"

Nora shrugged helplessly. "I don't know. Maybe. I haven't made any decisions."

"I think you have reason to be concerned, and I don't want you to think I'm judging that. But honey—" Maddie reached out and rested a hand on Nora's arm "—divorce is harder than you think."

"I know. I've seen what you've had to deal with. Other friends, too. I know it's not a choice you enter into lightly."

"That's not what I meant. It's not just the impact it has on your children or having to go through the hell of divorce court or even how lonely life can be. That's all awful enough. But the hardest part, or at least the hardest for me, was how suddenly my role in life changed. Before, I had what I thought was a firm place in the world. I was a wife, a mother, a homeowner, and suddenly... I wasn't any of those things. It just untethered me. Sometimes it feels like my entire life was just erased."

"You're still a mother," Nora protested.

"Yes, of course, but the kids are getting older and more independent with every passing day. One day in the not too distant future they'll leave for college, and I'll be truly alone."

"No way. You're gorgeous and smart. I'm sure you'll meet someone amazing."

Maddie shrugged. "Maybe I will, maybe I won't. But that's not even my point. This isn't about the presence or absence of a man in my life. It's that I used to know who I was, know what my place in the world was. Suddenly, all of that has changed."

"You're still you."

"Am I? Here's a fun fact—when you're single, a lot of your married acquaintances begin to view you as a potential adversary. As though Allen's leaving me means that I'm going to go after their husbands. I'm suddenly seen as dangerous while Allen got to just skate away to his happy new life."

Nora flinched at Maddie's reference to going after someone's husband. Wasn't that exactly what she was doing? If she and Josh were caught—this thought caused her a jolt of panic— how would she be viewed? As a bad person, or even worse—as some sort of immoral slut? Maddie had been the wronged one in her marriage, and she was being ostracized. Nora could only imagine how much worse it would be for her.

"You said you like being back at work." Maddie was a Realtor, although she'd stopped working when her children were born. She'd returned to her old real estate agency a few months earlier. "You've seemed happier since you started."

Maddie shrugged one shoulder. "I think it's definitely elevated my mood to have some structure to my days, especially on the weeks when I don't have the boys. But I'm a pretty long way from happy."

"I know. It's been a tough year."

"Am I interrupting?" Carter asked, breezing back into the kitchen. "All of the kids are demanding sodas. Apparently, I'm their waiter."

"No, come on in," Maddie said, breaking away from Nora's embrace. "I was just complaining to your wife about the woes of divorced life. I'm sure I'm boring the shit out of her."

"I'm sure you're not," Carter said. He walked over to Nora and wrapped an arm around her waist. "But it's good to give her the downsides of divorce. I've always been afraid that one day she'll leave me."

"What?" Nora asked.

"Kidding, honey." Carter kissed her on the cheek. "Just kidding. You and I will be together forever."

It took all of Nora's self-control not to shudder at his touch.

chapter eleven

gwen

A few weeks before Christmas, Gwen drove across the state to visit her sister. Christine, who had never married and shared her home with three pit bulls and a one-eared cat, lived in Clearwater. She worked as a court reporter, a job she hated, but which paid her well enough to afford a small house with a fenced-in backyard where her rescue animals sunned themselves. Gwen had never envied Christine's life. Her younger sister had always been sharp-tongued and short-tempered, and never seemed to take joy in anything.

Then again, Gwen thought, *when was the last time I felt joy? When have I felt any real emotion, other than regret?*

For that matter, did regret count as an emotion? Gwen wasn't sure it did. It was more a constant state of being.

However, suddenly Gwen found herself desperately jealous of her sister's freedom. Not that Christine ever went anywhere—

she thought kenneling her pets was on par with child abuse. In fact, the way her sister anthropomorphized her pets had always annoyed Gwen. Christine even dressed her dogs in outfits—including sunglasses—and took endless hours of video of them, ever hopeful that they'd go viral on YouTube, which they never did.

But at least Christine had the option to walk out her door, head off on an adventure. Which, from Gwen's current perspective, was the most liberating possible position to be in.

The drive across the state took just under three hours, and it was early afternoon when Gwen pulled her Jeep Grand Cherokee into Christine's driveway. Her sister lived in a tidy bungalow painted an unfortunate shade of turquoise blue. Her front patio was covered with terra-cotta pots filled with flowers and herbs. A set of wind chimes hung near the door. Gwen got out of her car and retrieved her suitcase from the trunk.

"I was starting to think you'd gotten lost. I expected you here an hour ago."

Gwen looked up to see her sister striding toward her, followed by a trio of dogs. Christine was a large woman who wore oversize T-shirts over leggings when she wasn't working. She refused to color the gray out of her hair as a point of pride. Christine gave her a perfunctory hug, then grabbed Gwen's suitcase from her.

"I've got this. Come in, I just made some tea."

Gwen suppressed a sigh. It was almost certain to be some sort of herbal tea that tasted like boiled weeds, no doubt. She'd have preferred to be offered a glass of wine, but she'd already resigned herself that putting up with her sister's affected bohemianism was the price she was going to have to pay for a few days of freedom. It would be worth it. Besides, she'd thought ahead and brought along a bag of groceries, including three bottles of wine, a box of petit fours, a selection of charcuterie meats and cheeses, and a baguette. At least she wouldn't starve.

Gwen sat at the table, petting one of the dogs who'd positioned himself beside her, resting his head heavily on her thigh and drooling on her jeans. Christine brought over a teapot, two mugs and a plate of fig bars, and sat down across from her.

"You don't take sugar, do you?" Christine asked. "If you do, I think I might have some somewhere."

"No, that's okay." Gwen sipped her tea, which was surprisingly good. "What is this?"

"Raspberry."

"It's delicious," Gwen said. She took a bite out of the fig bar. "Where did you get these? They remind me of the Cape."

"I had them shipped down from a bakery there."

"I've never thought of doing that! I always loved them when we were kids. I don't think I've ever seen them sold anywhere else."

Gwen's original family, which consisted of herself, Christine and their unhappily married parents, had lived for a time in Chatham, a small town in Cape Cod, Massachusetts. Their parents divorced when Gwen was a freshman in high school and Christine was in seventh grade, and the girls had moved with their mother to West Palm Beach to live with their grandparents. The plan had been that they'd stay there only a short time until their mother worked out her next move, but that had never happened. Their mother had still been living in her parents' home ten years later when she died in a car accident. As for their father, Gwen hadn't spoken to him since the day they'd left the Cape. She had no idea where he was now, but she assumed he was still alive. She and Christine would probably have been notified if he had died.

"I know. Me, too. They're one of the few happy memories I have of that place. That, and the beaches, although I don't know how we ever tolerated swimming in the water. It was freezing even in the middle of the summer," Christine said.

Gwen smiled. "And full of sharks."

"You're right. We were brave to even put a toe in."

"I don't think we thought about sharks back then. Not even after *Jaws* came out. Now, they tag them and monitor them, so you can see photos on the internet of how many there are out there, swimming just off the coast."

Christine shuddered. "I don't want to think about it."

"I don't know. At least getting eaten by a shark would make a good story. Better than being bored to death."

"Speaking of which, how's Josh?"

Christine and Josh didn't *not* get along, but they'd never been close. Christine had made it clear through comments she'd made over the years that she found it annoying Josh was such a people pleaser.

"Why is it so important that everyone likes him?" she'd asked more than once. "He's like that kid in high school who's always making jokes so that everyone thinks he's the greatest guy in the world."

Josh never criticized Christine, not even in private, but once after she'd departed from a Christmas visit a few years back, he had asked Gwen if her sister had always been so bitter. She supposed that could be viewed as a criticism, but the truth was, Christine had been in an incredibly sour mood the entire visit. She'd kept up a constant stream of barbed comments about the size of their house, the number of electronics they allowed their children to utilize and how rowdy Simon was, even though he was only ten at the time. Josh had seemed more curious than disparaging.

"You never liked Josh, did you?" Gwen now asked.

Her sister immediately bristled. Gwen should have anticipated this response. Christine had always been quick to become prickly.

"I never said that."

"I know," Gwen agreed. "You didn't. It's just a feeling I've always gotten."

"He's fine." Christine hesitated. "I mean, he's always been perfectly pleasant to me."

"That's why I've never understood why you don't like him."

Christine sipped her tea. After a few moments she said, "I guess I just never thought the two of you seemed right for one another. He wanted the whole suburban-dream life, while I always thought you…" Her voice trailed off.

"You always thought I'd what?"

"You always had such big dreams when we were kids. I always assumed you'd do something different with your life. Something more out of the ordinary."

"I may have talked a good game, but I was a paralegal when Josh and I met. I wasn't exactly setting the world on fire."

"That's just because Mom pushed you into being a paralegal, just like she pushed me into becoming a court reporter."

"I don't remember it like that."

"You don't? How's that possible? She would go on and on about how we needed to be smarter than she had been. By which she meant becoming proficient in a boring but high demand job so that we would never be in the position of having to rely on a man to take care of us."

"I know Mom was the one who suggested I go to the community college." Gwen had assumed she'd go away to college, but none of the schools she'd applied to had offered her a large enough scholarship. It had been—and probably still was—the most bitter disappointment of her life. "I don't remember Mom pushing me into being a paralegal. That was my choice."

Christine shook her head vehemently. "That's not what happened at all. You originally signed up for a photography class and another in journalism. Mom told you that if you were going to take throwaway courses, you'd have to move out of Grandpa's house to find a way to support yourself. She told me the same thing when it was my turn. I actually signed up for court reporting because it took less time to become certified. By then you were gone, and I didn't want to spend another minute living under the same roof as her."

"How do I not remember this?" Gwen asked.

"When you've had the sort of childhood we had, it's normal to suppress memories." Christine took another fig bar from the plate and bit into it. Once she'd chewed and swallowed, she continued. "It's why I've been in therapy for years and have repeatedly suggested that you do the same. We've both had a lot of shit to handle. I deal with it by, well, overeating." She smiled faintly, holding up the fig bar. "And by adopting dogs. And not knowing how to have normal relationships."

"And me?"

"You compensate by suppressing your memories, running obsessively and marrying a person you weren't in love with because he offered you security. Even though security was the last thing you actually wanted out of life."

Gwen let her sister's words—which, for once, were not barbed with acid, but which sounded almost kind—flow over her. She tried to remember the person she'd been at the age of twenty-three, when she met Josh. She remembered being bored in her job at the litigation firm. That was true. But she had never thought she'd made the decision to be with Josh, to marry him, with any sort of gold-digging calculation. He'd still been in dental school back then, so it wasn't like those early years were filled with luxuries.

I must have loved him once, she thought. *Right? Or as close to feeling love as I'm capable of?*

"Do you ever wonder why Mom stayed with Dad for as long as she did?" Gwen asked instead.

"What do you mean?"

"Christine. He *beat* her."

"You mean, *she* beat *him.*" Christine stared at Gwen. "Mom was the violent one."

"No, she wasn't. I mean, I remember her throwing plates at

him once, but I don't think she ever managed to hit him with one. Either she had terrible aim or he had excellent reflexes."

"You seriously don't remember this. Jesus, Gwen. I know you think I've indulged in too much therapy, but I probably should have strong-armed you into it years ago. It's seriously fucked up that you don't remember this."

Gwen shook her head as though that would somehow dispel what her sister was saying. "Mom had bruises on her face."

"She did those to herself."

"*What?* How is that possible?"

"She'd slam her head against a wall. She did it all the time. It was incredibly creepy." Christine shivered, and suddenly Gwen realized that her own skin was rising in goose bumps. "She'd bang it over and over again, and then laugh that horrible hollow laugh, and say to Dad, 'They're going to arrest you for that one. And this one, too.' Then she'd slam her head one more time."

"But...wait." Gwen suddenly felt like her memories had become slippery things that she couldn't grasp on to. "I clearly remember Dad pushing Mom up against a door...we were screaming at him to stop."

"You were screaming at him. He was trying to stop her from hurting herself."

Gwen thumped her own hand against her head, as if that would somehow unscramble her thoughts. Her father had abused their mother. It was something she had always known, a part of her history. A screwed up history, to be sure, but something she could at least point to as an explanation for why she'd made the choices she had. Had she somehow gotten it wrong?

"I don't remember it that way."

"That's weird," Christine said. "How could you forget it? I mean... I actually wish I could. It scarred me. I always assumed it scarred you, too, and that's why we never talked about it."

"I just remember Dad shouting...holding Mom against the

door…telling her that if she didn't stop, he was going to hurt her."

"No. He said if she didn't stop, she was going to get hurt. Meaning…she'd hurt herself. It frightened him when she got like that."

"But all those times the police came," Gwen said, and the same sickening shame she'd felt as a child spread through her now nearly fifty-year-old self. "They always arrested Dad."

"Right. Because Mom was the one who was bruised."

"But why would she do that?"

Christine sighed and lifted one shoulder. "She was fucked up, Gwen. And an alcoholic. She was probably bipolar, undiagnosed obviously, and self-medicated with alcohol."

"I don't remember any of this."

"And again, I wish I didn't remember as much as I do."

"But if you're right…why would Dad just let us leave with her?"

"What choice did he have? It was the eighties, when fathers were rarely awarded custody. Besides, by that point, Dad had a history of domestic violence arrests."

"But…he never called us. He never came to see us. He just let us go. Dropped out of our lives."

Christine hesitated. "I haven't told you this, but I've been in touch with Dad. He even came down to visit for a weekend."

Gwen could only stare at her sister, as a mixture of grief and confusion, and, yes, jealousy, washed over her. After so many years of learning to tamp down her feelings, learning to shut them off, this was suddenly too much all at once.

"He came to see you?"

"I invited him. It's not like he just showed up on my doorstep."

"When?"

"A few months ago. We've been talking on the phone for

about the past year. As I'm sure you can imagine, he has a lot of regrets."

"You mean, like abandoning his children to a woman who—if you're right—was violent and possibly crazy?"

Christine cupped her hands around her mug, looking imploringly at her sister. "Obviously, he has a different perspective on that. He felt like we were taken from him, and then never reached out to stay in touch."

"We were kids."

"We were teenagers."

"And the world was different than it is today. There weren't cell phones or social media. It wasn't as easy to stay in touch."

"It wasn't exactly the Dark Ages. We did have a telephone."

"And he could have called us or even written. He knew where we were."

"Dad says he sent us cards. Mom must have confiscated them."

Gwen stood suddenly to walk over to the counter where she'd set down the reusable grocery bag full of goodies she'd brought. She pulled out a bottle of merlot and turned to her sister. "Do you have a corkscrew?"

"In the drawer next to the sink."

Gwen rummaged around in the drawer until she found the corkscrew, then expertly popped the cork out of the bottle. "Do you want a glass?"

"It's a little early for me."

"It is for me, too, but this conversation seems to call for it."

"I'll have a small glass. The wineglasses are in that cupboard to your right."

Gwen knew her sister well enough to ignore the request for a small glass, and poured them each a generous portion. She set the glasses down on the table next to their tea mugs.

"What was he like?" she asked.

"Old." Christine smiled. "I hadn't seen him in thirty years, after all. I'd expected him to have aged, obviously, but I guess

I wasn't expecting an old man to show up. But he was fine. A little nervous, as you can imagine."

"Where has he been?" Gwen waved a hand in front of her. "What's he been doing for, oh, the past three-plus decades?"

"He still lives on the Cape. He's retired. Oh, he remarried a while back to a woman named Jean. She came with him. She seemed nice."

"I'm so glad everything's worked out so well for him."

"Everything's worked out well for you, too."

"You think so?" Now that her emotion chip had been activated, Gwen was finding it hard to get herself back under control. "Other than the fact that Abby has dropped out of school, thereby ruining her future, and makes it clear on a daily basis that she thinks I'm the worst mother in the world. That Simon cares more about playing video games than getting decent grades, so his future is probably fucked, as well. Then there's the fact that it's entirely possible that Josh is having an affair, and I'm not sure if I even care at this point. Other than that, my life is *great*. It's all exactly how I hoped it would turn out, minus, you know, small things like personal success and self-fulfillment."

Christine stared at her, picked up her wineglass and took an enormous gulp from it.

"I think you'd better start from the beginning," she said.

chapter twelve

---

abby

Abby hadn't made any progress in uncovering the identity of the wavy-haired blonde woman. It wasn't for lack of trying. Every day she'd drive toward downtown Shoreham, or what passed as a downtown in their small town. Her dad's orthodontic practice was located three blocks south, in a two-story office building that also housed several law practices and a store that sold health supplements. She'd circle past the building, hoping to catch him as he was leaving. It would have been preferable to just sit in the parking lot and wait him out, but the one day she tried that, a few of his assistants walked out heading downtown at lunchtime. Abby had to duck so they wouldn't see her. It was one of the problems of living in a small town—it made it hard to hide. She tried to think about it like a detective would, and figure out when would be the most opportune times for her father to sneak away.

His afternoons were always booked up with after-school appointments. Mornings were equally unlikely. Surely it would be weird for her dad to arrive at work, then leave immediately. Plus he usually blocked out his morning appointments for new patients who were having their braces put on. That left midday as the most likely time when he wouldn't be swamped by work, nor would it be odd if he left the office for a period of time. He could always say he was meeting a friend for lunch or had an errand to run before the afternoon rush.

"I'm like the Sherlock fucking Holmes of infidelity," Abby said to herself.

Except clearly she wasn't. If her dad was still meeting the blonde woman, Abby had yet to catch him in the act. Or to catch him again, she reminded herself. She had already caught him once, unless she really had lost her mind and imagined the entire thing, which was not a possibility she really wanted to dwell on. The truth was, she still wasn't sleeping well, and the medication she was taking continued to make her head foggy. Was it possible she had somehow dreamed up the entire interlude, in some sort of sleep-starved, betrayal-obsessed daydream?

No, she thought, gripping the steering wheel tightly. *I saw what I saw, 100 percent. Even if that does sound like a fucking Dr. Seuss book.*

Picking a midday window was logical, but again, it left her open to the chance of being spotted by one of her dad's employees venturing out at lunchtime. Abby was forced to slowly drive past the building, circling around side streets, then back again. It was brutally boring, but Abby was determined. She still wasn't sure what she'd do if she did catch her father or figured out who the woman was. Would she confront him? Abby had no idea.

Her mother had taken note of Abby's sudden daytime trips out, but she'd seemed pleased rather than suspicious.

"It's good to see you getting out," she'd said. "Where are you off to?"

"It depends." Abby shrugged. "Mostly, I just drive around."

"I think it's a good sign."

Her mother's forced cheeriness irritated Abby. "It doesn't mean I'm ready to go back to school or anything."

"All I mean is that it's a step in the right direction."

Abby had rolled her eyes and left without another word.

If only you knew what I saw, Abby thought as she angrily backed her car out of the Landon family driveway. She still didn't know why exactly her father's infidelity made her angry at her mother...but for some reason, it did. To an extent that almost frightened her.

After several weeks of unsuccessful stakeouts, Abby was starting to give up hope. Maybe she was just watching at the wrong times. Or maybe it had been a onetime thing. Did middle-aged people really do that? Randomly hook up with one another in beach parking lots? The idea made Abby feel faintly queasy.

But then her mother announced she was going out of town for a few days to visit Aunt Christine. This seemed odd. Abby's mother didn't particularly like her sister, and rarely went to see her, much less with almost no advance notice. But Abby instinctively knew that this was it. Her mother's trip would give her father a window of opportunity to see the blonde. She'd just have to be extra vigilant about watching him.

Her mother departed on a Thursday, just after her morning run. Abby waited in her bedroom until Gwen left, the better to avoid any last-minute lectures or queries into whether Abby had called the dean's office at school to see about registering for spring semester. But as soon as she heard the crunch of tires on the gravel driveway, Abby headed to the living room, where she could peer out the window and confirm that her mother was driving away. Izzy trailed after her, looking hopeful that Abby would take her on a walk.

"Not today, girl," Abby said, patting the Labrador's head.

Abby hurried out to her car and headed off to begin her usual routine of driving past her dad's office, occasionally parking across the street within view of the building. After an hour and a half of this, she was starting to get both bored and hungry. She was just about to give up…when she saw her father walk out of the office and head for his silver sedan. Abby checked the time. It was just after noon, so it was also possible he was just going to lunch. Then again, it was possible that he was finally, *finally* leaving for an assignation with the blonde.

She waited until her father had pulled out of his parking lot. He was halfway down the street before she drove after him. She couldn't follow too closely, she knew, but she also needed to keep his car in view. Her father left the downtown area and headed south toward US 1. Abby could feel her pulse pick up, her nerves jangling as she tailed him. She quickly learned it wasn't as easy to follow someone by car as it looked in the movies. There were traffic lights every few blocks, and she had to run two yellow lights in order to keep up with him before finally getting stopped at a red light. Abby hit her hands on the steering wheel in frustration. Had she lost him? But then the light turned green, and she saw that her father was still just ahead of her. He'd been stopped at the same light, but had been blocked from her view by a large Chevrolet Suburban.

Then, it happened.

Her father turned off US 1 onto Murray Street, and into the parking lot of a small motel Abby had never noticed before. There was a sign in front advertising it as the Seabreeze Hotel, along with another sign announcing that it offered free Wi-Fi and had vacancies. Abby pulled over on the shoulder of the road, not wanting to risk being seen, but she needn't have worried. Her dad parked his car, got out and headed into the hotel lobby without looking behind him.

Dumb move, Dad, Abby thought. You didn't live in a town the size of Shoreham without perfecting what Abby and her friends had always called the "small-town look around," which meant always checking over your shoulder to see who was nearby before you did or said anything controversial.

But what now? He was inside the hotel. What if the blonde was already inside waiting for him? Abby cursed herself for not paying more attention to the other cars that had been parked at the beach that day she'd seen them together, so she could compare them to the vehicles in the hotel parking lot. Obviously, her detective skills needed honing.

But just then, a blue Nissan Murano drove by Abby's car, and pulled into the Seabreeze Hotel's parking lot. While Abby watched, her pulse thrumming, a slim woman with shoulder-length wavy blond hair emerged from the SUV.

At least the woman had the sense to look around to see if anyone was watching. Abby quickly scrunched down out of view and waited for a full five beats before she peeked up again. The blonde woman was gone, presumably also having disappeared into the hotel.

Abby got out of her car and tentatively made her way toward the blue Murano. It didn't have any distinguishing bumper stickers like My Child Is an Honor Student at Shoreham Middle School. And when Abby worked up the nerve to look inside, she didn't see any useful clues, other than a bag from a sporting equipment store in the back cargo space, a pair of soccer balls and a duffel bag embroidered with a volleyball and the slogan, Hit Like a Girl. Abby deduced that the woman was either extremely sporty or, more likely, a mom.

This realization caused hot anger to snake through Abby. She didn't know why the woman being a mother made it worse, but somehow it did. They were both *parents*. They should know better.

Abby wasn't sure what she should do next. She could go into the hotel and ask the clerk at the reception desk about the two people who had just checked in, but she doubted the clerk would give her any information. She could wait in the parking lot and confront her father and the woman when they emerged. But the idea of standing there, while her father was inside, probably having sex, made Abby feel physically ill. Finally, she took out her phone, tapped open the notes app and wrote down the Murano's license plate. Then, she returned to her car and drove back home to plan her next move.

chapter thirteen

nora

Nora lay in Josh's arms, feeling both raw with emotion and more relaxed than she had been in months—years, even. She didn't know what it was about this man, but just being in his presence calmed her. The worries that constantly scrolled through her mind—*Is the content on my blog getting stale? Has the market for food bloggers become too crowded? Is Dylan going to ruin his life by getting a girl pregnant before he gets out of high school? Is Katie's self-importance a sign of a darker personality trait? Is Matt ever going to come into himself or will his shyness and tendency to retreat from the world cause him a life of loneliness? Will Carter start drinking again, get another DUI and end up in jail this time? Will I end up failing at everything in my life?*—were silenced.

"Are you okay?" Josh murmured into her hair.

"Yes, I'm perfect."

"That was incredible."

Nora nodded against his chest, feeling suddenly shy about the intimacy they had just shared.

"I'm glad you agreed to meet me here today," Josh continued.

The hotel room was small and utilitarian with dark taupe carpeting and drapes, and framed prints of bland beach scenes hanging on the walls. The air conditioner whirred loudly.

"Well, we can't just keep making out in cars all around town."

"No." Josh laughed softly. "That was starting to get frustrating."

"And...here's the thing." Nora pulled away a little so that she could look up at him. He was smiling at her, his eyes soft. "If we keep doing that—or this—we're going to get caught."

Josh's expression immediately sobered. "I know. I've been thinking about that."

"You have?"

"Of course. It's pretty much all I think about. Well. You're pretty much all I think about."

"Oh." Happiness unfurled inside Nora, and she curled back toward him, tucking her head into the crook of his shoulder. "I can't stop thinking about you, either."

"I'm starting to think I'm a little obsessed."

"Me, too. But in a good way."

"The best way. The feelings I'm having for you have made me realize just how miserable I've been. For years, really."

"Yes." Nora exhaled. "I know exactly how you feel."

"Do you ever wish that Gwen and Carter would just disappear? Vanish off the face of the earth?"

Nora stilled. She had wished that. She just wasn't sure she was ready to admit it out loud. Instead, she said, "You were saying that you've been thinking about what will happen if we get caught."

"Yes. I think it's time to tell Gwen."

Nora's heart skittered around. "About me?"

"No, of course not. I wouldn't do that to you. I just think

it's time I told her I'm not happy, and we need to separate. I honestly don't think it will come as that much of a surprise to her. I don't think she's any happier in the marriage than I am."

"Have you talked to her about it before?"

"Separating? No. But, again, I don't think she'll be shocked. Our relationship hasn't been working for a while. Years, really. I've just been hoping that Abby's situation will get sorted out first. I know there's never going to be a perfect time to make the break, but it would be adding more stress to an already high-pressure situation."

"Has she agreed to go back to school for the spring semester?"

Josh shook his head. "No. She's adamant that she's not going back."

"What will her next step be?"

"I want her to enroll in the community college and take courses there for now, so she doesn't get too far behind on her degree. But she won't talk about that, either. Gwen's running out of patience with her. She thinks we should give Abby an ultimatum—go back to school or start looking for a job. But Abby's been emotionally fragile. I'm not sure how hard we should push her."

"Is she still spending all of her time in her room?"

"Actually, no. Gwen said that Abby's been leaving the house every day for hours at a time, but she won't say what she's doing or where she's going. I don't know if that's a good sign or not."

"I know what you mean. When any of my kids start getting secretive, it sets off alarm bells. A certain amount of that is normal for adolescents. But still. It's scary."

"Abby's twenty. Shouldn't she be getting beyond adolescence at this point?"

Nora lifted one bare shoulder. It occurred to her that this entire conversation had been taking place with the two of them naked and curled around one another. It should have felt awkward, but instead, it was remarkably comfortable.

"I've read that kids don't reach mental maturity until the age of twenty-five," Nora commented.

"That would explain a lot." Josh hesitated. "What about you?"

"What about me?"

"I hope this doesn't come across as too intrusive, but…have you thought at all about leaving your husband?"

"Only every day for the past decade."

"Wow. Okay. What's stopped you?"

"The usual. The kids, the house, the difficulty of going through a divorce. My best friend and her husband—well, ex-husband, now—just went through it. It's not easy."

"No, I don't imagine it will be. But you also reach a point where staying is harder than going."

"Are you at that point?"

"I think so, yes. You?"

Nora had often wondered what her twenty-five-year-old self would think of where she would end up in twenty years. She was sure the younger Nora would be horrified, disgusted, to know that her future would be tied to a self-destructive man she didn't love and sometimes had good reason to fear. But that younger Nora lacked perspective and wouldn't understand that you didn't just lose your sense of self overnight. It eroded by tiny grains of sand over the years until you were suddenly in a place where you no longer recognized yourself.

Nora shook her head. "Past it. I wish I'd left years ago."

Nora's family had decorated the house for Christmas a few weekends earlier, and so she returned home to the woodsy scent of their fir tree. Something about the sight of the Christmas decorations—the stockings hanging in the living room, the mercury glass nativity scene set up on a sideboard, the twinkle lights wound around the stair banister—caused her stomach to sour. Nora had always loved Christmas, despite how exhausting it always proved to be, but this year she was already sick to death of it. Was that guilt over her affair, she wondered, or a sign that her marriage really had reached its breaking point?

She went upstairs to shower and change into yoga pants and a T-shirt. Her mind was racing, full of thoughts of Josh—the afternoon they'd spent together, the conversation they'd had. Nora finally decided the only way she'd ever be able to calm down would be to work. She went to the kitchen and pulled out the ingredients for a blueberry slump. It wasn't very Christmasy, but that suited her current mood perfectly.

A slump was similar to a cobbler, but cooked entirely on the stovetop, so the dumpling top was steamed rather than baked. Before Nora started cooking, though, she had to stage the ingredients for photographs, which always took time. The key was to make the assorted ingredients look organized, rather than haphazardly bunched together, which was especially difficult with baked dishes. Flour and sugar were not particularly photogenic, although the whipped cream she'd top it with always looked pretty, rising in white peaks on the whisk of her industrial stainless-steel mixer.

Nora puttered around the kitchen, taking photographs, checking them, and then rearranging the ingredients to see if she could improve on the composition. Finally, when she was satisfied that she had enough decent photos for the blog post, she began to cook. She made the dumplings first, which involved stirring together the flour, sugar and a pinch of salt. Then she folded in a mixture of milk, egg and melted butter until just combined. She stopped several times during this process to take more photographs, and once satisfied, turned her attention to the blueberry filling, which she made in her favorite copper pot. The process of measuring out ingredients, stirring them over a low heat and watching the blueberry mixture gradually turn into a thick syrup was deeply satisfying. Nora could feel herself relax as she worked.

After the slump was complete, Nora was taking a few last shots of it—a few where the dish was set on a blue-and-white-striped dish towel, another few set next to a bowl full of whipped cream—when the back door slammed shut, causing Nora to jump.

"Sorry, the wind blew it." It was Carter, home early from work. "Where is everyone?"

Nora turned away, realizing as she did so that it was her default reaction to her husband these days. He'd walk into a room and she'd instinctively move away, avoiding his gaze. Sitting across the table from him at dinner had become almost intolerable. She could only make her way through it every evening by focusing all of her attention on her children.

"Katie and Dylan are both at practice. Dylan's going to pick her up on his way home, although I should probably send him a text to remind him about that. Matt's up in his room."

"How was your day?"

"Fine."

Carter had moved up behind her without Nora realizing, so when he rested a hand on her waist, she jumped again.

"Are you okay?" Carter turned her gently to face him. He looked anxiously down at her, his eyebrows furrowed. "You haven't seemed yourself lately."

"I haven't?"

"No. You've been...distant."

You have no idea, Nora thought. She felt distinctly uncomfortable at how close her husband was standing to her. She was also suddenly very aware of how much larger he was than her. Panic flickered somewhere deep in the primitive part of her brain that would never, ever forget what he had done to her. She stepped aside, away from his touch.

"I'm fine," she said again. "I just have a lot on my mind. The kids, work, the holidays."

"I was thinking it might be nice to get away for a few days.

Maybe over New Year's. We could head down to the Keys for a few days. How does that sound?"

Nora stared at Carter. He had started wearing a goatee a few years earlier, and she'd always hated it. Or maybe…maybe she just hated him.

"I think it's way too late to try to plan anything like that. New Year's is only, what? Three weeks away?"

"We could still look into it. Why don't you check to see how much a rental would cost? Or maybe we could stay at a resort. You're much better at planning that sort of thing than I am."

"No." The word left Nora's mouth before she could stop herself. But…*no*. The idea of going anywhere with Carter was anathema to her. Especially to a small rental house, where it would be even harder to avoid him.

"What?"

"No, I'm not going to look for a rental. I'm a little busy at the moment, what with doing all of the Christmas shopping and the wrapping, mailing packages and the ten thousand activities the kids have to attend, not to mention my job. I don't have time to plan a vacation on top of everything else."

Carter leaned back against the counter and folded his arms over his chest.

"I know that you've been stressed out. That's why I thought it might be good to get away for a few days. I think it would be good for us, too. It would give us a chance to reconnect."

"I think it's a little late for that." The words were again out of Nora's mouth before she could think through the implications. But wasn't it the truth? It was too late. There was no fixing what had broken between them.

"What are you saying?"

"I don't know. I think we should just try to get through the holidays right now."

"I think this is something we should talk about."

Nora threw down the dishcloth she'd been using to wipe

the counter and looked at Carter. "You want to talk now? You
certainly didn't all those times I suggested we go to marriage
counseling. Nor were you interesting in talking after you—"

"Are you guys fighting?" Matt had appeared in the kitchen
without Nora having noticed his presence.

"No," she said automatically at the same time Carter said,
"No, buddy."

It was the one thing she and Carter had always been in solid
agreement on—the need to hide as many of their problems from
the kids as possible.

"Everything's fine," Nora added.

"It doesn't seem like it's fine," Matt said.

"We're just having a conversation," Carter said. "Nothing to
worry about. How was school today?"

Matt looked from one parent to the other, clearly not believ-
ing them. Finally, he shrugged in a weary way that made Nora's
heart squeeze. She tried to remember the last time she had seen
her younger son seem lighthearted or even smile and couldn't.
The transition to high school had not been easy on him. Matt
hadn't found his footing at his new school yet, and—even more
concerning—was spending even more time alone in his room,
isolated from the world.

It was another tick in the Stay box of the constant stay-or-go
tally Nora mentally kept. The affect it would have on Matt. A
divorce would affect all her children, of course, but Dylan would
be off to college soon, and nothing would keep Katie down for
long. She was a force of nature. But Matt… He would struggle.

"Hey, did you ever look into joining the golf team, like we
talked about?" Carter pressed him. "After all of those lessons
you took, you shouldn't have any problem getting on it."

"No," Matt said. "I told you, I don't like golf."

"Okay, it doesn't have to be golf. But there's got to be some
sport you're interested in playing," Carter continued. "Track?
Crew? I'd bet you'd be a great rower."

"When's dinner going to be ready?" Matt asked.

"In about an hour," Nora said. "I made a blueberry slump for dessert."

"What's a slump?"

"It's like a cobbler. You'll like it."

Matt nodded without enthusiasm and disappeared out of the kitchen as quietly as he'd entered.

"Good talk." Carter raised an ironic fist in the air. "Nothing like great communication between father and son."

"He's not Dylan. He's probably never going to be into sports."

"I know, but he has to do something other than sit by himself in his room all of the time."

"I agree. But he's going to have to figure out his path. All we can do is keep encouraging him."

They were on familiar footing now, discussing one of their children. It was one area where they almost always agreed, and rarely had conflict over. It was yet another tick in the Stay column. But the fractures in their relationship were becoming harder to ignore. She didn't know if it was inevitable or linked to her affair with Josh. Now, she'd inadvertently signaled her unhappiness to her husband, without truly thinking through the consequences of having done so.

Nora realized, her stomach lurching, that had been a mistake. She'd long ago learned that Carter could be a very dangerous enemy.

chapter fourteen
---
abby

As it turned out, it was easier than Abby would have thought to track down the blonde woman's identity using just her license plate.

It wasn't as easy as just logging on to the website for the Florida Department of Highway Safety and Motor Vehicles. They didn't allow the public to simply run searches on license plates. That made sense, Abby thought. The authorities wouldn't want a nutcase to be able to track down the person who cut her off in traffic, or for some pervert to find out the address of a woman he was stalking.

However, there were plenty of websites that basically worked as virtual private investigators. All Abby had to do was pay fifty dollars, which she did using the credit card her parents had given her when she first went off to college, type in the license letters and numbers and within mere moments, she had the basic background information on the woman who drove the blue Nissan Murano.

Her name was Nora Holliday, age forty-five. She was married—*Aha!* Abby thought—to Carter Holliday, age forty-nine. Their marriage took place on June 20, 1998, in Palm Beach County, Florida. The Hollidays owned a home at 742 Laurel Drive, which was currently valued at $475,800. Nora was not involved in any litigation, past or present, and didn't have a criminal record.

Abby ran a search on Nora's name, and was immediately able to access her Facebook page, which—luckily—didn't have any privacy settings.

Idiot, Abby thought.

Abby scrolled through Nora's photos first, but the woman clearly wasn't into selfies. She did have a profile photo. Abby looked at it for a long time, taking in Nora's oval face, wide blue eyes, closed-lip smile and, yes, wavy shoulder-length blond hair. It was definitely the same woman she'd seen at the Seabreeze Hotel. And, Abby suspected, very likely the woman she saw her father kissing in his car.

Nora posted only sporadically on Facebook, but she was just active enough for Abby to learn that she was the mother of three children. She had two sons, Dylan and Matt, who were both students at Calusa County High School, the same school Abby had attended. Her daughter, Katie, was enrolled in Shoreham Middle School. Abby studied all of their photos. She thought that Dylan might look familiar, but then, he would have been a freshman when Abby was a senior in high school. It was entirely possible she had passed by him in the hallway every day at school.

There was a link on Nora's Facebook page to her website, *Scones and Jam*. Abby clicked over to it. It was a food blog with a focus on baking that looked like it was updated two to three times a week. The posts were heavy on photographs that were well lit and artistically taken. Abby thought it looked ridiculously pretentious. Nora didn't just use regular store brand vanilla extract, for example, or at least didn't include it in the photograph of ingredients for the apple tart recipe she'd posted. Instead, she used a bourbon vanilla extract in an expensive-looking bottle. And the butter wasn't just regular old sticks that came in boxes of four, but a block of fancy European butter.

Who the hell does she think she is? Abby wondered indignantly. *It's so pretentious. And so fake. She's pretending to be some sort of perfect domestic goddess, while she's sneaking around, ruining other people's families. She's just as horrible as Lana. Worse, even, because she's a mother. She should know better. She should care more.*

The thought of Lana—which, of course, immediately brought Colin to mind—caused Abby an unexpected and unsettling jolt of grief. She realized that she'd been so focused on tracking down the woman her father was having an affair with, that it had been a while since she'd really thought about her ex-boyfriend and despicable ex-friend. She grabbed her phone and pulled up Lana's Instagram feed, and yes, there they were. Picture after picture of Lana, or Lana and Colin together, every photo followed by the usual cloying comments, heart emojis, and lots and lots of hashtags. Abby stared down at her phone, scrolling through the posts slowly, each new picture causing her a fresh stab of pain.

Why did people like Lana and Nora think they could get away with doing such horrible things? Did they really believe they could wreak havoc in the lives of those around them, and not suffer any consequences?

Abby set her phone down and turned back to her laptop, where Nora's face was smiling out at her. It wasn't until Abby blinked that she realized her vision was blurred by the tears that were now streaming down her face.

"You're not going to get away with this," Abby said quietly to Nora's picture. "I wonder what your husband will think when he finds out what you've been up to?"

chapter fifteen

---

gwen

Christmas was not a happy day in the Landon household.

Just as she wasn't a fan of Thanksgiving, Gwen had also never particularly enjoyed Christmas. It took too much effort to keep up with the never-ending good cheer required. She found it easier to keep up the facade at the cocktail parties they usually attended during the holiday season, but she couldn't muster any enthusiasm for attending any of the soirees they were routinely invited to. She'd RSVP'd "no" to all of the invites they'd received. If Josh had noticed the lack of activity on their social calendar, he hadn't mentioned it.

It had been easier to play her part when the kids were young and still believed in Santa Claus. But as they grew older, and Abby became an expert at scrutinizing her failings, Gwen lost the motivation to make Christmas the magical greeting card all the television commercials insisted it should be. This year, the idea that they were all supposed to playact at being a happy family exhausted her. Josh was still distracted and distant. There was no discernible improvement in Abby's depression, or any indication that she was going to return to school or move forward with her life in any meaningful way. Simon had basically disappeared, and spent most of his time in his room or at friends' houses.

What's the point of putting on the show if there's no one around to watch it? Gwen wondered.

She did put up the Christmas tree—by herself—but left most of the other Christmas decorations in their storage boxes. Gwen didn't even bother reminding Josh to string up lights on the house. He didn't think to do it on his own. No one in the Landon family seemed to notice or care that the regular holiday celebrations and traditions had been downsized.

On Christmas morning, Gwen was up early, drinking coffee in the living room. She stared at the Christmas tree and wondered how soon she could take it down. Josh wondered in, coffee mug in hand.

"Should I get the kids up?" he asked.

"What's the point?"

"So they can open their presents. Celebrate the holiday. Fa-la-la-la-la and all that."

"I didn't get you anything," Gwen said abruptly.

"Oh…okay."

"What's the point? It seems silly to buy each other presents out of our joint account."

"Okay, it's no big deal."

"Why, did you get me something?"

"Yes, but—" Josh shrugged "—it's fine that you didn't get me anything."

"Good." Gwen returned to studying the tree. She could feel Josh's eyes lingering on her, but then he turned and disappeared into the home office without another word.

Simon and Abby finally emerged from their rooms in the late morning, both yawning.

"Why didn't you wake us up?" Simon ran a hand through his hair, which was flattened on one side and sticking up on the other.

"I assumed you'd rather sleep in," Gwen said.

Abby and Simon exchanged a look.

"Aren't we going to open presents?" Abby asked.

"Sure. Go get your father."

Once the family was gathered, Gwen and Josh watched while Simon and Abby first went through their stockings, then turned their attention to the wrapped gifts under the tree. Gwen had bought almost all their presents online, mindlessly adding clothes and books to her virtual shopping cart, then paying extra for everything to be wrapped for her. Simon and Abby gave her running clothes and their father a book. Josh had bought her a wallet, which Gwen didn't particularly like or need, but she thanked him anyway with a tight smile. Everyone seemed strained, and Gwen wondered if her own sour mood was infecting the entire family. If so, she didn't particularly care.

"What's this?" Abby asked, pulling a small square box that Gwen didn't recognize from underneath the tree.

"I have no idea. What does the tag say?"

"'To Abby. Merry Christmas! From, Tara Edwards.' Who's that?"

"Tara Edwards got you a present?" Gwen gave Josh a cutting look. "What's that about?"

"I have no idea," Josh said. "Her sons are patients of mine. That must have been among the presents I brought home from the office. Deirdre put all of the ones for me in a bag. I didn't look through it to see what was in there. Just brought it home."

"Why would she get me something? I don't even know her. Look, here's another one with the same wrapping paper." Abby checked the tag. "It's for Simon."

"Cool." Simon took the package from her.

"Go ahead and open them," Gwen commanded. "Let's see what Tara Edwards got you."

Abby tore of the wrapping paper, uncovering a set of high-end lip glosses. "Wow."

"I got a video game," Simon said. "Awesome. I don't have this one."

"Those are pretty expensive gifts for kids she doesn't even know," Gwen commented.

"Most of my patients who even bother with presents just drop off cookies or something like that. I have no idea why Tara would buy the kids presents," Josh said.

Sure you don't, Gwen thought. But that was hardly a conversation they could get into right then.

That afternoon, Abby took Simon to the latest blockbuster superhero movie. Gwen had been surprised that Abby had offered, but suspected both wanted to escape the stressful atmosphere permeating the house.

Maybe that's the trick, Gwen thought. *Maybe if I can ratchet up the tension enough, it will motivate Abby to run all the way back to college.*

They were having spiral-sliced honey ham for dinner, which Gwen had purchased at the store, and only required reheating in the oven. It would be accompanied by mashed sweet potatoes, and a green bean casserole she'd made the day before. Gwen decided to take advantage of the free time this allowed her and began stripping the ornaments off the tree, setting them in a pile on the living room carpet. She'd always found it deeply satisfying to de-Christmas the house, but especially so this year. Tomorrow, it would be like the holidays had never even happened, and it would be a whole year before she'd have to deal with them again.

"You're taking down the tree already?" Josh asked, appearing in the living room.

"Yes."

"Do you want some help?"

"No."

"Do you want a glass of wine?"

"Sure."

Josh went to the living room and returned with two glasses of pinot noir. He handed one to Gwen.

"What's going on? You seem upset," he said.

"I'm fine."

"You've been in a bad mood all day."

"Have I? Well, maybe I think it's inappropriate that the woman you're possibly having an affair with bought Christmas presents for our kids."

Josh's mouth actually dropped open, which Gwen almost found amusing. It was one of those mannerisms you read in books but rarely see in real life. He also seemed to be struggling to speak.

"What?" he finally said.

"Tara Edwards. The lip glosses, the video game. Surely you remember."

"I'm not having an affair with Tara Edwards."

"You know what?" Gwen turned to face her husband. "I really don't care one way or the other if you are."

"You wouldn't care if I had an affair?"

"No. Does that surprise you?"

Josh looked at her, his expression unfathomable. "No, I guess it doesn't. I think it would surprise me more at this point to learn that you care about anything or anyone other than yourself."

"That's not true."

Josh sighed heavily. "I know you care about the kids."

"That's not what I was referring to. What I care about is making a change. Because I'm pretty sure this—" Gwen swished a hand around "—was not the life I was meant for."

Josh closed his eyes briefly. "Are you saying you want a divorce?"

"I don't know. Maybe. Why, would that upset you?"

"I just didn't think we'd be having this discussion on Christmas Day. But I suppose we can, if that's what you want."

"What I want." Gwen laughed without amusement. "What I want is to go back in time and pick a different path. Live a different life."

"That's not actually possible."

"No, it's not," Gwen agreed. "But I could have been so much more. I was smart. I was a good student. I could have done anything. Instead, I've spent my life catering to three people who don't even appreciate me."

"This is what life is for most people. It's work and errands and taking care of what you need to. It doesn't matter how smart you are. It helps, of course, but everyone still has responsibilities. Life isn't exciting and glamorous for most people."

"Maybe not. But some people create their own rules."

"What exactly is this life you think you were deprived of? I truly want to know."

"I could have been a travel journalist. I was always a good writer. Excellent, even."

"Gwen." Josh held out his hands, palms facing upward. "You were a paralegal when we met. You weren't exactly on a career path to become a travel journalist."

Gwen could feel her rage building. It had been a constant friend over the past few months, ready to uncoil and strike out at the slightest provocation. "That's just it! Everyone stood in my way. First my mother, then you. It kept me from realizing my potential. I should have had a very different life. An extraordinary life."

"It's always about you," Josh said quietly. "Gwen the great. Gwen the victim."

They stared at one another, both breathing a bit heavier than usual. Gwen thought they probably looked a bit like two box-ers squaring off. Josh was the first one to break eye contact and turn away.

"Do what you want," he said. "I won't stop you."

"That would make everything easier for you, wouldn't it? If I leave, you get to retain your status as Mr. Nice Guy. Poor Josh, whose mean wife deserted him. It's harder to pull off being the good guy when you're the one walking out the door."

Gwen knew she had landed her blows with pinpoint preci-sion. That was exactly what Josh was hoping. He shouldn't have been surprised that she'd already figured that out. After all these years, she knew him better than he knew himself.

"I'll let you know what I decide, when I decide it," Gwen said. "Until then, please keep your girlfriend away from my children."

"Our marriage difficulties aside—and, yes, that's clearly an issue we need to address in the near future—I barely even know that woman. I have no idea why she bought those presents for the kids."

"So you said," Gwen replied. "But whatever happens, I prom-ise you this. I will not ever allow you to make me look like a fool. Is that clear?"

Josh was silent. Finally, he sighed and said, "You know this isn't healthy, right? This relationship, this marriage? Things can't continue on like this."

No, Gwen thought. *They certainly can't.*

Gwen waited until the week after New Year's, when life had finally returned to normal and school was back in session. Or it was for everyone other than Abby, who still wasn't showing any signs that she'd ever go back to college. Gwen got in her Jeep and drove to Tara Edwards's house.

Getting the address had been easy. Gwen had simply called Deirdre, Josh's office manager. Deirdre had always loved Gwen, and had the added benefit of being a dolt, so she didn't think to question her request for Tara's home address.

"I'm writing thank-you notes to all of Josh's patients who gave him Christmas gifts," Gwen had explained.

"How nice! I probably should be doing that, but if you want to handle it, I'm more than happy to let you," Deirdre had chirped before reading off Tara's address, along with a few others on the list Gwen had given her, just to make her request seem less targeted.

Gwen had no intention of writing thank-you notes to anyone, least of all Tara. Instead, she pulled into Tara's driveway and strode up to the front door. She rang the bell, then waited for Tara to appear. When she answered the door, she was wearing her usual yoga gear. Today, Tara's face was scrubbed bare, and her long brown hair was piled on top of her head and secured with a green scrunchie.

"Gwen!" Tara exclaimed. "What a nice surprise! I wasn't expecting you."

"No," Gwen agreed. "I'm sure you weren't."

Tara's face scrunched into a frown. "Is something wrong?"

Gwen held out the grocery bag.

Tara took it and looked inside. "I don't understand. Those were gifts for Abby and Simon. Didn't they like them?"

"It doesn't matter if they liked them or not. What matters is that they're completely inappropriate."

Gwen was amused to see that Tara went pale. "I didn't mean anything by it. I just…Josh…Dr. Landon, I mean…has been so kind to the boys. To all of us. I just…I was trying to say thank you."

"Writing him a check for services rendered is all the thanks Josh needs." Gwen's voice was cold and clipped. "Then we use that money to buy our own gifts for our kids."

"I didn't mean to offend you."

"Didn't you?"

"Of course not!"

Gwen leaned forward slightly, baring her teeth in a faux smile. Tara took an involuntary step back, which pleased Gwen. She'd always found it satisfying how predictable people were. Step into their space, and they almost always moved aside for you. Or maybe, they just did it for her.

"I'm going to be as clear as possible," Gwen said, biting each word out. "Whatever it is you're doing, whatever agenda you may have, I want you to leave me and my children out of it. Don't contact us, don't stop by our house, don't bring us gifts. Got it?"

Tara's mouth formed an O of unhappiness. She nodded mutely.

Gwen straightened her posture, nodded. "Good." She turned to leave but glanced back over her shoulder at Tara. "Oh, and happy New Year."

chapter sixteen

nora

"I should get back to the office," Josh said.

They were lying in bed at the Seabreeze Hotel, which had become their standard meeting place, both because it was out of the way and because the regular daytime desk clerk was a stoner who seemed supremely uninterested in the couple who checked in for a few hours at a time.

Nora and Josh met as often as they could. They tried to see each other at least once a week, although sometimes life conspired against them. For example, it had been harder to steal time to be together over the holidays, which had been difficult for both of them. They texted back and forth every day, however, and Josh called her as often as he could. It was hard for him, working in an office and surrounded by people for most of the day, or else at home. Nora worked alone, and it was easier for her to find a few minutes here and there to chat, just not in the late afternoon once the kids and Carter were home.

Every time they met, every single time, Nora always thought the same thing. *This can't go on.* And yet, she did nothing to end it, nothing to stop what was starting to feel like a runaway train. Seeing Josh, touching him, talking to him had become so precious to her, she couldn't let him go.

"I should get back, too." Nora stretched luxuriously, enjoying the feel of the crisp sheets against her naked skin. Who would have thought she'd turn into such a hedonist? Afternoon trysts, lying naked in bed with a man who wasn't her husband. But it felt wonderful. "I wish we could just stay here for several more hours."

"I do, too. I've been thinking about it a lot."

The day after Christmas, Josh had called Nora and filled her in on his talk with Gwen, and how for the first time, the subject of divorce had been raised.

"Was she upset?" Nora had asked.

"She didn't seem upset. She was the one who brought it up. I'm starting to think that there's something seriously wrong with her."

"Because she wants a divorce?"

"No, not that. Truthfully, I'd be thrilled if Gwen were the one to initiate the divorce proceedings. No matter what she says, she will not take kindly to my leaving her. It would be too much of a blow to her ego."

"Is that fair? She must have some emotions about your marriage ending. Even if the marriage has broken down irrevocably, it's still sad."

"That's just it. I don't think Gwen is capable of feeling anything for anyone, other than herself. She's a narcissist. It all makes sense. Her grandiosity. The way she's charming to other people in public, but cold to her family in private. Her lack of empathy. I truly don't think she cares about anyone or anything in the world. Now she's insisting that she's been robbed of some sort of special life that she was meant to live."

At the time, Nora wasn't sure how to respond. Even as she and Josh grew closer, which they were with every passing day, she still felt uncomfortable when the conversation turned toward either one of their marriages. She didn't like picking apart his problems with Gwen or hers with Carter. She wanted their time together to be special and apart, although she supposed this was a foolish and unrealistic wish.

Several weeks had passed since then—it was already late January—and both Nora and Josh remained in a sort of uneasy stasis in their marriages.

Now, Nora looped an arm over Josh's chest to curl closer to him. "How's Abby doing?"

She could feel Josh shrug, his shoulder moving beneath her head. "Not great. She's closed herself off from everyone. She won't even talk to me about it, and we've always been close. Maybe I should take her out to dinner, just the two of us. See if she'll open up then."

"That's a good idea."

"I have to try, at least. She refused to sign up to take classes at the community college this semester, and she obviously didn't complete any of the courses she was taking last semester. At this rate, she'll never get her degree." He sighed and ran a hand over his face. "What they say is true. Life does actually turn out to be harder than you think it's going to be when you're young."

Nora smiled against his shoulder. "Back when we thought we had all the answers."

"As it turns out, we knew nothing at all." Josh turned Nora toward him and kissed her deeply. "I hate to say this, but I really do have to go. I hate leaving you."

"I know. This is a weird and difficult situation."

"We'll figure it out. I mean, I've already made the decision that I'm going to leave. I just need to figure out when and how I'm going to make that work."

Nora nodded. Leaving Carter wasn't going to be easy, either. Just the thought of it caused a knot of dread to form in her stomach. Gwen might be as cold and self-centered as Josh had described her, but as far as she knew, his wife had never been violent.

She couldn't say the same about Carter.

Josh kissed her again and stroked her face gently with the tips of his fingertips.

"I love you," he said.

"I love you, too."

Nora and Josh always staggered the times that they arrived at and departed from the hotel, so Nora stayed in the room for a short time after Josh left. She dressed and checked her messages. When enough time had passed for Josh to have safely driven away, Nora headed out herself.

She was walking toward her car when a voice called out. "Nora?"

Nora froze. *It's finally happened*, she thought. *I've been caught.*

Her heart pounding, she turned slowly to face the person who might be the one to bring her world crashing down around her.

"Oh. Hi, Olivia. How are you?"

Nora's potential downfall had appeared in the unlikely form of Olivia Hudson. She was in her late forties, had a chin-length blond bob and a square, stocky build. She was walking a large boxer who had a similar, square stocky build. The dog took the opportunity of Olivia's abrupt stop to raise his leg and urinate on the hotel's signpost. Nora had known Olivia for years, ever since Olivia's daughter, Peyton, was in a baby music class with Dylan. All the mothers would sit in a circle, holding their children in their laps, and try to coax them into banging on a drum or shaking a bead-filled egg. Nora and Olivia had never been close friends, but would stop to chat about their kids when they bumped into one another in the grocery store. They usually marveled about how many years had passed since that baby music class, which they both agreed seemed like it had just been yesterday.

"How are you?" Nora tried to sound as normal as possible.

"What are you doing here?" Olivia asked. She glanced up at the hotel signage, and then back at Nora.

Nora remembered now that Olivia's overly direct personality was one of the reasons she'd never been interested in developing a closer friendship with her. Olivia could be blunt to the point of rudeness.

"I was looking for a place to take some photos for my blog and was told that this hotel has a pretty lobby with good light." This would be an obvious lie to anyone who'd ever stepped into the hotel. The lobby was utilitarian at best, and there was nowhere remotely suitable to take photographs. "It was a bad tip, though. I think the person who told me that must have mixed it up with another hotel."

Olivia snorted. "I would imagine so. This is just one of those places tourists on a tight budget stay at. You should try the Reef Hotel over by the beach. They have that gorgeous ballroom that opens up onto a patio with a view of the water. Or how about the sculpture garden at the Winston Museum? There have to be better places than this dump."

"Good tip," Nora said brightly. Too brightly, she thought. "Like I said, I think the person who told me about this place had it confused with somewhere else."

"How's Dylan doing? Can you believe that he and Peyton are in their senior year? I don't know where the time has gone," Olivia said, launching into the same conversation they always had when they saw one another.

"He's great. Just waiting to hear back on his college applications."

"Oh, did you hear? Peyton got into Tulane on early admission. Isn't that wonderful?" Olivia asked aggressively.

"Congratulations," Nora said dutifully.

"She didn't get as much of a scholarship as she was hoping for, though, so we're waiting to see where else she gets in. It's a stressful time, isn't it?"

Dylan hadn't seemed the least bit stressed about any part of the college application process, but then, that was his personality. Dylan never worried about anything. Besides, he'd already been scouted by several schools with strong soccer programs, so he was on solid footing there. She decided not to share any of this with Olivia, as it would just prolong the conversation. Nora was also fairly sure that Olivia was the sort of woman who would have strong views against athletic scholarships that she wasn't particularly interested in hearing.

"It is, indeed," Nora said. "Well, I should get going."

"Where's your camera?"

"What?"

"You said you were here to take pictures. Don't you need a camera for that? Or do you just use your phone?"

"Oh. No, I do use a camera. But, as I said, I was just scouting it out as a possible location. I wasn't planning on taking any pictures today," Nora said, starting to feel a twinge of nerves.

"I thought your blog was about cooking. Don't you need a kitchen for the sort of pictures you take?"

"Yes, but I'm in the middle of expanding," Nora lied, "into other lifestyle areas, beyond just cooking. Hopefully, it will attract sponsors interested in product placement. That sort of thing."

Nora wondered if she sounded as completely full of shit as she thought she did. It was a warm day, and she suddenly felt almost unbearably hot. She could feel sweat beading on her forehead.

She wondered if she smelled like sex.

"Oh, that's good," Olivia said. "How's everyone else doing? The kids? Carter?"

"Everyone's fine. Your family?" Nora was forced to ask, even though what she really wanted to do was flee. What if someone else came along? She didn't want to be standing in the middle of a hotel parking lot, while anyone she knew could traipse by.

Olivia nattered on for a few minutes, in what was essentially a mom brag about both Peyton and her younger son, Peter, who were apparently both exceptional in every way. Nora nodded along, while letting Olivia's commentary slide over her without taking in one word.

"Well, it was so nice to see you," Nora said when Olivia had finally paused to draw in a breath. "But I should get going. I have a few errands to run before I pick up Katie."

Nora escaped to her SUV and pulled out, waving to Olivia, who was still standing in the parking lot, now waiting for her boxer to evacuate his bowels. She drove down US 1, through several lights, then pulled into a strip mall and parked her car. She pulled her phone out and noticed as she held it that her hands were shaking. She sent a text to Josh.

We need to find a new place to meet.

abby

Abby had spent the weeks since learning Nora's identity compiling as much information as she could on the woman and her family. She kept the information in a spiral-bound notebook, which she kept either on her person or tucked under the mattress. Abby didn't trust her mother not to snoop.

The Hollidays were all—save the younger of her two sons—remarkably unconcerned about keeping their online information private. Still, Abby had to do a little work to get access to their social media accounts.

She created a fake Facebook account under the name Ella Davis. She copied a bunch of Lana's many selfies off her Instagram account and used them to set up the fake Facebook account. She dropped in a profile photo and added others to the dozen or so posts she made over a month. It was a tad risky. If someone who knew Lana saw it, they might flag the account as fake. But Lana was from Clearwater and didn't know anyone from Shoreham, other than Abby. Besides, it amused Abby to use the photo of one morally bankrupt cheater to trap another.

Once Abby thought that her account looked adequately established, she scrolled through Nora's friend list and started to send friend requests to both Nora's friends and, when possible, their children who were close to her in age. It took only one or two days before her requests were accepted, and there was quickly a snowball effect. Once people saw that she was Facebook friends with their acquaintances, others readily accepted her requests in turn.

As soon as Abby had friended enough people in Nora's circle, she put in friend requests to Nora, Carter and their three children, staggering the requests over a few weeks. She didn't want the Holliday family to be sitting around the dinner table and have one of them casually mention they'd gotten a friend request from someone named Ella Davis. All she needed was one of them to wonder out loud who that was and have the rest of the family chime in that they, too, had gotten the same request. Her patience paid off. In the end, Abby-Ella was soon friends with almost all the members of the Holliday family, and had access to all of the information they posted.

Abby had already been able to access Nora's account, but through her new "friendships," she learned that Carter worked at a commercial real estate firm called Pool and Associates, and that they often employed summer interns. He'd posted several photos of company events where the interns were treated to crawfish boils or taken to baseball games. Dylan, the elder Holliday son, was an infrequent poster, but he was often tagged in photos with the high school soccer team or out fishing with friends on a boat. The youngest Holliday, Katie, was on Facebook constantly, mostly posting selfies of herself—there was a touch of Lana in her, Abby thought—making silly faces and referring to her group of friends as The Queens.

No shortage of self-confidence there, Abby thought.

Abby also learned that her father had been Katie's orthodontist. Katie had posted before and after pictures on the day she had her braces taken off, including a photo taken with Abby's dad in the office. Even though Abby had seen her father pose in a similar way with other patients when they got their braces off, seeing him there, with that woman's daughter, made her stiffen with rage.

Matt, the middle child, was the only one who didn't accept the Abby-Ella friend request. Abby wondered why but decided it didn't really matter. She had more than enough information on the family to make her next move.

Abby looked up the number for Pool and Associates on her phone, then hit the call button.

"Pool and Associates, how may I assist you?" a chirpy female voice said on the other end of the line.

"Hi, I'm calling for Carter Holliday, please."

"Who may I say is calling?"

"Abby Landon."

"Hold one minute."

Abby listened to a brief musical interlude while she held, trying to take deep calming breaths in through her nose and out through her mouth, like she'd learned in the one yoga class she'd ever attended.

"This is Carter Holliday," a male voice suddenly said into her ear.

For a beat, Abby couldn't speak. She knew she had to say something—this might be the only chance she had to talk to him—but the words were stuck in her throat. Part of it was that Carter Holliday didn't sound like she thought he would. From his pictures, she'd assumed he'd have a deep baritone, not this slightly nasally tenor.

"Hello?" He sounded irritated. "Is anyone there?"

"Yes…sorry. We must have a bad connection. You were breaking up for a moment," Abby said.

"That happens. Who am I speaking to?"

"Hi, Mr. Holliday, this is Abby Landon."

"Please, call me Carter. Landon…that sounds familiar."

"Yes, my dad is an orthodontist in town. Your kids were patients of his." Abby wasn't sure if all three of the Holliday kids had been treated by her dad, but at least Katie had. Chances were the others had, too.

"Oh, right, of course. I know your dad. We work out at the same gym."

Abby hadn't known this, but she jotted down a note about it in her spiral binder.

"So how can I help you?" Carter continued, sounding much friendlier now.

"I'm a student at FSU. I'm taking a semester off, but I'll be returning in the fall," Abby lied. She still had no intention of ever returning to FSU. "I was looking into applying for internships during my semester off, and saw that your company has a really highly rated program."

Abby was quite pleased with herself for thinking of this cover on the fly. She hadn't been entirely sure what she was going to say when she called Nora Holliday's husband, but it was quite a good reason for making an initial contact.

"We do accept several interns every year, but to be honest, it's usually over the summer months. We don't normally start accepting applications for those positions until April," Carter said, which doused Abby's short-lived sense of victory. But then he continued. "However, considering our family connections, why don't you come in for an informal interview? I'm pretty booked up for the next few weeks, but maybe we can set something up for late February or early March."

"Great!" Abby didn't have to fake her enthusiasm. This was exactly the opening she'd been hoping for.

"I'll transfer you to my assistant and she'll set it up. Make sure you bring a copy of your CV with you."

Abby didn't have a CV, or even know what exactly that was, but how hard could it be to figure out how to get one? She'd accomplished the much more difficult task. She'd arranged a face-to-face meeting with Carter Holliday.

"That would be great," she said. "Thank you again."

Abby was sitting on her bed, working on her CV—which, she discovered, turned out to be just a fancy word for a résumé— when there was a knock on her door, which was closed, as usual.

"Come in."

The door cracked open. Her father stood there.

"Hi," he said. "What are you doing?"

"Nothing," Abby said, shutting her laptop before he could see what she was working on.

"I'm taking you out to dinner tonight. I thought we'd go to Bello Italiano."

"Why?"

"Because I want to. We haven't spent much time together lately. Not just the two of us."

"I'm not hungry," Abby said curtly.

"It wasn't up for discussion. Get dressed. Let's go."

Abby looked up at her father, startled by his commanding tone. Her dad didn't normally give her orders.

"I'll be waiting in the car," he said.

After he'd left her alone, and Abby heard the front door close, she weighed her options. She could let him just sit in the car. Did he deserve more from her at this point, after what he'd done? And yet, despite her anger at him, the profound sense of disappointment she had in him, there was still a part of her that wanted to please her father. Maybe it was time they did talk. She wasn't ready to discuss what she knew about his affair—just the thought made her sick to her stomach—but maybe she'd glean some insight into what he was thinking. Or what was going on between her parents.

Abby changed into shorts and a T-shirt and slipped on flip-flops. She could hear Simon rattling around in his room, the constant soundtrack of video games and YouTube videos blaring, but she didn't run into Gwen as she headed out of the house. It occurred to Abby that she hadn't seen much of her mother lately. Pretty much only at family meals, and even those had been few and far between. Gwen had stopped cooking, and dinner was usually takeout from somewhere, with everyone helping themselves when they felt like it. Abby had been glad—less exposure to her parents meant fewer questions about her future. Now she wondered if this was symptomatic of a more serious problem. Was her parents' marriage breaking down? If so, how did she feel about that? No one wanted their parents to get divorced, she decided, no matter how fucked up their relationship appeared.

Abby got into her father's car, slamming the door behind her. He glanced over at her and smiled. "I'm glad we're doing this."

"What about Mom and Simon?"

"They'll manage without us for one evening, I think. I told Simon I'd bring him back spaghetti and meatballs. He gave me a thumbs-up."

Abby nodded, and felt a stab of envy at how uncomplicated her brother's life was. A Styrofoam container of pasta was all that it took to make him happy. Or maybe she was underestimating him. He lived in the house, too. He couldn't have completely missed the constant undercurrent of tension.

They drove to Bello Italiano in silence. The Landon family had been going there as long as Abby could remember. The owner, Angelo, greeted them warmly and sat them in a booth near the back of the restaurant. Josh ordered a glass of wine; Abby opted for a coke. Then they both studied their menus as though they weren't going to order the same thing they always did. Abby always got the chicken piccata, and her dad always had the *zuppa di pesce*. The waitress returned with their drinks and a basket of crusty bread, took their orders, then bustled off, leaving Abby and Josh alone. Abby's stomach tightened, and she suddenly realized that she was nervous.

That's weird, she thought.

"How've you been?" her dad asked as he tore off a piece of bread and dipped it in a shallow bowl of olive oil.

Abby shrugged. "Fine."

Josh raised his eyebrows.

"Okay, not totally fine," Abby admitted. "But I really don't want to get into the whole when are you going back to school talk. Again."

"We don't have to have that conversation, if you don't want to."

"Good."

"I actually meant, how are you doing emotionally? You've seemed like you're feeling a bit better lately."

"I have?"

Josh nodded. "Less lying in bed and staring into space. Your mom said you're spending a lot of time on your laptop."

Abby realized that her Little Project, as she'd come to think of it, had been keeping her occupied. No, it was more than that. It had been consuming her. The pain over Colin and Lana that had so completely flattened her when she first arrived home hadn't receded, exactly. But it had been pushed to the side, slotted into a separate compartment in her mind while she focused on learning all she could about Nora Holliday and her family. She'd stopped spending every spare moment brooding over Colin's abandonment and Lana's betrayal. When it did pop into her thoughts, she still experienced the now-familiar spasm of pain, as sharp as ever. Surprisingly, it had stopped dominating every minute of her every day.

"Did you ever look into taking online classes?" her dad asked. "Or the community college is still an option."

"No, it's not. The semester has already started. I thought we weren't going to have this conversation."

"We're not. We're going to have a tougher conversation. Along the lines of, if you're not going to go back to school, what are you going to do instead? Do you have an alternative plan?"

Abby sighed, her shoulders collapsing forward. "I thought this was Mom's line of interrogation."

Josh shrugged. "She has a point. You've been home for over three months. You can't stay in limbo forever."

"Actually, I'm applying for an internship."

"Really? With a local politician?"

It took Abby a few beats to realize what her father was referring to before it clicked. She'd been a political science major at FSU before dropping out. It wasn't a subject she had any passion for, since she wasn't interested in politics or public policy. She'd chosen it as her major mainly because she'd liked the professors who taught in the poli sci department and the classes had been highly rated. She'd been considering changing her major at the end of her sophomore year to something that would suit her better, whatever that might be. She actually didn't have a clue.

It had always seemed odd to Abby that after a year or two in college, she was supposed to know what she wanted to do with the rest of her life. She had known students who did, friends who were already set on a premed track, ticking off the required classes each semester. Or others who were intent on careers in architecture or graphic design, which required hours of their time spent at the respective studios. Abby had only vague ideas of what she wanted her future to look like. For a time, she thought she might want to go into public relations, but she had a feeling that was just because she'd seen a movie where the heroine was in PR and had the unrealistic glamorous movie life to go along with the job. She'd also considered going on to business or law school. Although, again, not because she had any real passion for either, but because graduate school would allow her to put off the real world for a few more years.

In any case, then she'd met Colin. Her relationship with him had taken precedence over everything else in her life, including figuring out what to do with her future. Even as she experienced the familiar stab of pain that thinking of Colin always brought her, this time it was mixed with a dose of shame. How could she have been so stupid? She'd completely lost all sense of the course of her future life for someone who had jettisoned her out of his without a backward glance.

"Not anything related to politics. I've already decided that's not what I'm going to do."

"I have to admit, I never could picture you going into politics."

"Why not?"

"You're too honest and decent. I figured if you stayed on that course, you'd end up at some sort of a think tank. Or maybe become a lobbyist."

Abby considered this and shook her head no.

"What are you interested in?"

"I like researching things," Abby surprised herself by saying.

"Now that, I can see. You always did well on research projects in high school. You excelled in all of your classes, but you seemed like you especially enjoyed writing papers. Is that what this internship is? A research assistant?"

Abby shook her head. "Not exactly."

"What is it, then?"

"I don't want to say. Not until I see if I get it," Abby lied. She wasn't interested in interning at Carter Holliday's commercial real estate firm. That was just a ploy to meet him face-to-face. Besides, she certainly wasn't going to announce who she was interviewing with to her father. He'd probably choke on the piece of bread he was chewing.

"Fair enough. But I'm proud of you, kiddo."

"For what?"

"For taking steps in the right direction." Their food arrived. Josh paused while the waitress set their plates before them. Once she departed, he continued. "Getting work experience while you're taking the semester off is a great idea."

Abby's anger at her father, at Colin and Lana, at the sorry state of her current life, bubbled up as it always did when the topic of her leaving school inevitably came up.

"What if I never go back to school? Would that really be the worst thing in the world?"

"The worst thing? No. But it would certainly limit your options going forward. The sort of career you can one day have."

"What if I don't want to have a career? Besides, this is all just so hypocritical. Mom doesn't have a career."

Abby knew she was lashing out, but she couldn't seem to stop herself. The thing was, she did want a career, even if she was less clear on what she wanted that to be. And her mother certainly wasn't her role model in anything.

Abby's father set down the fork and spoon he'd been using to eat the mussels in his *zuppa di pesce*. His lips twisted in a bitter expression Abby couldn't remember having seen before.

"Yes, and apparently that's all my fault."

"Mom blames you for her not having a career?"

"Forget it. I shouldn't have said anything." Her dad looked weary as he held up his hands, palms facing outward, in a placatory gesture. "I—we—both just want you to have options. Having a good job where you can support yourself and not have to rely on someone else is always the best option to have."

"If I don't have some sort of amazing career? What then? Will that define me as a failure forever and ever, amen?"

Abby's father stared down at his plate of food before pushing it aside. "Why does everything always have to be so dramatic with this family?"

"What is that supposed to mean?"

"I don't think that you'll be forever defined as a failure by not getting a college degree. But I do think it's a mistake that you will come to regret later in your life. And, yes, I absolutely do believe that it's a valid choice for a man or woman to be a full-time parent. But there are consequences to every decision. It's perfectly possible that if you chose not to get credentials and pursue some sort of a career, that ten, twenty years down the road from now, you may come to deeply regret that."

"Like Mom? She regrets not having a career?"

"I'm speaking generally."

"What you're saying is that Mom is upset that she had us instead of a career."

"That's the unnecessary drama I was just referring to. Of course your mother doesn't regret having you. We both love you and Simon very much."

Abby stared down at her chicken piccata. The lemon-butter sauce had oozed over onto the pasta, which was normally her favorite part of the dish. But right now, it looked oily and unappetizing. She followed her father's lead and pushed her plate to the side.

"Sometimes I wonder if that's true," she said quietly.

"Again, drama."

"I don't mean you. I know you love us. But...what if Mom isn't capable of loving anyone? Has that ever occurred to you?"

When her father didn't say anything, Abby looked up at him and took in his stricken expression.

"You have thought that," she said accusingly.

"No."

"Yes, you *have*. I can tell."

Her dad just shook his head.

"Are you and Mom getting a divorce?" Abby asked.

"What? Where's this coming from?"

Abby took note that while her father didn't answer the question, he also didn't deny it.

"I live in the same house. It's pretty obvious there's something wrong."

There's also the not so small fact that I know you're having an affair, Abby silently added.

"Okay. That's fair. But if your mother and I were having problems, it wouldn't be appropriate for me to discuss them with you."

"Why? I'm not a child anymore."

"That's not the point. Whatever issues your mother and I may or may not have are our private business."

"Which affects Simon and me."

"I'm not getting into it with you, Abby."

"Fine. But will you answer one question?"

"That depends on what the question is."

Abby stared at her father. "Do you think there's something wrong with Mom? Because I do. I've thought that for a long time."

Abby's father was silent for so long, she didn't think he was going to answer her question. He even signaled to the waitress for the check, and pulled out his credit card so he could hand it to her when she brought the bill over. Finally, he sighed and rubbed a weary hand over his face.

"Honestly, Abby, I don't know what I think at this point."

chapter eighteen

---

gwen

Josh and Gwen were mostly silent on the drive to the Reef Hotel, where the Red Cross Heart Ball was being held. Gwen had successfully managed to avoid most of the party circuit over the past few months, but she couldn't get out of going to the Heart Ball. They'd committed to attending months ago, when Andrea Young had called and invited them to sit at her table. The Youngs had paid thousands for the table, so the Landons' absence would have been noticed and noted. Gwen resigned herself to a boring night surrounded by boring women who would talk about nothing other than their Pilates classes or tennis lessons. She'd have to nod along as though she gave a flying fuck, while silently screaming inside.

When did everyone become so boring? Gwen wondered. She knew she was smarter than most people, but at least when she was younger and in school—even at the pathetic community college she attended—she'd been in contact with people who were interested in ideas, in conversation, in the greater world. Now all anyone wanted to talk about was their tiny privileged world.

"How long do you think we have to stay at this thing?" Gwen asked.

"Through dinner," Josh replied.

"Great. Let me guess. A limp salad overdressed with sour vinaigrette, followed by a rubbery chicken breast and a side of rice pilaf?"

"If you're dreading this so much, why are we going again?"

Gwen shrugged off the question. They hadn't revisited their Christmas Day conversation about whether or not to separate. For Gwen, though, it was now a foregone conclusion. She just needed to make a plan and execute it, in her own time and on her own terms. She'd spent enough of her life taking care of everyone else's needs. Now she was going to focus on her own.

"Maybe I like rubbery chicken," she said flippantly.

"Let's just get through the evening."

Gwen glanced at Josh, surprised by his curt tone, which was unlike him. Perhaps the strain in their marriage was getting to him.

Good, Gwen thought. *He should be upset at the idea of losing me.*

It wasn't her fault that after twenty-four years of marriage, he'd never fully appreciated her for who she was, for what she could have been. If he was only figuring that out now, when it was too late, that was his problem. Gwen turned to stare out the window so that he wouldn't see her lips curving into a satisfied smile.

One of Gwen's natural gifts had always been her ability to shine at social events. It was a useful skill that gave her a surprising power over other people. She could still remember when she was in second grade. She'd informed Jenny Robinson that she wouldn't be attending her birthday party, mainly because

she was sick to death of hearing Jenny brag about the bowling party she was having, and the pink Barbie cake her mother
had ordered. Gwen had told Jenny that she hated bowling and
hated Barbie even more, that she wouldn't be caught dead going
to such a babyish party. This had prompted tears from Jenny,
then a phone call from Jenny's mother pleading with Gwen's
mother to talk her into attending the party. Gwen had eventually agreed, but only after Jenny promised that she'd ditch the
Barbie cake in favor of something less pink.

As Gwen had matured into womanhood, she'd learned to
hone this natural talent into a true art form. Whenever she was
in a group, she would sparkle. People would flock to her. She
wasn't sure why, but it had always worked that way. It was why
Andrea Young had invited her to sit at her table at the ball so
many months in advance. Gwen's presence was always in demand.

Josh pulled up to the valet parking stand outside the hotel.
The valet opened Gwen's door. She stepped out of the car, then
waited for Josh so she could tuck her hand into the crook of his
arm. It was the first time she had voluntarily touched him in
months, but she knew it would make a better appearance for
them to walk into the event looking like the happy, charmed
couple everyone believed them to be.

The hotel ballroom was already teeming with people. The
Heart Ball was always a popular event on the Shoreham social
calendar, partly because it was the only black-tie event. The
wealthy women in town were thrilled to have an opportunity
to buy long, poufy ball gowns. It was almost like they were
reliving their prom nights, which Gwen had long ago figured
out had been a life-defining event for many of them, second
only to their weddings. In contrast, Gwen had opted to wear a
mid-length black slip dress, like a chic flapper in the twenties
might have worn for a dinner out on the town. The simple lines
of the dress set off her lean frame and pale skin. Her short dark

hair was slicked neatly back. The only makeup she'd bothered with was a slash of dark red lipstick. Sometimes less was more, and she knew she'd stand out among the flock of overly coiffed, overly made-up women.

"Gwen! You're here!" Andrea swept toward her in a slim dress of ill-fitting red satin that had been designed for someone thirty years younger, affirming Gwen's adult prom theory. Andrea had long flat-ironed hair in a frankly unbelievable shade of blond. She sported the sort of dark tan that had been out of fashion for several decades. Andrea air-kissed first Gwen then Josh. "I'm so glad you two made it!"

"Thank you for inviting us," Gwen said.

"You look amazing as ever." Andrea tilted her head back to scan Gwen's dress, then turned to Josh in mock disbelief. "Does she ever not look gorgeous? Please tell me she doesn't wake up looking like this. Life is so unfair."

"You look lovely, too, Andrea," Josh dutifully chimed in.

Gwen nodded in agreement. "I love your dress," she lied. "You should always wear red. It's perfect with your complexion."

Andrea glowed at the praise.

"I'm going to go get a drink. Can I get you ladies anything?" Josh asked.

"I'll have a glass of wine," Gwen said.

"No, you have to try one of these." Andrea held up her martini glass, which contained a bright pink liquid. "It's the signature drink tonight. They call it a Cupid Crush. I have no idea what's in it, but it's yummy. Josh, will you get us each one?"

"Will do," Josh said, and headed off to stand in line at the crowded bar.

Gwen was mildly irritated that Andrea had overruled her drink choice. She wasn't a fan of mixed drinks. Especially not sweet ones. But she had just spotted Tara Edwards across the room, standing with a loose knot of couples, including a man who Gwen supposed must be Tara's husband, as he had his hand resting on the small of her back. Gwen vaguely recognized him from other social functions. She tried to remember his name. Kyle, maybe? Kurt? No, that didn't sound right. It wasn't surprising he wouldn't have made much of an impact on her. He looked like a bore with his doughy face and bobblehead nodding along with the conversation. More interesting was Tara, who was now staring in Josh's direction, her face alight.

"Our table is right over there," Andrea was saying, although Gwen was only half listening to her. "Let me show you where, so you can sit next to me. I'm dying to catch up with you."

"Do you know Tara Edwards?" Gwen asked.

"Tara. Hmm, I'm not sure. Is she here?"

"She's over there." Gwen tipped her head. "Long brown hair, wearing the light pink dress."

Andrea's interest was instantly piqued, as Gwen knew it would be. She had always loved gossip. Gwen hadn't known Tara would be at the ball, but here she was. The opportunity it offered to cut her down almost seemed fated.

"No, I don't think I've ever met her. Why, is she a nightmare?"

"Total nightmare," Gwen said, rolling her eyes for added effect. "Think desperate social climber."

"The worst. I wonder how she got in here? This party used to be somewhat exclusive. Now I guess they'll let in anyone who can buy a ticket. How do you know her?"

"I don't, really, although she seems determined to get to know me. I think her kids are patients at Josh's practice, but please." Gwen waved a dismissive hand. "That doesn't mean she and I are going to be best friends."

Tara suddenly stepped away from her husband and the people they'd been chatting with. She headed toward the bar, her gaze still locked on Josh. Gwen watched with interest, wondering how this would play out. For his part, Josh had glanced back over his shoulder and seemed to spot Tara heading toward him. Even from across the room, Gwen could see that he'd turned pale, his expression unfathomable.

And you said you barely knew her, Gwen thought. *Liar.*

"Look, she's making a beeline for your husband." Andrea clutched at Gwen's arm, which was irritating, but Gwen let it pass. "Maybe you're not the one she's determined to be friends with."

Gwen forced herself to smile. "You're terrible."

"I know. I am, aren't I?"

While Gwen and Andrea looked on, Tara finally reached Josh. She plucked at his sleeve to get his attention. Josh turned toward her, away from where Gwen and Andrea were standing, which was unfortunate. Gwen would have dearly liked to have seen his expression.

"Poor Josh has been cornered," Andrea commented. "Do you want to rescue him?"

"No, he's a big boy. He can handle himself."

"I wonder what her agenda is?"

"She's probably harmless, but I have to admit, something about her pings my radar."

"I'll find out what I can about her," Andrea promised. "That's the sort of woman who needs to be put in her place."

Gwen nodded, feeling pleased. Andrea wouldn't just dig up information, although she'd certainly do that. But in the process, she'd also start spreading the rumor that Tara Edwards was trouble. Soon everyone in town would view the woman as suspect.

chapter nineteen

---

nora

Nora and Carter didn't usually attend the Heart Ball, but this year his firm had bought a table. All the senior management was expected to attend.

"You look very nice this evening," Carter commented as they walked into the ballroom at the Reef Hotel.

"Thank you," Nora said. She was wearing an A-line navy blue sheath with low-cut Vs in the front and back. She wasn't sure if it was appropriate for a ball, but she'd been far too distracted by all the complications in her life to have any time or interest in dress shopping.

"Is that a new dress?"

"No, I wore it to Macy Baldwin's wedding a few years ago."

"I don't remember it, but it looks great on you."

It was the sort of stilted polite conversation that two strangers might have.

You don't remember it because you spent Macy's wedding knocking back bourbon after bourbon and passed out in the car on the way home, Nora thought.

Nora and Carter had reached a détente of sorts. They hadn't discussed their marital problems again, not since the day Matt had walked in and interrupted their conversation. Nora hadn't brought it up because she was still trying to figure out what she should do. The damn pro-con list that ran constantly through her thoughts was confounding her. She didn't know why Carter hadn't wanted to discuss it again, but suspected it was because he didn't want to address his past behavior and how it had contributed to the erosion of their marriage. So instead, they lived like polite roommates, avoiding one another when possible, unless they needed to discuss their schedules or something involving the children.

Nora knew that this could not continue indefinitely. There was Josh pulling her in one direction, her responsibilities pulling in the other. The net effect of this was to cause her to feel trapped in indecision.

Carter checked the seating chart set up on an easel by the front double doors that led into the ballroom. "We're at table eight." He pointed. "Over there, I think."

Nora followed Carter to their table, where a few of his coworkers were already gathered.

"Hey, buddy." Harrison Monroe slapped Carter on the shoulder. "How are you doing? Hey, Nora."

"Hi, Harrison." Nora smiled tightly. She was going to be in for a long night of forced conversation with Carter's coworkers.

"If we're going to have work obligations on the weekend, I guess this beats being at the office," Harrison said. He was holding a short glass tumbler of clear liquid, with a lime slice bobbing around inside among the ice cubes.

Nora was suddenly desperate for a drink. She glanced around the room to see where the bar was located...when she saw him.

Josh.

He was in line at the bar, looking straight back at her. Nora immediately felt off balance, as though she were already drunk. She hadn't known he was going to be there. She wondered why he hadn't told her, but realized she hadn't mentioned she would be attending the ball, either.

Nora immediately swiveled her head, searching for the person she knew must also be there. Gwen Landon, glamorous with her short gamine dark hair, wearing a sophisticated slip of a dress. She looked vivacious and animated. Even though she wasn't a great beauty, there was something about her, a luminosity, a presence, that made it hard to look away from her.

I hate her.

Nora was instantly shocked by this unbidden thought. But it was true. She did hate Gwen, with a ferocity that took her breath away. Nora didn't know if her enmity was a result of how Josh had described their marriage, or—and this was far worse—if it stemmed from an intense jealousy that this woman was married to Josh. Even if it was an unhappy marriage, even if it was going to end sometime in the future, he still belonged to Gwen.

"Honey?"

Nora looked up at Carter and realized that he'd been saying something. She hadn't heard a word. Her husband looked perplexed, and Harrison looked from one to the other, with undisguised curiosity.

"I'm sorry, it's loud in here." Nora recovered. "What did you say?"

"I asked if you wanted something from the bar."

Nora looked back at the bar, where Josh was still in line, now talking to a pretty woman with long brown hair and wearing a very short pink dress. She had her hand on his arm, and was chattering excitedly up at him. Nora tried to figure out which option was worse—her getting in line behind Josh or allowing Carter to do so?

"Yes," Nora said.

"What would you like?"

"A vodka and soda. Thank you."

Normally, Nora would be the one to fetch the drinks. Carter had been sober for three years. Usually sending him over to an open bar would make her anxious. *I can't go over there*, she realized. *If I do, and Josh and I see one another, we might not be able to hide how we feel. And let's face it…if Carter's going to fall off the wagon, there's nothing I can do to stop him. I've never been able to make him do anything.*

"Coming right up," Carter said. "Do you need a refill, Harrison?"

"I'll come with you," Harrison responded. "This gin is shit. I want to see what else they have. You'd think at the prices they charge for tickets, they'd have better booze to offer."

Nora couldn't just stand there and watch her husband queue up behind her lover. Josh had reached the front of the line by this point, still accompanied by the pretty brown-haired woman. Carter would be within a few feet of him.

"I'm going to go find the ladies' room," she announced, and turned and strode out of the ballroom.

She didn't go to the ladies' room, though. Instead, she circled the room, making sure to keep her distance from where Gwen Landon was deep in conversation with Andrea Young, whom Nora had always found to be an insufferable busybody. She headed out the back door to the patio, which overlooked the Intracoastal Waterway. As soon as she was outside, Nora gulped in deep breaths of air, trying to stave off the panic she could feel rising inside her. Unfortunately, the party had spilled out onto the patio, so there were still too many people around, laughing and talking loudly as they downed their open-bar drinks.

She turned to the right, to find herself on a walkway that skirted the edge of the hotel. Nora followed it blindly, with no idea where she was going except to get away from the crowd.

Just past a clump of palm trees, she saw a parked golf cart. There were several waitstaff members standing around it, a few smoking cigarettes. She realized that she'd stumbled upon the employees' break area.

"Sorry," she said, and started to turn away, but it was too late. The waitstaff all hurried to stub out their cigarettes and return to their posts inside, muttering apologies as they left.

"Really, please don't go on my account," she said again, but it was too late. She was left alone with the lingering smell of cigarette smoke and the sound of the cicadas chirping in the trees. Nora had no interest in returning to the party, so she sat down on the slightly grubby seat of the golf cart. She wasn't used to wearing heels, much less the unusually high ones she'd opted for that evening. It was an immediate relief to be off her feet.

Now what? Nora wondered. *How long can I hide out here before I'm missed? Probably just a few minutes.*

Yet, she wanted nothing more than to stay hidden in her isolated spot, rather than have to go back inside and deal with the intense discomfort of being in the same room as her husband, her lover and his wife, surrounded by throngs of people they all knew.

I'm not this person, Nora told herself for what—the hundredth, thousandth time since her affair with Josh had begun? *I can't live like this. It's too much drama, too many emotional peaks and valleys. It's too much for me to bear.*

"Hey."

Nora glanced up. When she saw Josh standing there, she felt a jolt of electricity pass through her. She'd been so caught in her thoughts, in her anxiety, she hadn't heard him approach.

"What are you doing out here?"

"I could ask you the same thing."

He smiled. "I saw you leave. I followed you out."

"What if someone saw you?"

Josh shrugged. "What if they did? Why did you sneak away?"

"I don't know. I guess I just…" Nora smiled weakly, then shook her head. "I saw you, then I saw Gwen. I freaked out a little."

"Tell me about it." Josh walked around the golf cart to sit next to her. Their shoulders brushed. It took all of Nora's strength not to lean against him. "I wasn't expecting to see you here tonight."

"Believe me. I wasn't expecting to run into you, either."

"Do you normally come to this shindig?"

"No, but Carter's firm bought a table in exchange for being listed as one of the sponsors. They're making a push to be seen as a philanthropic presence in town. Do you?"

"Usually. Gwen always manages to wrangle some invites. She used to love going to these sort of events, but I'm surprised she bothered this year."

"Why?"

"Because Gwen likes people to envy her. With the troubles we've been having, both in our marriage and with Abby, that puts her at risk. She'd rather die than have anyone feel sorry for her. She's been turning down invitations for months."

Nora stood abruptly. For the first time since their affair had begun, Josh's presence was making her feel almost claustrophobic. She didn't know if it was worry over being caught together or him talking about his wife when she was so nearby. But suddenly, she felt the urge to escape from Josh, too.

"I should go inside."

"I know. I just couldn't *not* talk to you. When I saw you walk out here, I thought I'd take my chances on getting a moment alone with you."

"This feels dangerous."

Josh shook his head. "I'm sick of this. I'll go inside right now and tell Gwen it's over. We've already talked about it before, so it's hardly going to come as a surprise."

"No!" Nora exclaimed. Then, realizing she was being far

too loud, she lowered her voice. "You can't tell your wife you want a divorce in the middle of the Heart Ball."

"There's never going to be a perfect time."

"This is pretty much the opposite of perfect. You just said that she abhors being pitied. You'd be humiliating her in front of everyone she knows."

"She's never cared about my feelings. Why should I offer her the same courtesy?"

"Because you're a better person than that."

Josh and Nora stared at one another for a long moment.

"Look." Nora sighed. "I have to get inside. Carter is going to wonder where I am. This is dangerous."

She saw Josh register that it was the second time she'd used that word. *Dangerous.* He looked at her carefully.

"Has Carter ever hurt you? Physically hurt you."

Emotions began to flood over Nora, recollections she'd done her best to suppress. The memory of the physical pain was easier to bury. There was also the shock and betrayal that accompanied that pain, and which caused more permanent damage. The all too familiar tendrils of anxiety began to creep up, winding their way through her.

"I can't do this right now. I'm sorry, I just can't."

Nora turned abruptly, and strode away back down the walkway until she reached the patio. She walked through the crowd, which had swollen to an even larger size in her absence. She thought she heard someone call her name, but she didn't stop to see who it was. Instead, she headed straight toward the edge of the patio, which overlooked the ocean. Once there, she gripped the iron safety railing with both hands, tipped her head forward and closed her eyes. She tried to force her breath to steady, to return to normal.

"Nora! I was calling your name. Didn't you hear me? Here, I got this for you." Carter appeared next to her. He was holding two glasses. One was a pink cocktail, which he handed to her. The other was something clear, possibly club soda. There was a time when Nora would have checked to make sure it was. Not tonight. "I know you asked for a vodka, but the bartender talked me into having you try the specialty drink of the night. It's a Cupid something."

"Thank you," Nora said.

Thank you. Yes, please. No, thank you. These were the words that passed for their marital communications these days. Nora took her cocktail and gulped a hefty swallow. It was too sweet, too potent, but she didn't care.

Let me go numb, she thought. *Numbness would be a gift right now.*

"Where did you go off to?"

"I just needed some air." Nora took another large sip of her drink and was startled that she'd nearly emptied the glass in two gulps.

Is this how all alcoholics begin? she wondered. Stress combined with a free flow of alcohol? She'd always assumed she was inoculated against the disease. Living with an alcoholic, and all of the shittiness that surrounded it, would make anyone think twice before finding solace in a bottle. Yet, here she was, at a social event she hadn't even wanted to attend, in the midst of a full-blown panic attack. The only thing she could imagine that would remotely help was to consume as much alcohol as possible.

"Easy there," Carter said. He tipped his head to one side and assumed what Nora privately thought of as his Concerned Carter face.

Nora was, for the second time that evening, surprised at the level of antipathy that coursed through her. *Go away,* she wanted to say. *Go away, and leave me alone, forever and ever. Is that too much to fucking ask? I cleaned your vomit off the stairs. I hid your crippling hangovers from the kids. I picked you up from the drunk tank at the police station in the middle of the night. Now you're going to give*

*me that look, that annoyingly sanctimonious expression, just because
I consumed one drink faster than you'd have liked? Fuck the fuck off.*

Nora took one last rebellious drink of the pink cocktail. It
tasted of strawberry and vodka and something unpleasantly sour.

"I want another one," she said, handing her glass back to
Carter.

"Are you sure?" he asked.

The fucking hypocrite.

"Yes," Nora said. "I'm sure."

chapter twenty

abby

Abby's nerves were jangling as she sat in the waiting room of Pool and Associates, the commercial real estate firm where Carter Holliday worked. She'd been surprised to find that the firm was officed in a converted cottage, complete with a porch and flowering bushes planted around the front entrance, rather than in a more modern office building. The front room had a row of uncomfortable wooden captain's chairs, with a matching coffee table piled high with glossy magazines of commercial real estate for sale. To distract herself, Abby flipped through one or two of the magazines, looking at photos of golf courses and large office buildings listed at staggeringly high prices. It didn't help. Her palms were sweating. She felt almost lightheaded from the stress of being there.

What was she going to say to Carter Holliday? Abby had no idea. She was fairly sure she shouldn't have gone there without having worked out some sort of plan of action. But she couldn't resist the opportunity to meet him. She felt an almost kinship to the man. They were both being betrayed by people they loved.

The receptionist—a nice older lady with close-cropped gray hair and bright orange lipstick—had disappeared into the back of the office shortly after Abby arrived for her ten o'clock appointment.

When she returned to her desk, she said to Abby, "Mr. Holliday will be right out."

"Thank you."

Abby obviously had no interest in being an intern at Pool and Associates, but she wondered what the job entailed. Did the interns ride along when clients were being shown the properties for sale? Were they left behind in the office to collate files and sort through paper clips? Internships were supposed to provide valuable work experience, but from what Abby had heard from friends who'd had them, a lot of companies just stashed their interns in back offices and either ignored them or assigned them the boring tasks none of the paid employees wanted to touch.

Abby wondered if private investigators took on interns. Maybe that was something she could look into. Imagine being able to shadow a PI for a few months. Although, real life private investigators probably did most of their work online, and Abby had already learned that stakeouts involved hours upon hours of boredom.

A door to the back office opened, and Carter Holliday appeared. Abby recognized him immediately from his pictures on Facebook. She felt another flurry of nerves. He was tall and in decent shape, especially for a guy his age. He'd combed his light brown hair back in a way that she supposed was an attempt to disguise the fact that it was thinning, and he sported a hideous soul patch–style goatee.

"Abby, right? I'm Carter Holliday." Abby stood and they shook hands. His grip was very firm. "Come back to my office."

Abby managed to fix a smile on her face. "Thank you for meeting with me."

"Of course." Carter chuckled. "Although after all the money I've paid your father over the years for three sets of braces, I really should be sending my kids to apply for internships with him."

Carter led Abby to his office, which was spacious enough to accommodate a large wooden desk, a pair of chairs facing it, several filing cabinets and a leather couch pushed up against one wall. His work space was not tidy. There were stacks of paper everywhere—piled on his desk, on top of the filing cabinets, taking up almost all the room on the couch. Carter even had to clear papers off one of the chairs positioned in front of his desk so that Abby would have somewhere to sit.

"Officially, we're trying to become a paperless office," Carter joked as he deposited the stack to his already cluttered desk. "You can see how well that's going. Anyway, take a seat. Did you bring a copy of your CV?"

"Yes," Abby said, handing over the document, which she'd polished in the weeks since first contacting him.

He glanced over it, then looked up at Abby.

"It says you're majoring in political science," he commented. "Most of the kids who apply for internships here are business majors."

"Actually, I'm planning to change my major when I return to school. I'm not really interested in politics."

"Smart girl. Do you mind if I ask why you're taking time off from school?"

Abby hesitated. This was a question she should have been prepared for. But, then, she hadn't prepared herself for this conversation at all. What had she been thinking? Why hadn't she come in with a plan? Or at least anticipated the sort of probative questions to ask to elicit evidence and control the conversation.

But then, Abby thought, *I'm not a detective and I'm not investigating a crime. I just know something terrible about his wife.*

"My boyfriend and I broke up."

"I'm sorry to hear that."

"Yeah. I guess I needed some time off."

Carter frowned. "Can I offer you some advice?"

"Sure."

"I know that you're only applying here for an internship position, but part of interning is learning how to conduct yourself in a professional setting. A breakup is probably not the sort of information you'd want to share in a real interview. Especially if you left school over it. Your main goal in an interview is to impress potential employers. You certainly don't want them to think that you're flighty or unreliable. Which I'm sure you're not, but you know the saying—you only get one chance to make a good first impression."

Abby flushed with embarrassment and immediately felt defensive.

"So I should have lied? Made up a reason?"

"Don't get me wrong." Carter held up his hands in a placating gesture. "I appreciate your honesty. But if you were my kid, this is information I'd want you to have. Sometimes it's more important to finesse the details in order to put your best foot forward."

Abby didn't know what to say. *What am I doing here?* she wondered. *What could I possibly have hoped to accomplish by meeting him?*

Carter smiled. "It's nothing to worry about. This is just part of the learning process. It's rare for someone to instinctively be good at interviews. But it's something you can practice and work on. For example, it's never a good idea to share information that's too personal. Instead of saying you're taking time off from school because of a breakup, maybe instead say you decided it was important to gain some real-world experience.

For you to better tailor your studies going forward. Does that make sense?"

Even though Abby knew Carter Holliday was trying to be helpful, there was something about him that put her on edge. What right did he have to be so smug and condescending? His wife was having an affair with her father, and he had no idea. In fact, if Abby was going to blame her mother in part for the affair—and she did—why didn't this man also bear some of the responsibility? Maybe he was a shitty person, too. Maybe he was a horrible husband.

Who knows? Abby thought. *Maybe his wife hates his stupid soul patch, too.*

As she sat there, listening to him blather on as though he was some sort of expert on everything, she realized that there was something off about Carter Holliday. Something unpleasant. If Abby believed in auras—which she did not—his would be dark, possibly even malevolent.

"Young people always think they know more than they do." Carter was still talking, oblivious to the fact that Abby was no longer listening. "It's not just you, it's your entire generation. You all think that you're owed something. You have no appreciation for how hard you have to work to compete. Life isn't easy. You have to learn that in order to succeed, you have to have a gladiator mind-set. You have to—"

"Your wife is having an affair with my father," Abby blurted out.

She hadn't meant to say it. Or, she didn't think she did. But she had. Now it was out in the open, impossible to take back.

chapter twenty-one

nora

"Where have you been? I've been trying to get ahold of you for days," Maddie said as soon as Nora picked up her call.

"I know. I'm so sorry." Her hands were floury from the dough she'd been kneading, so Nora tucked the phone between her ear and shoulder. "I've been crazy busy."

"I know you have a lot going on." Maddie still sounded disgruntled. "I've just missed you. You're my rock, remember?"

Nora was immediately flooded with guilt. She'd been so distracted by her relationship with Josh, she'd been ignoring other areas of her life, including Maddie, who needed her support right now.

"I'm sorry," Nora said again. "What are you doing tonight? Do you want to come over for dinner?"

"I can't tonight. I have the boys."

"Bring them along. I'm making chicken potpie. It will be fun to have you."

"I wish we could, but Leo has a basketball game and James has Cub Scouts. I'm not sure how I'm supposed to be in two places at once, but I guess I'll have to figure it out. Allen and I used to divide and conquer, each taking a kid. But he's too busy with Sabine to help. They have dinner reservations in Palm Beach. Apparently, that's more important than his sons. He was kind enough to point out that it's my week to have them. That I shouldn't expect him to be around to help out on his off weeks."

"What an asshole."

"Yep. He pretty much defines asshole. I can't believe I was married to him for fourteen years and never realized it."

"People do change," Nora said. "He probably wasn't an asshole when you married him."

"I think he just hid it better back then. Anyway, when can I see you? Are you free for lunch next week?"

"Definitely." But even as she made plans to have lunch with Maddie the following Tuesday, Nora found herself hoping that wouldn't be the one day Josh could get free to see her. Her call-waiting beeped. "Hold on one second. Someone's calling in." She checked the caller ID. It was her bank. "Hey, it's the bank calling. I'd better grab it."

"No worries. See you Tuesday."

Nora said bye before hitting the flash button to pick up the incoming call.

"Hello."

"Is this Nora Holliday?"

"Yes, speaking."

"Mrs. Holliday, this is Sharon Conway at Calloway Bank. I'm calling because there's been some unusual activity on your account that was flagged by our fraud department. I wanted to make sure the charges to your account were authorized."

"Oh, no." This had happened before. The last time, someone had stolen Nora's debit card number and made purchases at several gas stations and a big-box electronics store in Miami before the bank caught it and turned off the card. The bank had issued a refund to their checking account, but it was an account that Nora frequently used to pay online bills. It had taken hours to update her new card information on all of the websites. "The only time I've used my card today was at the grocery store. If it's anything other than that, the account probably was compromised."

"The charges were actually made on the card of your account's joint holder."

"That's my husband."

"I tried calling Mr. Holliday but wasn't able to reach him. As I said, the activity was unusual, so I wanted to get in touch with one of you as quickly as possible."

Nora felt the familiar sensation of a sick tightening in her stomach. She was about to hear something she didn't want to know. It was a sixth sense she'd developed over the years of her marriage, always waiting for the next catastrophe. Like the time Carter had called from the police station after he was arrested for drinking and driving. Or when the hospital called to tell her he'd been admitted to the emergency room after falling at a bar and hitting his head. Just last week, she'd gotten a letter from the bank informing her that their account was overdrawn, and she still hadn't gotten a straight answer from Carter about that. She'd learned over the years that sometimes it was easier to let things go, to not examine them too closely. The strategy clearly didn't work. Nora just ended up blindsided.

"Where were the charges made?"

"Several offshore companies, which was the first red flag. I did some research, and they appear to be gambling websites. The charges are fairly significant. There's one for two thousand seventy-five dollars, another for three thousand thirty-two dollars. Do you think it's possible that your husband made those charges?"

Yes, Nora thought. *Yes, it's not only possible, it's likely.*

"I don't know if my husband authorized the charges or not." Having to admit this was humiliating. Nora pressed her hand, which was suddenly ice-cold, against her forehead. "I'll call him now and have him get in touch with you. Can you give me the best number where I can reach you…?"

After Nora hung up with the bank, she immediately dialed Carter's number. He didn't answer his phone. She sent him a text asking him to call her back as soon as possible. Then she turned her attention back to the bread dough. At least punching it down would relieve some of the tension that was now knotting her shoulders and neck. Although it did nothing to end the sickening feeling in her stomach that something was very, very wrong.

Carter never called Nora back. He also didn't arrive home from work at his usual time.

He was occasionally late, so his tardiness alone wouldn't have caused her to be alarmed. It happened sometimes, if he got busy with a client or if his coworkers decided on an impromptu get-together after work. But he usually remembered to send a text, letting her know where he was. She hadn't heard from him all day. Her sixth sense was now clanging with alarm.

What have you done? she wondered. *What will it be this time? Just the gambling debts, or is it something more? Something even worse?*

"Dinner's ready," Nora called up the stairs. "Will you guys come down and set the table?"

Katie was the first to appear. "Where's Dad?"

"I'm not sure. He must be working late."

Dylan and Matt ambled in behind their sister. The kids set about getting the plates and silverware out while Nora used thick kitchen mitts to pull the steaming chicken potpie out of the oven.

"I texted Dad, like, an hour ago, asking if he'd stop at the office supply store on his way home," Matt said. "He never responded."

This caused Nora yet another jolt of concern. It was also unlike Carter to ignore a text from one of their children.

"I'll call him," Nora said, reaching for her phone. "Here, will someone butter the peas, and put the bowl on the table? I'll serve the potpie from the counter. It's too hot to touch."

Nora dialed Carter's number and waited. The phone rang once before almost immediately switching over to his voice-mail message. *You have reached Carter Holliday with Pool and Associates. Your call is very important to me. Please leave a message with your name and telephone number. I will return your call as soon as possible. Thank you.*

Nora hung up without leaving a message.

Did he just reject my phone call? she wondered. It sounded like he had. Maybe his phone was just low on power. Carter was forever forgetting to charge it.

She sent him a text: We're about to have dinner. Please check in ASAP.

Nora sat down with her children at the table. None of the kids seemed particularly concerned by their father's absence. In fact, other than Carter not being there, it was a typical Holliday family meal. Dylan teased Katie about a selfie she'd posted on Facebook, which quickly devolved into a squabble until Nora intervened and told them to cut it out. Matt reported that the biology test he'd taken that day had gone well. Nora listened to their chatter and picked at her food, while all three of her kids went back for second helpings.

"Can I have the last piece of potpie or should we leave some for Dad?" Katie asked.

Nora checked her phone. Carter still hadn't responded, although there was a text from Josh: Are we still on for tomorrow?

Yes, she typed back quickly.

"Go ahead. Your dad must have gone out for dinner," Nora replied.

"I wish he'd text me back," Matt said. "I need some mechanical pencils."

"Are you out again?"

"Yep."

"Okay, well, I can pick some up for you tomorrow," Nora said.

"Thanks," Matt said.

The kids miraculously offered to do the dishes. Nora was more than happy to leave them to it. She headed upstairs, lugging a laundry basket of clean clothes with her. She set the basket on the bed in the master bedroom and began folding. The mindless busywork soothed her a bit, but the worry was still there, gnawing away.

Where is he? she wondered. Carter still hadn't called, hadn't texted her or their kids. Did he know she'd spoken to the bank? Was afraid to face her? If so, what did that mean? Just how much trouble was he in?

She had sorted out the folded stacks of laundry, when Katie came in.

"Here…take your laundry," Nora said. "Will you ask your brothers to come get theirs?"

"Sure," Katie answered. "Dad finally texted me."

"He did? What did he say?"

"Just that he was at a work thing. He's going to be late."

"Can I see?"

Katie shrugged as she handed over her phone. Katie had sent Carter a series of several videos featuring Cats or Otters being silly. When he hadn't replied to those, she'd finally texted him, Wut up?

Carter had finally responded a few minutes later: Wirking lare c u soonz.

Nora stared at the text. It reminded her of the texts she used to get from Carter during his drinking days, vague and riddled with typos. Was it possible he was drinking again? Well, of course it was possible. Carter was an alcoholic. His sobriety was and probably always would be precarious. She could feel Katie watching her. She had to be careful not to register any concern. Children were always quick to pick up on any parental strife.

"I'm sure he'll be home soon." Nora placed her daughter's phone on top of the stack of laundry, and handed the whole bundle to her. "Don't worry."

"I'm not worried," Katie scoffed, shooting Nora a strange look.

I am, Nora thought.

Carter still wasn't home when Nora went to bed. She didn't think she'd be able to sleep, so she picked up the novel she'd been reading and tried to focus on it, but found herself just re-reading the same paragraph over and over. All the while, she listened for the sound of the door squeaking open, signaling Carter's return. It never came.

Nora drifted off at some point. When she woke up a few hours later, she was disoriented and still alone. The light was on. Her book was resting against her chest. She turned to check the clock, which glowed 1:42 in blue numbers. Nora got up. Between the stress of the day and the awkward position she'd fallen asleep in, the back of her neck was sore. She gently stretched it, trying to work out the painful knot. She padded downstairs, still holding her hand to her neck when she heard it.

Snoring.

It was coming from the direction of the living room, so Nora headed there. The lights were still on, or rather, had been turned back on. Before she'd gone to bed, Nora had switched off all the lamps other than the overhead in the kitchen so that Carter wouldn't return to a dark house.

But there he was, stretched out on the couch, still wearing the suit he'd had on when he left for work that morning. He hadn't even kicked his shoes off. Carter was lying on his back, his mouth slack and open. He was snoring so loudly, Nora was surprised she hadn't been able to hear him all the way upstairs. His coloring looked odd, ashen with an almost green pallor. Nora took a few steps closer toward him, preparing to wake him, when she smelled it.

The unmistakable scent of alcohol. He reeked as though he'd doused himself with it.

Carter wasn't just asleep. He was passed-out drunk.

chapter twenty-two

gwen

In the weeks following the Heart Ball, Gwen's thoughts kept returning to Tara Edwards. Both the way she'd made a beeline for Josh and his look of shock at seeing her there. It confirmed what Gwen had already suspected. There was definitely something going on between the two of them. Was it just a flirtation? Or was it a full-blown affair? Gwen didn't know—not yet, anyway—but she was surprised by the intensity of her reaction, especially since she'd been wondering for months how much she'd care if Josh was having an affair.

Gwen was enraged.

She supposed that was a normal reaction. No one would respond positively to finding out that their spouse was possibly cheating on them. But for Gwen, it wasn't the thought of Josh having sex with someone else that caused the fury to bloom inside her. That aspect of their marriage had withered years ago.

She had no interest in her husband physically, so this was not the unhinged anger of a spurned lover.

It was worse than that.

Ever since her visit to Christine before Christmas, Gwen hadn't been able to stop thinking about the choices she'd made as a young adult. She was particularly struck by Christine's revelation that she'd always believed Gwen was destined for a bigger, more vibrant destiny than the suburban mediocrity she'd settled for. It encapsulated everything Gwen had been feeling for the past few years. This idea that she'd been manipulated into a life she wasn't meant for, only to have Josh cheat on her after twenty-four years of marriage, was unacceptable. After all she had given up, all she had sacrificed, he was going to turn her into a stereotype of the cast-aside wife?

It was deeply and unforgivably insulting, and Gwen would not allow it to go unpunished.

First, though, she needed to find out all she could about what exactly was going on between her husband and Tara Edwards. A few weeks after the Heart Ball, Gwen called Andrea Young.

"I just wanted to thank you again for inviting us to the ball," Gwen had said brightly. "And I wanted to invite you to lunch. My treat."

"How fun! I'd love to get together! We need to catch up. There were so many people around the other night we hardly got to gossip at all. Although—" Andrea lowered her voice "—I was going to call you anyway. I asked around about that certain person we were discussing that night. I have some dish for you on that front."

Gwen smiled to herself. She'd known that Andrea would be the perfect accomplice to enlist in her fact-finding mission. Gwen hadn't even had to steer their conversation back to Tara Edwards.

"I can't wait to hear everything," she said.

★ ★ ★

"Why are you so dressed up?" Abby asked.

Gwen was standing in the foyer, applying lipstick in the mirror that hung by their front door. She glanced over at her daughter, who had been acting even odder than usual lately. Abby wasn't as listless as she'd been when she first dropped out of school, true, but now she seemed jittery and always on edge. Maybe it was time to schedule a follow-up with Dr. Thomas to see if the antidepressant she was taking was working.

"I'm going out to lunch." Gwen capped her lipstick and dropped the tube into her handbag.

"By yourself?"

"No. With a friend."

"Who?" Abby was playing with the ends of her hair, twisting them around her fingers. At least she was wearing something other than her pajama pants for once, although the leggings and T-shirt she had on weren't much of an upgrade.

"Andrea Young. Why the sudden interest in my social life?"

"I just thought...never mind." Abby turned away, her shoulders hunched up.

"What did you think?"

"That maybe you had a meeting with someone. Like...a business meeting or something."

Gwen laughed without humor. "Unfortunately, I don't have business meetings, because I was too foolish in my younger years to understand how important it was to have a career. Which is advice I've been trying to impart to you, and which you seem intent on ignoring."

Abby slunk off back to her room. Gwen let her go without further comment. Her daughter didn't realize how lucky she was to have had the advantages they'd given to her. When she was Abby's age, Gwen would have killed to have had the opportunity of a college education handed to her. Instead, here Abby was, throwing it all away. It was infuriating, really. Unfortunately, her daughter would have to figure it out for herself eventually. The days when she could count on her parents to take care of her as though she were still a small child were rapidly coming to an end.

Gwen had arranged to meet Andrea at an intimate bistro in downtown Shoreham. Andrea was already there when Gwen arrived, sitting at a table covered in white linens and sipping a glass of white wine. Another stroke of good luck, Gwen thought. Andrea was always more loquacious when she'd been drinking.

"Hello there, beautiful girl." Andrea stood and air-kissed Gwen. "This is such a treat."

"It is for me, too. I'm thrilled to get out of the house. What are you having?"

"Chardonnay. Do you want a sip?"

Gwen tasted the wine. "Oh, that's good!" Gwen leaned forward conspiratorially. "We should order a bottle."

Once the waiter had poured the wine, they ordered their lunches, both opting for the Cobb salad. Gwen hoped that Andrea would immediately tell her what she'd found out about Tara Edwards. Andrea, however, was all aflutter about some drama involving her landscapers, which had resulted in several valuable palm trees dying. Gwen tried to appear interested but found herself quickly losing patience with the subject.

"Then they tried to tell me that the trees were already diseased!" Andrea prattled on. "I told them, 'Look, those trees were absolutely healthy before we hired you. We're supposed to believe that it's just a coincidence that as soon as you took over our landscaping, everything started dying off?' I swear, customer service is a lost art."

"I know what you mean," Gwen said. "We're having our driveway paved. The company we hired said they can't start work until mid-April. We had to go with them because every other company I called said they wouldn't be able to start work until May at the earliest."

"That's ridiculous. What, is there some sort of rush on driveway paving services?"

"I guess there must be," Gwen said. She poured more wine in Andrea's glass. "Here, you look like you're ready for a top-up."

Andrea laughed. "You're going to get me in trouble. At this rate, I'll be completely hammered by the time David comes home from work."

"So, you said you had gossip to tell me," Gwen said, hoping to nudge the conversation back on course.

Andrea gasped, and dramatically covered her mouth with her hands. "Oh, my God, I can't believe I didn't tell you this right away! It's about that Tara Edwards. The one who was all over Josh at the Heart Ball."

Finally, Gwen thought. She toyed with the stem on her own wineglass, careful not to drink too much herself. She needed to stay sharp and focused for this conversation.

Andrea leaned forward. "You are *not* going to believe this."

"I can't wait to hear."

"Josh isn't the first husband Tara Edwards has gone after."

"We don't know that she's after Josh," Gwen demurred.

"Just wait until you hear what I found out. You may change your mind about that. I asked around. Apparently, Tara has quite the reputation for this sort of thing."

"Doing what exactly?"

"Get this. I found out that she and her husband scored an invite to the Heart Ball through Leslie Carr. You know Leslie, right? Pretty brunette, but she overdoes it on the fillers."

Gwen smiled. It was an apt description. "Yes, of course. Her daughter was in the same year as Abby. They were on a travel volleyball team together."

"That is the one. I've known Leslie for years, so I called her and asked her how she knew Tara. She said she barely does. But

Leslie's youngest son is friends with Tara's twin boys. Anyway, Tara called Leslie up one day and basically begged her for an invitation to the Heart Ball. Leslie said she totally felt put on the spot, but someone at her table had just dropped out, so she offered the tickets to Tara and her husband. She said it was the worst decision she's ever made."

Gwen thought that if that was actually true, Leslie had lived a remarkably easy life. She didn't want to interrupt Andrea's flow of chatter, however, so she just nodded encouragingly.

"The husband—his name is Kynan—is an aerospace engineer and supposedly very smart, but apparently he's basically incapable of carrying a conversation. Leslie said it was like trying to talk to a wall. He just sat there all night and hardly said a word," Andrea continued.

Gwen wasn't sure what any of this had to do with Tara's reputation for going after other people's husbands, but nodded again, hoping Andrea would eventually get to the point.

"So, I asked Leslie what she knew about Tara. Here's the part you're not going to believe. Leslie told me that two years ago, Tara had a *huge* crush on Mark Lambert. Do you know Mark and Casey Lambert? No? They're very sporty. In fact, they own one of those CrossFit places where people go and torture themselves flipping tractor tires and whatnot, and the women all end up looking like linebackers. But Mark also volunteers a lot of his time coaching, and one—or maybe both, I don't know the exact details—of Tara's sons was on a basketball team Mark coached through the county league. Anyway, that's when Tara became *obsessed* with Mark. First, she joined his gym and would show up there all the time, just so she'd run into him. Then they became Facebook friends, and that's when the trouble really began."

Gwen perked up. "Trouble?"

"Mark apparently posts on Facebook a lot to advertise the gym. Every time he'd post something, Tara would immediately like it and comment on it. She was the first commenter on every single post that he put up. It was like she was stalking him online, just waiting for him to post something so she could engage with him."

Gwen was starting to find Andrea's story anticlimactic, especially after she'd built it up as being some sort of a scandal. So far, it just sounded like two people who spent too much time on social media. Was that what passed as noteworthy gossip anymore?

Andrea continued. "Then it started to get really weird."

"Weird how?"

"Tara started showing up at the gym with presents for Mark. Homemade energy bars, granola, things like that. At first, both he and Casey thought it was sweet, that she was just being friendly. But she always made a point of saying that whatever she brought in was for Mark. Not for Casey, or their staff, but specifically for *him*. Then she started buying things for their kids. One of the Lamberts' sons lost his practice basketball, so Tara bought him a new one, even though it didn't have anything to do with her."

Andrea now had Gwen's full attention. This was starting to sound familiar.

"What did they do about it?"

"At first, nothing. They were busy running a business, and they didn't want to risk alienating a client. But her behavior just kept escalating. She started texting Mark constantly. She would do it under the pretext of saying she wanted to make sure that he was teaching whatever class she was planning to attend that day. That he was her favorite trainer. But it got to the point where she was texting him multiple times a day. I guess you don't know Casey, but she's a tough cookie. She got fed up. She told Mark it was time he put an end to it."

"What did he do?"

"He basically sat Tara down one day and told her that he was happily married. That while they welcomed her business, he was uncomfortable with the amount of attention she was paying him. He told her it had to stop."

"Was she upset?"

"Apparently. She tried to say he'd misunderstood her intentions, that she had just been trying to be friendly. Mark said he was glad it was a misunderstanding, and that was the end of it."

"And was it?"

"Not entirely. Tara stopped going to their gym, and unfriended both of the Lamberts on Facebook. They also had an issue for a while with someone leaving anonymous bad reviews about their gym on different websites, but they were never sure if it was Tara who was behind that. They'd had an issue with a client who felt he'd been overcharged, so he could have been the one leaving the bad reviews."

"Still," Gwen mused. "It is an interesting story."

"I knew you'd think so." Andrea looked pleased. "Do you think she's targeting Josh now?"

Gwen shrugged. "Honestly, I'm not sure. I didn't tell you this before, but..." Gwen paused for full dramatic impact. "Tara Edwards bought Christmas presents for Abby and Simon."

Andrea gasped. "She didn't."

"She did," Gwen confirmed. "They were inappropriately expensive, too, especially considering she doesn't even know my kids."

"What did Josh say?"

Gwen had already decided that while she wanted Tara Edwards's reputation to take another hit, she didn't want to make her own marriage the subject of town gossip. That might eventually be unavoidable. But if and when she did divorce Josh, she wanted no one to be in doubt that she was the one leaving him, not the other way around.

"He was oblivious, of course." Gwen waved an airy hand. "You know Josh. He's nice to everyone. I can see how someone who's predisposed to developing crushes on married men would take that the wrong way. Except Josh would never cross the line. Especially not with the parent of one of his patients. He's far too ethical for that."

"No, he would never," Andrea agreed. "Plus Josh absolutely adores you."

Gwen smiled. "I know. I'm very lucky."

"No," Andrea cooed. She'd had several glasses of wine by this point. Her eyes were starting to look glassy. "He's the lucky one. Everyone always says that. How could he possibly ever be interested in a nobody like Tara Edwards when he has you? It's incomprehensible."

"That's sweet of you to say."

"So what happened with the presents?"

"I stopped by Tara's house one morning, thanked her and told her we appreciated her for thinking of us, but that we really couldn't accept the gifts. Our kids already have so much. I suggested that she should instead donate them to one of the charities that provides for less fortunate kids."

"Did you really?" Andrea pressed a hand to her chest and laughed. "God, Gwen, you are so poised. I doubt I'd have been that magnanimous with the little hussy, but it sounds like you handled it perfectly. What did she say?"

"I think she was embarrassed, but I made it clear it wasn't a big deal. She does have to bring her boys into Josh's practice, after all. I don't want that to be awkward for her. To be honest, at the time, I thought she was just trying to make friends with both of us. She'd once asked me about going out to dinner as couples."

"Except now we know she's done this sort of thing before."

"Right." Gwen shook her head and took a tiny sip of her wine. "I almost feel sorry for her."

"I don't." Andrea snorted. "She's pathetic. In fact, if anyone brings her name up to me, I'm going to be sure to let them know what kind of a person she is. Pretty soon, no one's going to want to deal with her."

"Just please keep Josh and me out of it. You know what this town is like when it comes to gossip."

"Don't worry, I won't mention you. Besides, Josh is clearly blameless. You couldn't have been nicer about it. She's lucky she wasn't sidling up to my husband and dropping off presents for my kids." Andrea shook her head. "If she was targeting my family, I'd make sure her life was no longer worth living."

chapter twenty-three

abby

Abby had made a terrible mistake telling Carter Holliday about the affair. She knew it as soon as the words had left her mouth. Now, weeks later, she was still waiting to find out the consequences her rash decision would bring.

After she'd told him, Carter had stared at her for several long beats. Then he'd abruptly stood, set her résumé on his desk and strode angrily out of his office. Abby hadn't been sure what she should do. Was she supposed to leave, too? Wait for him to return? She had sat frozen in place, staring down at her hands clenched in her lap.

He was gone for so long that Abby finally decided she should go. She was just standing to leave when Carter suddenly returned, thumping his office door closed behind him. He was carrying a lowball glass that was two-thirds full of a clear liquid. He returned to his seat behind his desk, took a long drink from his glass and only then did he look at her again. There was something in his expression that Abby found deeply unsettling.

What have I done? she wondered.

"Tell me," he said.

"I just... I found out... I thought... I guess I thought you had a right to know, too," Abby stammered.

"No. I mean, tell me the details. Tell me what you know."

Abby sat back down and told him everything. She told him about seeing her father kissing a blonde woman in his car, and how she'd spent weeks trying to figure out who it was. She told him that she'd followed her father to the Seabreeze Hotel, how a blonde—the same woman she believed she'd seen in the car with him at the beach—had arrived a few minutes later and how she'd copied down the woman's license plate number. She told him about her subsequent internet sleuthing that had revealed the woman to be Nora Holliday. While she talked, Carter had steadily drained the liquid from his glass.

"But you can't be sure it was her," he said when she'd finished. "Basically, you saw your father with a woman whose face you couldn't see. Later you saw him arrive at a hotel at around the same time my wife was there. But there was never a point when you saw them together and could identify Nora as the woman he was with."

"No," Abby admitted. "But, I'm pretty sure it was her."

"Pretty sure," Carter repeated. His tone was scornful. His words were now slightly slurred. "You made an appointment to see me under false pretenses, to tell me one of the worst possible things a husband can hear about his wife, only to be *pretty sure.*"

Abby felt her face go hot. She didn't know how she'd expected him to react, mostly because she hadn't thought any of this out carefully enough to have expectations. If she had, she would have assumed he'd be upset, or possibly angry. But she hadn't expected him not to believe her.

"Why else would they both be at the hotel?"

"I don't know. Maybe they were both having lunch there separately."

"The hotel doesn't have a restaurant. I checked."

"Okay, maybe your father was there meeting some other woman to fuck, because the only thing you're actually sure about is that he's screwing around. My wife could have been there for some completely unrelated reason."

Abby had flinched at the ugliness of his words, the vehemence of his anger.

"It was her," she said evenly.

"How do you know?"

"I could tell by the way she looked around when she got out of her car. She was nervous, like she was worried about being seen. I recognized her hair. I know she's the woman my dad was with in the car that day."

"I think it's time for you to leave."

Abby had already come to the same realization, and she stood quickly, her arms stiff at her sides. She took a few steps toward the door to his office before glancing back. Carter was staring at his now empty glass.

"I'm sorry," she said, although the words seemed completely inadequate.

He hadn't responded.

But then, nothing happened.

Abby kept waiting. She knew she had set something in motion with no way to undo it. Carter would confront his wife, or possibly even her father. Gwen would find out, and there was no way she would ignore the situation. But the days kept passing, and Abby waited and watched. Still…nothing happened.

Her parents behaved exactly as they always did, like polite strangers who didn't particularly like one another. But there weren't any loud blowups or even strained conversations. Once,

Gwen got more dressed up than usual to go out, and Abby was sure she must be on her way to meet with a divorce attorney. Except she was apparently just having lunch with a friend.

Abby continued to monitor the Hollidays' social media pages. Neither of the parents were posting very much, other than Nora's regular entries on her cooking blog, but that wasn't unusual for them. Dylan and Katie were more active, although none of their posts indicated any sort of familial discord. Matt still hadn't accepted her friend request.

It was almost as though Abby had dropped a bomb into the lives of their two families, and no one had even noticed.

"This isn't normal," Abby said out loud, staring down at her laptop.

She was just about to switch over to Instagram when her phone rang, startling her. Abby had become so isolated from her friends and previous life that she rarely heard from anyone. Besides, even before, she and her friends never called one another. They communicated almost exclusively via text. She'd had a few concerned messages in the weeks after she'd left school, but those had dwindled before stopping completely after the holidays had passed and the second school semester had begun. She picked up her phone and was even more surprised to see who the caller was.

It was Zara. Her roommate. Or more accurately, now ex-roommate. Abby hadn't heard a word from Zara since she left FSU. This hadn't surprised her. She and Zara had never been particularly close and had only ended up as roommates because they both knew Lana. Also, Abby had always found Zara too intimidating to try to get close to. Still…she was curious why her ex-roommate was reaching out now.

Abby hit the accept call button. "Hi, Zara."

"Hey there." Zara sounded like her usual self, her voice deep and languorous. "I guess that answers my first question. You are still alive, which is good. You know, you could have let us know that you weren't coming back."

"Right. I probably should have."

"I mean, I know you hate Lana. Which is totally understandable." Abby could hear the flick of a lighter as Zara lit a cigarette and exhaled deeply. "But you could have kept me in the loop."

"Sorry."

"So what's going on? Are you ever coming back? Because you left most of your stuff here."

"I don't think so."

"Why not?"

"You know why."

"No, I don't," Zara said, sounding almost disinterested, even though she was the one who had initiated the phone call. "Why?"

"Because of Lana. And Colin. You expect me to live there with her? And with him coming over to see her?" Abby could hear her voice turning shrill, but...seriously? What did Zara expect?

"Huh," Zara said, a response Abby found highly unsatisfactory.

"What do you mean?"

"I just never thought you'd turn out to be such a wuss."

"What? I'm not!"

Zara took another long drag on her cigarette. Abby had always found it odd that Zara smoked, considering her dance background. Weren't athletes supposed to be into clean living and treating their bodies like temples? Zara always seemed like she'd been plunked down in the current day from a different generation. One where cigarettes and cocktails were cool.

"Yeah, you pretty much are. Dropping out of school and running away, and why? Because Colin's fucking Lana? She's as deep as a puddle and about as interesting. She's not the kind of person you ruin your life over."

"I thought you two were friends."

"We are, sort of. I seriously doubt I'll be in touch with her ten years from now. Frankly, I was always surprised you were such good friends with her."

"You were?"

"Yeah. You always seemed like you had more going on than that. You know, a soul."

Abby laughed, which surprised her. She couldn't remember the last time she'd laughed.

"Anyway," Zara continued, "if you're not coming back, do you mind if I store some of my stuff in your room? I could use the extra space."

"Go ahead." Abby paused. "And I may be back at some point. Not to the apartment, although I guess I will eventually have to pick up my things. But...I might come back to school." The words surprised her as she spoke them. Maybe it was bravado in reaction to Zara calling her a wuss. But suddenly, the idea of returning to school didn't seem so impossible. What was she going to do, spend the rest of her life cloistered in her childhood bedroom? "I'll be back at some point."

"Good. If you'd left to go volunteer in South America or something like that, that would be one thing. But making life-altering plans because you finally realized that Colin and Lana are assholes would be tragic."

"You think they're assholes?"

"Everyone thinks they're assholes. It's not even a subjective opinion. They are, in fact, assholes. Frankly, it's better you found out now before you wasted any more time on either of them."

After Abby and Zara hung up, Abby sat on her bed, running one hand over the soft quilt her grandmother had made her. She thought about their conversation for a long time. She'd always assumed that everyone adored Lana. The idea that Lana wasn't as well-liked or well-thought-of was startling. Except maybe Zara was right. She should have stuck it out at school, rather than running away. At the time, it hadn't felt like a choice. But that was stupid. Of course it had been.

Maybe it really was time to consider going back to school in the fall. Colin would graduate and be gone by then, anyway. Even if she did bump into him at some point, would that really be the end of the world?

No, she decided. It probably wouldn't. Annoyingly, her father had been right. The more time that passed, the less it all hurt. What had once been a pain so intense it knocked the breath out of her body, now felt more like a dull throb of unhappiness. She could live with that.

But, I don't have to make any decisions right this moment, she decided. After all, anything could happen between now and the fall semester. The bomb she'd dropped might still detonate. *Who knows what will happen then?*

chapter twenty-four

nora

Carter was drinking heavily. If anything, it was worse than it had been the last time.

He wouldn't tell Nora what had triggered the relapse. In fact, he hardly spoke to her at all. He began arriving home late at night, usually after she and the kids had gone to bed. When he woke up in the mornings, he was groggy and obviously hungover. More often than not, he'd have left his car at a bar somewhere, and would call for an Uber to collect him before heading into the office. She supposed that was one silver lining. At least, he wasn't drinking and driving—that she knew of anyway.

"Have you called your sponsor?" she asked him one morning. She'd managed to corner him in the kitchen before he'd left for the day while the kids were still upstairs getting ready for school. "Or gone to a meeting?"

Carter had just stared at her blankly over his mug of coffee.

Then, without saying a word, he'd set the mug on the counter, picked up his suit jacket and briefcase and walked out the door. Nora looked down at her hands. They were shaking.

"Are you driving me to school today? Or am I taking the bus?" Katie asked as she roared into the kitchen with a level of energy Nora could only marvel at. She couldn't remember the last time she'd had an unbroken night of sleep, much less woken up feeling energetic.

"The bus," Nora said. "Make sure you eat something. Are the boys on their way down?"

"No idea. I do my best to avoid ABC whenever possible."

"ABC?"

"All Brotherly Contact," Katie replied as she slotted an English muffin into the toaster.

"Nice. Just think, I was going to offer you a ride to school," Dylan said, sauntering in.

"Oh, come on! Mom! Make him drive me!"

"Can I please consume at least one cup of coffee before you all start rioting?" Nora pleaded.

Once the kids had left for school, and the house was almost eerily quiet, Nora picked up her phone. She scrolled through her contacts until she found the person she was looking for. She called his number, waiting for him to pick up.

"Paul? It's Nora Holliday. Carter's wife. Are you free to meet sometime? Today, if possible?"

Nora waited for Paul Miller at a coffee shop in downtown Shoreham. She ordered a latte and a blueberry muffin, but only picked at the pastry. Her appetite had vanished over the past few weeks, which she supposed was somewhat ironic, considering her line of work. The pastry chef who couldn't bear to eat.

"Nora, I'm so sorry I'm late," Paul said, even though she'd only been waiting for a few minutes. He was a tall, gangly man with shaggy dark hair and a prominent Adam's apple. With his heavily lined face and red-veined nose, Paul looked at least ten years older than the fifty-one she knew he was. Nora and Carter had attended his fiftieth birthday party the previous year. But, then, Paul had not led the easiest of lives. At his birthday party, he'd announced that he was celebrating his eighth year of sobriety. He'd been Carter's sponsor in Alcoholics Anonymous ever since Carter joined three years earlier. Nora had met Paul several times over that period, but this was the first time she'd arranged to see him alone.

Nora stood and hugged Paul. "Do you want anything? Coffee, something to eat?"

"I'll get it, don't worry."

Paul went to the counter to order a coffee while Nora tried to figure out the best way to tell him about Carter's relapse as she waited for him to return. She realized that there was no way to soft sell it. The only option was the blunt truth. For once, she wasn't going to hide anything.

"How have you been?" Paul asked as he settled himself in a chair across the table from Nora.

"Not good," she admitted. "That's why I needed to see you. Carter's started drinking again."

Paul nodded as he took a sip of his coffee. "I know. He told me."

"He did?" Nora was surprised. "I guess it's good that he's reaching out for help."

"It's a first step, but he was pretty drunk when he called me. He's been dodging my phone calls ever since."

"He won't talk to me, either. I tried again this morning. Asked him if he'd reached out to you or gone to a meeting, but he wouldn't even answer."

"Well." Paul looked uncomfortable for the first time since he'd arrived. "You do know that the anonymous part of Alcoholics Anonymous means that we're not supposed to share what is said in private. However..." He paused and looked thoughtful for a moment. "I will tell you he said that he—or I suppose the two of you—have been having marital problems."

"He did?"

Nora was certainly aware of their marital troubles. She was surprised that Carter was using that one discussion they'd had several months ago, when she'd finally admitted how unhappy she was, as the excuse for why he had started drinking again.

Unless.

Was it possible Carter had found out about her affair with Josh? It would explain why he'd been so cold, why he was refusing to speak to her. She'd assumed his silence stemmed from not wanting to discuss his drinking and gambling. But what if she'd been wrong?

This thought caused Nora to turn cold with fear.

"Did he go into any detail with you?"

"No. And, like I said, he was pretty trashed at the time we spoke. He wasn't making a whole lot of sense. He just said he thought his marriage was over." Paul looked anxiously at her. "I feel like I'm overstepping here."

"Not at all. I asked you."

"Okay, good. Look, whatever is going on in your marriage is certainly none of my business. But everyone has tough times. Part of what we learn in recovery is that we can't use rough patches as an excuse to relapse."

"Carter has always been self-destructive. In fact, there are a few other things you should probably know."

Paul nodded, waiting for her to speak. Nora realized that he was probably an excellent sponsor. He had a very calm, very still way about him, and he listened attentively.

He's probably heard it all before, she thought. *He's probably beyond being shocked at this point.*

"The first is that I believe Carter also has a gambling addiction," Nora said. "I don't know how bad it is, but there have been several large withdrawals made from our joint bank account. They were for debts he incurred on online gambling websites. I don't know if it goes further than that. If he owes more, and if so, to who. But I think it's become a serious problem."

Paul sighed and rapped his knuckles against the table. "I'm sorry to hear that, Nora. I'd like to tell you it's uncommon, but I'd be lying if I did. As I'm sure you are well aware, some people just have addictive personalities. They might sober up, but then they move on to drugs or overeating, any myriad of other self-destructive behaviors."

Nora knew she had to tell him the rest. She had to tell him everything, so that Paul would know what they were dealing with. But the idea of baring this last secret, the one she'd kept from everyone, was almost physically painful. She could feel her breath go shallow as her pulse started to slowly tick upward.

"There's something else. I don't want to tell you, but I think I have to," she said. Paul nodded again, his eyes intent on her. Nora leaned forward slightly and lowered her voice. "There was one time…when Carter was drinking… He became violent."

Paul didn't seem surprised. Nora wondered if Carter had talked about it at the AA meetings.

"The night it happened, we were fighting about his drinking. Of course. That's what we always fought about. He'd say he was fine, and I'd point out all the ways it wasn't fine. That night—this was a little over three years ago—he was supposed to meet the kids and me at a soccer tournament Dylan was playing in. We had plans to all go to dinner after. Instead, Carter went to a bar after work and got lost in a bottle. That's what I used to call those days—lost days. He'd just disappear. But that night, Dylan was really upset that his dad had missed the game, and Dylan never gets upset about anything. All of the kids were freaked out when Carter got home that night, so drunk he could barely walk. He knocked over a lamp trying to walk across the room. I sent all three of them up to their rooms, and I just lost it. I lit into him. I don't lose my temper very easily, but that night I did."

"Nora. That's a normal reaction to have. You had a right to be angry."

"I know. And, like I said, it wasn't the first time we fought about his drinking. But that night…there was something in his expression." Nora held up her hand and circled her index finger in front of her own face. "Something just changed. It was like the man I'd been married to for all of those years was gone. Like there was this stranger standing there." She looked up at Paul. "He scared the hell out of me."

"What happened then?"

"He hit me." Nora had never said the words out loud before. Not to a friend or a therapist, or even the nurse at the hospital who had looked at her so pityingly. Nora had nearly been sick from the shame. "Just once, but…it was bad. He punched me in the stomach really, really hard. As it turned out—" To her horror, she could feel the hot prick of tears beginning. She used a paper napkin to dab at the corners of her eyes before they could spill out onto her cheeks. "I was pregnant at the time. He didn't know. I didn't even know until I miscarried. But… it happened. Carter felt terrible, of course. It was what motivated him to go into recovery. He finally realized that he had a severe problem that was officially out of control. But it's not something I've ever gotten past."

On her Should I Stay or Should I Go list, the most important entry in the Stay column—and, really, the only one that truly mattered—was that if she left, Carter would have partial custody of the kids. She'd never filed a police report against him—so there was no evidence of domestic abuse. Florida law dictated that parents shared equal custody of their children after a divorce, barring evidence that one of the parents was unfit. If she left him, Carter would continue to live with her children 50 percent of the time, time when she wouldn't be there to protect them from him. If it had terrified her before, it was even worse now that he was drinking again. Carter had never been physically abusive toward the kids. Then again, Nora had never imagined that he would have been capable of hurting her. That, above all else, was the main reason she hadn't left.

"No, I don't imagine it would be easy to ever get past that."

"I told him at the time that if he ever hurt me again—or worse, one of our children—that it would be the end. He promised he wouldn't. To be fair, he's never been violent since that night. But now that he's drinking again…"

Paul leaned forward. "Nora. If you have even the slightest fear that he's going to hurt you, you have to leave. Take the kids and walk out the door. It's really that simple."

"No," Nora said. "It's really not."

"Why not? What's more important than your safety? Your children's safety?"

Nora balled her hands into fists. "Seeing that stranger wearing my husband's face scared the hell out of me. There are days I think I don't know the man I'm married to."

"That's even more reason to leave."

"But you don't understand. What if he falls even farther down this hole and becomes even worse…and I'm not there to see it? To monitor him, at least as best I can?"

"What do you think is going to happen?"

Nora stared at Paul and shook her head. "I don't know, but I do know this—if I leave Carter, and he becomes worse…if he becomes violent again and possibly ends up hurting someone—I could never live with myself for allowing that to happen."

chapter twenty-five

gwen

Gwen didn't ruin Tara Edwards's life overnight. It took her most of the month of March to accomplish the task.

Looping Andrea into her plan had been a stroke of brilliance, Gwen realized. She turned out to be more of an asset than Gwen had even imagined. Within a few days of their lunch, Gwen was leaving the high school after dropping off Simon's gym uniform, which he'd managed to forget at home for about the twentieth time that year. She was just crossing the concrete sidewalk toward the parking lot when someone called her name.

"Gwen! I thought that was you. Wait up!"

Gwen turned around to see Chrissie Calhoun hurrying to catch up with her.

"Hey, Chrissie." Gwen automatically adjusted her features into her public face, even though she didn't really feel like stopping to chat. It was blindingly bright outside, and she'd left her sunglasses in the car. She could already feel a headache coming on. Gwen shaded her eyes, and waited for Chrissie to reach her.

"I'm so glad I ran into you!" Chrissie exclaimed. She was a gregarious redhead with a smattering of freckles over her nose and cheeks. "I talked to Andrea the other day. She was filling me in on your conflict with Tara Edwards."

Gwen wondered what exactly Andrea had told Chrissie, and felt a flash of irritation. Andrea had promised she wouldn't bring Gwen's or Josh's name into any conversations she had about Tara Edwards. Gwen supposed that was the downside of enlisting the help of an unabashed gossip. Andrea probably couldn't help herself. Adding her pursuit of Josh onto Tara's list of misdeeds made it a juicier story.

"I'm not having any conflict with Tara," Gwen demurred.

"Oh, no, that's probably the wrong word. Andrea just told me that Tara has been inappropriate with several married men in town. She mentioned that Josh was one of her targets."

"To be fair, I'm not sure that's true." Gwen had no interest in being fair, but it was important that she appear to stay above the fray. "She's just a little overfriendly. I'm sure she's harmless."

"That's what I wanted to talk to you about." Chrissie looked delighted. "I have a story about her. It's one of those crazy small world things. One of my sorority sisters from the University of Alabama lives in Atlanta now. She knows Tara from when she lived there. When Marcella heard Tara was moving to Shoreham, she actually called me to warn me about her."

"For behaving inappropriately with men?"

"No, it was something entirely different. Back then she was stalking *women*. Tara became obsessed with one of Marcella's friends. Like, *obsessed*. They met at a playground, so it must have been when their children were little. Their kids played well together, so the two moms exchanged numbers and made plans to meet up again. Suddenly Tara was texting and calling Marcella's friend all the time."

It was an interesting insight into Tara's personality, Gwen thought, but not exactly the sort of gossip she could weaponize. Overly friendly moms were a common pitfall of playgrounds. It's why Gwen had always brought a book along with her when she used to have to take her kids to the playground.

"I have to admit, she does come on a little strong," Gwen agreed. "I've always found it off-putting."

"There's more. This went on for a few months. Marcella's friend was getting tired of having to constantly make up excuses for why she couldn't get together with Tara every single day. Then Tara started *copying* her. Like, if the friend had a new bag or pair of sandals, Tara would ask her where she got them, go out and buy the exact same thing. She even started to copy the way Marcella's friend braided her hair."

"That sounds borderline clinical."

"I know! By that point, Marcella's friend was totally over it. She tried to be polite and distant, hoping Tara would take the hint. It didn't work. She was finally forced to bluntly tell Tara that she didn't want to be friends with her."

"That must have been an awkward conversation."

"I know, seriously. She basically had to break up with her. The old, it's not me, it's you routine."

Gwen smiled. "How did Tara take it?"

"That's the craziest part. She went out and did the exact same thing with another mom she met at the same playground. She got such a reputation for glomming onto people, that Marcella and her friends nicknamed her the Clinger. She basically became a pariah. Marcella told me that she thinks that's part of the reason why Tara and her family moved to Florida."

The Clinger, Gwen thought. It was almost too perfect.

"Yikes. Did you tell Andrea about this?"

"Of course. She said she could totally see Tara pulling that kind of crap."

Good, Gwen thought. *If Andrea knows, soon everyone in town will hear all about the Clinger.*

After that, Tara Edwards's name seemed to come up nearly every time Gwen bumped into someone she knew. Every time, they'd pull her aside to grill her on what she knew about Tara's bizarre behavior. Gwen started to suspect that many of the stories were being embellished or even completely made up. Like the one where Tara and her husband were supposedly secret swingers. But who cared if the truth was getting blurred? Gwen certainly didn't.

One night, in mid-April, Gwen was in the kitchen stashing Chinese take-out containers into the refrigerator. She'd completely stopped cooking since the Christmas holidays. The family had fallen into the habit of helping themselves to the takeout of the day, then migrating to the living room to watch television while they ate. No one had even mentioned this abrupt change in Landon family protocol, which suited Gwen just fine.

My days as a domestic goddess are over, she thought as she stacked a container of pork lo mein on another containing orange peel beef. *Why did I even bother all these years? No one cares one way or the other. No one in this family has ever appreciated me.*

"Tara Edwards came into my office today."

Gwen glanced up to see Josh, whom she hadn't heard enter the kitchen. He had changed into a T-shirt and sweatpants after work. He was looking at her with the grim, unhappy expression she'd grown used to over the past few months.

"Is this confession time?"

"Confession?" The grim look morphed to one of first surprise then mild irritation. "You still think I'm having an affair with Tara. I don't know where this is coming from."

"I don't know what I think. I do know she seems to spend an awful lot of energy trying to get your attention."

"I barely know the woman. However, she brought in her boys today to have their bands changed. She asked if she could speak to me privately. I said fine. As soon as we stepped into my office, she burst into tears. She seems to think that there's some sort of a whisper campaign going on about her."

"A whisper campaign?" Gwen couldn't help smirking. It was more like a shouting campaign at this point, but she was hardly going to admit that to Josh. "That seems overly dramatic."

"Are you behind it?"

"Excuse me?"

"Are you the one behind this supposed whisper campaign?"

"I'm not going to dignify that with a response. You're the one who's apparently having an affair with her. How exactly is it that I'm the one being vilified?"

Josh sighed heavily. "I am *not* having an affair with Tara Edwards. I don't know how you got that idea, but it's not true. It's not even remotely close to being true."

Gwen considered whether she should throw away the last egg roll. They always got soggy in the fridge. She picked up her large chef's knife, and with a whack slashed it down the middle. She picked up one half and ate it. It wasn't bad, she decided, even though it was cold and greasy. She chewed and swallowed it before replying.

"On the night of the Heart Ball, nearly everyone we know in town saw that woman make a beeline for you, then hang off of you the entire night. She followed you around like a love-sick puppy. If people are talking about her in connection with you, I'm sure that's where they got the idea from. The two of you were not discreet."

"I have no control over what Tara Edwards does. As for my part, I was just being polite. What was I supposed to do, tell her to stay away from our family, the way you did?"

"She told you about that?" Gwen tossed the other half of the egg roll in the garbage can.

"Yes. When I saw her today."

"To answer your question, that's exactly what you should have done. You're not the first married man she's targeted. Other men—and apparently, women, too—have had to tell her to back off."

Josh ran a weary hand over his face. "I hardly have any contact with her, so I don't need to tell her to back off. Anyway, I feel sorry for her."

"You feel sorry for *her*?"

"Yes, I do. She was distraught when we spoke. She said she knows she's been the subject of some very nasty gossip. That people she thought were friends are now giving her the cold shoulder. She seemed fragile."

"What about me?" Gwen stared coldly at her husband. "What about the fact that those same people are also gossiping about me? About you, anyway. Me by extension. Why aren't you worried that I might be fragile?"

Josh held her gaze. "You're the least fragile person I've ever met. I think you can handle yourself just fine. I'm still not convinced that you're not the one behind Tara Edwards being targeted."

"Based on what evidence?"

"Evidence?" Josh gave a humorless bark of laughter. "This isn't a court of law. But I know you, Gwen. Everything about this story has you written all over it."

"Charming." Gwen folded her arms over her chest and narrowed her eyes. "I wasn't the one who spread the story around town that Tara Edwards chases after married men."

"No, I bet you arranged it so that others did. You made sure that woman's life was ruined. Why? Because you thought she might have a crush on me? Why would you even care? You've made it clear enough that you don't even like me, much less love me."

"No," Gwen agreed. "I don't. But I also don't like being made a fool of. I suppose that I should be glad that for once, at least, you're not underestimating me."

"I'll certainly never again underestimate your capacity for cruelty."

"Fuck off," Gwen snarled. "Actually, please do more than fuck off. Drop dead."

Josh stared at her with an expression Gwen had never seen before. It was a look of pure, unadulterated hatred.

"You first," he said.

chapter twenty-six

abby

Abby sat huddled on the ground, her arms wrapped around her bent legs, listening to her parents' conversation through her cracked open door. She didn't have to try very hard. For once, they weren't bothering to lower their voices. *Fuck off? Drop dead?* Abby knew her parents had never had the ideal marriage, but she'd never heard them speak like that to one another. The harsh, ugly words made her feel vulnerable. Like she was a young child again, and her entire world existed between the walls of this house.

And who the hell was Tara Edwards? Abby had no idea, not the slightest hint of an idea, who they were talking about. Apparently, some woman her mother was convinced her father was having an affair with? But that wasn't right. It couldn't be right. Could it?

Was it possible that Abby had gotten it all wrong? That her

father wasn't having an affair with Nora Holliday, but with this Tara Edwards person instead? That Carter Holliday had been right? That his wife had been at the Seabreeze Hotel that day for an entirely unrelated reason? The horror of this thought made Abby's stomach curdle, and she hunched into herself until her head was resting on her knees.

Abby finally stood, closed her door softly and climbed onto her bed. She pulled out her laptop and flipped it open. She ran a search on "Tara Edwards" and "Shoreham," and immediately found Tara Edwards's Facebook page, which had the privacy settings set to public. Abby shook her head. What was it with people and their complete lack of concern when it came to online security? Tara Edwards's page was open for anyone—perverts, creeps, stalkers—to see.

She'd posted literally hundreds of photos of her twin sons, who looked to now be in their early teens, although there were pictures going back to the time they were little.

There were also photos of Tara Edwards, who did not have blond, wavy hair. Instead, she had long, dark, straight hair with severe bangs. There was even a recent photo of her from St. Patrick's Day, posed with a twin boy on each side, all three dressed in green. As Abby scrolled through her photos, which dated back years, there was no point where Tara had ever been a blonde.

Abby had no idea who this Tara Edwards was to her father, but she did know one thing… It was not the woman Abby had seen him kissing in the beach parking lot that day.

"The paving stones are here," Gwen announced.

Abby had practically crawled out of bed after another nearly sleepless night. Her emotions felt like they had been scraped raw, and her brain was like a sluggish machine with gummed up, sticky gears. She was sitting at the table, eating cereal and staring at the opaque orange pharmacy bottle that contained her antidepressants.

Are they helping? Or are they making me even foggier? she was wondering, when her mother breezed in after her morning run.

Even damp with sweat and her hair scraped back in a headband, Gwen looked refreshed, even buoyant. She didn't seem at all affected by the fight Abby had overheard the night before.

"What paving stones?" Abby had no idea what her mother was talking about.

"We're having the driveway paved. They're going to start work next week, but they dropped off the stones this morning. They're stacked on the side lawn."

"Oh."

"What's up with you?" Gwen asked.

"What do you mean?"

"You look like the world is coming to an end. Like there's been a nuclear holocaust and you're left facing a life in a grim postapocalyptic dystopia." Gwen pulled out a bag of granola and dumped it into a bowl. She added a dollop of Greek yogurt and began to eat with a relish that irritated Abby.

"Postapocalyptic dystopia?"

Gwen rolled her eyes. "I was joking."

"I heard you and Dad fighting last night."

"Oh? I thought you would have outgrown eavesdropping by now. Do you still sit on the floor with your door cracked open?"

Abby was taken aback. She hadn't realized her mother knew she did that. When Gwen saw her expression, she actually laughed.

How the hell can she be so cheerful? Abby wondered. It was weird, even borderline scary. Her mother had been in a sour mood for months. Now that she'd been caught spreading rumors, she was positively jolly. *This can't be normal.*

"Oh, Abby," she said. "I know you better than anyone else

in the world. Do you really think you can hide anything from me at this point?"

Abby felt her fury rise, pulsing at her temples. "Actually, yes. I think can. I think I've gotten quite good at hiding things."

"Like what exactly? Your inability to cope out in the real world? If you can call college the real world, which it isn't. Not even close."

"I coped," Abby sputtered. "I was going through a tough time."

"You had your future handed to you on a silver tray. Signed, sealed and paid for. Instead of making the most of it, you dropped out at the first sign of adversity. I did not raise you to be weak."

"How would you know?" Abby demanded. She hated how shrill her voice became, but she didn't seem to have any control over it. She was starting to think that she didn't have control over anything. "You think you've led some sort of a troubled, difficult life as a suburban stay-at-home mom?"

"You mean other than being deserted by my father, raised by an alcoholic mother and not having even one-tenth of the privileges you've enjoyed? Yes, Abby, please tell me how my life has been so easy, while yours has been so difficult."

Gwen shook her head with dismissive disgust as she turned toward the sink. Abby was shocked at how much this casual indifference enraged her.

"I know Dad is having an affair."

The words were like a whip in the air, cracking through the open-plan kitchen. At first, Gwen didn't respond. She rinsed out her yogurt bowl, then opened the dishwasher and placed it inside. Only then did she turn back toward her daughter. Gwen's expression was impassive, other than the slightly arched eyebrows.

"Yes, I know you were eavesdropping on our conversation last night. You're well aware of my suspicions."

"Yes. But you're wrong." Abby knew she should shut up—

this conversation hadn't worked well when she'd had it with Carter Holliday—but she couldn't seem to stop herself. There was something about Gwen's smug superiority that made Abby want to lash out, to hurt her mother, this person who cared so little about anyone else's feelings.

"Darling girl," Gwen said with such condescension it was clear that the *darling* was not meant with any genuine affection. "You may have overheard part of a conversation. But trust me, you know nothing about it."

Abby watched her mother pull the headband out of her hair and toss it on the counter. It was clear that she was done with the conversation, as dismissive as always.

"I saw Dad with another woman."

Gwen stopped so suddenly, Abby felt a triumphant jolt of victory. Now she had her mother's attention. Gwen pivoted slowly, her running shoes squeaking on the tile floor, to look at her daughter.

"Tell me," she said.

"Now you're going to listen to me?"

"I don't know. It depends what you have to say. You could be full of shit. Most people are."

Abby tried not to flinch. Gwen might love her—as much as her mother could love anyone—but Abby instinctively knew she didn't like her. Instead, Gwen had always seemed to take it as a personal affront that Abby hadn't taken after her. Gwen said it all the time—Abby was too emotional, too insecure, too wrapped up in worrying how other people thought of her.

But it turned out Gwen was wrong. Abby did take after her mother, at least in one way. Whenever Gwen felt someone had slighted her, she always, *always* got revenge. Abby realized with a sickening horror that she'd inherited this same trait. Look at how she'd reacted to Lana's betrayal. Abby had spent hours upon hours wishing for all sorts of terrible things to happen to

Lana. She'd reveled in those fantasies. If she hadn't been such a coward, she might even have acted upon them.

Abby was more like Gwen than either of them had ever imagined. Maybe it was time she embraced that.

"Dad's having an affair," Abby said. "I saw him with another woman. But it wasn't Tara Edwards."

For once, her mother didn't have a snappy comeback. Instead, she stared at Abby, her expression inscrutable. The silence was broken by the chime of the doorbell. Gwen glanced at the clock.

"It's a bit early for visitors," she said. "Maybe it's a delivery."

"I'll go see." Abby pushed her chair back, stood and headed toward the front door. When she opened it and spotted who was standing on their front porch, she stopped breathing.

It was Carter Holliday.

Abby had wondered when the bomb she dropped was finally going to explode.

Apparently, that day was today.

chapter twenty-seven

nora

Nora was climbing up the stairs, carrying a bin of cleaning supplies, when she stumbled over something and nearly fell. "Damn it!"

She managed to right herself at the last minute, but even once the danger had passed, her heart thudded heavily. She was two-thirds of the way up the staircase. Falling from that particular spot would have been dangerous. She could have broken her neck.

She looked down to see what had tripped her up. It was one of Matt's sneakers. Nora let out a huff of exasperation. Her children were constantly scattering their things around. How did only one shoe get left on the stairs? Nora picked it up and took it up with her.

The kids were at school, so Nora went into Matt's room and opened his closet door. She hoped the other sneaker was inside, or if not, that Matt at least knew where it was. It wouldn't be the first time one of her children managed to lose their shoes. She set down the cleaning supplies and began poking around inside his closet, looking to see if the sneaker's mate was there. That's when she heard the sound of clinking glass. Frowning, Nora pulled out a duffel bag and moved aside some of Matt's sweatshirts that had fallen to the floor...but no, they hadn't fallen, she quickly realized. They'd been placed there deliberately to cover something.

Vodka bottles.

Nora's entire body went cold. Matt was drinking? How was that even possible? She tried to think if she'd ever seen him acting the least bit drunk. She was sure she hadn't. But then, she'd been so distracted lately, and Matt spent so much of his time sequestered away in his room. Was it possible she'd miss something so huge?

As much as she didn't want to admit it, she realized it was entirely possible.

Nora gathered up the vodka bottles and headed downstairs, where she lined them up on the kitchen counter. She stood and stared at them for a long time, trying to picture Matt tipping the contents of one of the bottles into a glass and then throwing it down his throat. Then she thought about the time she'd taken him to the zoo when he was small. It had been just the two of them. She couldn't remember now where Dylan and Katie had been. After they'd toured the animal exhibits, she'd bought him a ticket to ride the creaky old carousel. Matt had sat astride a wooden zebra and chortled with delight for the entirety of the ride. How had that small happy boy turned into this unhappy teenager, drinking secretly in his room?

The sight of the vodka bottles, lined up like a row of soldiers, was making Nora nauseous. She could feel her stomach begin to churn, and she realized she was on the verge of throwing up.

She had planned to spend the day making and photographing a glazed lemon pound cake, but right now she needed to get out of the kitchen. Out of the house altogether.

Nora picked up her phone and sent a text: Can u meet?

"It's normal for kids to experiment with alcohol," Josh said. "I know we don't want to think about that as parents, but hell, I did when I was in high school. Didn't you?"

They were sitting in his car at the beach parking lot, their old haunt. Now that it was April, and the weather had turned warm and sticky, there were a lot more beachgoers. The parking lot was practically full. If she and Josh kept meeting here, it was only a matter of time before they ran into a person one of them knew, Nora realized. They'd have to pick a new spot.

Or stop this altogether.

They hadn't planned to meet that day, but Nora had needed to talk to someone. There had been a time, long ago now, when she would have turned to Carter with her problems. Later, when Carter became so unreliable, Nora would seek out Maddie. These days, Josh was the person she went to, and Nora found herself relying on him more and more. It made their relationship that much more dangerous. When their affair did end, she wouldn't just be losing her lover, but also the person who had become her closest confidant.

"Not a whole lot," Nora admitted. "The occasional beer at a party. But, Josh, this wasn't a few beer cans I found. There were seven large empty vodka bottles hidden at the back of his closet. Seven! I can't even imagine how long it would take to drink that much alcohol."

"That's definitely troubling," Josh admitted. "But you said you've never seen him acting drunk?"

"No, never. But what if I just missed it?"

"You would have noticed."

"Would I? I've been so distracted lately. The thing that scares me the most is that his father is an alcoholic. A severe one. What if Matt is going down the same path?"

"You need to talk to him. Get him to open up, find out what's going on," Josh said.

"I know. I'm going to talk to him after school today. It's just... I'm so scared for him."

"This parenting gig is not as easy as they make it out to be. It's like what I'm going through with Abby. Not with alcohol— not that I know of anyway—but she's just not herself anymore. I don't know what to do about that. She's completely closed herself off from me, which she's never done before."

"It's so much easier when they're little. When they're three or five or seven years old and have a problem, you can solve it for them. Once they get older and start hiding things...that's when it gets complicated."

Josh and Nora sat quietly for a few minutes. They were holding hands. The silence, and Josh's presence, had a calming effect on her.

"Gwen and I got into an argument last night," Josh finally said.

Nora had the usual stirrings of misgivings she always experienced when Josh brought up Gwen or Carter. She wondered why the subject made her so squeamish. At this point, with Carter drinking the way he was, and the possibility that Matt had inherited his father's self-destructive tendencies, it wasn't like she felt protective about her marriage. Paul Miller's words echoed through her thoughts every day.

If you have even the slightest fear that he's going to hurt you, you have to leave. Take the kids and walk out the door. It's really that simple.

As always, the memory caused goose bumps to rise on her arms.

Was it that simple? Leave to keep her children safe? She'd always thought the opposite would be true. Leave and she wouldn't always be there to protect her children from their father. Now, after discovering the bottles in Matt's closet today, Nora realized that there were unforeseen consequences to every choice. If, three years earlier, she had filed a police report for domestic violence, then left, she might have been granted full custody of their kids. Maybe then she could have prevented Matt from following his father's self-destructive path.

"Gwen accused me of having an affair," Josh continued.

Josh's words snapped Nora's attention back to their conversation. "Wait, *what*? She found out about us?"

Josh shook his head. "No, no, don't worry. Not about you. She thinks I'm having an affair with someone else."

"Okay, you need to back up and tell me the whole story. From the beginning, please."

"Do you know Tara Edwards? She has twin sons, but they're probably a year or two younger than Katie."

Nora shook her head. "No, I don't think so."

"It all started because Gwen began to suspect that Tara has a crush on me."

"Does she?"

Josh shrugged helplessly. "I have no idea. I barely know the woman, other than to say hello to her when she brings her boys into the office."

"So where did Gwen get the idea that she has a crush?"

"Tara did a few odd things. She baked me brownies and dropped them off at the house. She bought the kids—my kids, I mean—Christmas presents."

"Okay, that is weird," Nora admitted.

"It is, but honestly, I just thought she was trying to be friendly in her own awkward way. I don't know her very well, but Tara's always struck me as being one of those people who desperately wants to be liked, but doesn't know how, so ends up trying too hard."

"But Gwen doesn't believe that?"

"First there were the gifts. Which, like you said, were weird. Then, on the night of the Heart Ball, Tara was there, and she was being very...friendly. Probably, overly so."

"Oh, wait... I remember her. Long brown hair? Pink dress?"

"I have no memory of the dress." Josh smiled. "But probably. She was sort of..."

"She was hanging all over you." Nora smiled faintly. "I noticed."

"I wasn't encouraging that. Not at all."

"No, I know. I could tell. But I can also see why someone— why your wife—would be irritated by how much attention another woman was paying you."

"That's just it. Gwen doesn't care about me, not like that. We haven't had a loving or intimate relationship on any level for years. But the one thing Gwen can't stand is looking foolish in front of anyone. That's how she'd view my infidelity."

"But, you *are* being unfaithful to her."

"I know." Josh banged his head against the car's headrest. "That's why I have to end it."

"Oh." Nora exhaled. She'd come to the same conclusion— that it was time, past time really, for them to end this affair. But she'd been completely unprepared for how devastating it would be to hear Josh voice the same thought. The pain cored her, hollowing her. *Will this be what it will feel like for the rest of my life? Will I spend every day missing him?* "It's probably for the best. Before anyone gets hurt, I mean."

"What?" Josh turned to look at her. "What are you talking about?"

"I thought you were saying you wanted us to stop seeing one another."

"No. God, no." Josh brought Nora's hand to his mouth and kissed it. "You're the one thing that makes me happy. I can't lose you."

"But…you just said you wanted to end it. What did you mean?"

"My marriage. I've been putting it off, hoping that Abby would get back on track and back to school before I left, but I think if anything, the tension in the house is making everything worse. No, it's time I left. I'll tell Gwen tonight, and then…"

"And then?"

"I'll pack a bag and go."

"What about your kids?"

"I don't expect that Gwen is going to take this very well. I'll have to talk to them later. Separately."

"Why are you so sure she'll be angry? You said she's talked about wanting a divorce."

"Yes." Josh rubbed Nora's hand. "But it's one thing for her to leave me. It's an entirely different thing for me to leave her."

"What's the difference?"

"Perception. Gwen's a narcissist. In her mind, who would ever want to leave her? She'll be punitive. She'll make sure I pay for this. Do you want to hear something terrible?"

She smiled faintly. "I don't know. Do I?"

"Last night, Gwen told me to drop dead. And I said, 'You first.'"

Nora's smile faded.

"Here's the worst part. In that moment, I meant it. It would make my life so much easier if Gwen just disappeared. No divorce, no punishment, no turning the kids against me. Because Gwen is capable of doing that and more. She'll hurt me however she can."

"You don't mean that," Nora protested. But she knew exactly how he felt. Hadn't she had the exact same thought before about Carter? She'd lie in bed alone, while he was out drinking himself into oblivion yet again, and think maybe this time he'd wrap his car around a tree. Just like that, all of her problems would be solved.

Josh looked at Nora, his expression unfathomably sad. "What if I do? The truth is, my life would be easier if Gwen died."

chapter twenty-eight

gwen

As soon as Abby left the kitchen to answer the front door, Gwen leaned on the counter with both hands, struggling to regain her composure. She hadn't wanted her daughter to know she'd landed a blow with her announcement that Josh was having an affair.

What does Abby know? she wondered. *And how?*

She could hear her daughter talking to a man at the door. The conversation went on for longer than it would normally take to accept a package delivery. Gwen wanted to ignore whatever was going on—she needed time to come up with a plan for how to deal with Abby—but then she started to pick up on the conversation taking a strange turn. Abby's voice became high-pitched, like it always did when she was upset. The male voice sounded not angry, exactly, but stern. Almost as though he were lecturing Abby about something.

What the hell is going on? Gwen wondered. She strode toward the front door, ready to deal with whoever was there. The last thing she wanted to deal with was some religious freak handing out literature, but she certainly had no problem shutting a door in the face of someone she didn't want to speak to. It was annoying Abby couldn't take care of it herself. It wasn't that she'd ever approached motherhood with the expectation that her child would be a duplicate of herself. When Abby was little, Gwen had never cooed about how she had a "mini-me," or dressed them in those revolting matching mother-daughter outfits. But she certainly wished Abby had inherited some of her grit, her confidence, her resolve.

Gwen looked down the hallway and could see Abby standing there, her shoulders slouched, her fingers playing with her hair as she spoke to a man. He was backlit with sunlight so bright Gwen had to squint to see who it was. He looked familiar, but for a moment she couldn't recall how she knew him.

"Did you think you could just tell me what you told me without there being consequences?" the man asked aggressively. He seemed to be holding something that looked like a thick stack of papers.

Abby shrank away from him. "I didn't think... I wasn't trying to..."

"Abby, who is it?" Gwen asked. She walked down the hall and stood next to Abby, although unlike her daughter, she squared her shoulders and fixed the man with her coldest gaze. "Hello, I'm Gwen Landon. Have we met?"

"Actually, I believe we have. I'm Carter Holliday."

"Holliday." Gwen's memory was stirred. "You're Nora's husband, right? She's the food blogger. Our sons are both freshmen at the high school."

"Yes." Carter grimaced. "I'm Nora's husband. For the moment, anyway."

Gwen supposed he was about her age, and somewhat attractive, if the over-the-hill Frat Boy look appealed, which it never had to her. He had sandy hair, combed back to unsuccessfully cover his balding pate, and a horrible little goatee. His most attractive features were his square jaw and light blue eyes, although they were looking a little red at the moment.

Allergies? Gwen wondered. *Or...* Then suddenly she smelled it. *Alcohol.* Was he drunk? It was—Gwen glanced at the table clock that lived on the hallway sideboard—ten in the morning. Which meant he either hadn't recovered from last night's drinking session or he'd started early—possibly both. Well, that partly explained why he was behaving so oddly. Gwen recalled that Carter used to have quite the reputation for partying. She also now remembered hearing that he'd sobered up, but that clearly wasn't the case. She supposed it would make for a good story, if she ever needed some dirt on the Holliday family.

"For the moment," Gwen repeated, his last words just now sinking in.

Then suddenly it all clicked into place. Carter's aggressive behavior, Abby's announcement that she knew her father was having an affair. Josh's growing distance and, lately, hostility.

Was Josh was having an affair with Nora Holliday? Gwen couldn't quite picture it. Nora had always seemed so proper, almost to the point of prudishness. But as she swiveled to look at her daughter, and saw the expression of horror and shock on her face, she suddenly knew that this was what Abby had been talking about.

"What's going on, Abby?" Gwen asked. "What did you do?"

"This isn't my fault!" Abby protested.

"Mr. Holliday accused you of meddling in his life. What did he mean by that?"

Gwen had been addressing her daughter, but Carter Holliday was the one to answer.

"She told me that my wife and your husband are having an affair," he said. Now that Gwen knew to listen for it, she could hear the slight slur to his words. "That's why I'm here. I thought it was about time you and I had a talk."

Gwen showed Carter into the living room, then asked Abby to step into the kitchen with her so they could speak alone.

"Go to your room," Gwen said, as though Abby were still small and had drawn on the walls with crayons. Which, actually, Gwen reflected, Abby had never done. She'd almost never been naughty. It wasn't in her nature.

"I want to stay. This affects me, too," Abby whispered.

"I think you've done enough." Gwen drew in a deep breath, stealing herself to go face Carter Holliday and his sordid revelations.

"Wait!" Abby grabbed Gwen's arm, stopping her, even pulling her closer. Gwen couldn't remember the last time her daughter had voluntarily touched her. Abby cupped a hand over her mouth and whispered in Gwen's ear, "Something about him scares me."

Gwen pulled back and studied her daughter quizzically. Abby could sometimes be overly dramatic, but usually only about her own problems. Gwen couldn't remember Abby ever saying that someone *scared* her—and she could tell that Abby meant it. Her skin had gone ashy and pale, her eyes were so round, they were rimmed with white.

"Stay in your room, but keep your door open," Gwen decided. "I'll go see what he has to say."

Abby nodded. Gwen headed back toward the living room, carrying two glasses of ice water with her. Carter had declined her offer of a beverage, but Gwen was thirsty after her run and he was obviously in need of hydration. Carter was sitting on one end of the L-shaped couch, still clutching the papers he'd brought with him. He accepted the glass when she handed it to him. Gwen chose a chair opposite of where he sat, purposely putting the heavy brass coffee table between them. Abby was right. There was something off—and off-putting—about Carter Holliday.

"We've met before, I believe," Gwen said. "Remind me where. The school auction? Or maybe at a party?"

"The Stewarts' Christmas party two years ago," Carter said. "We talked about sailing camp. One of your kids had gone and loved it. I was trying to find an activity that might interest my son Matt." He smiled thinly. "I'm actually still working on that."

"Right." Gwen remembered now. Carter Holliday had struck her as the sort of man who liked to talk just to hear his own voice. The sailing camp conversation had gone on for far too long. Gwen had felt cornered, and she'd been forced to invent an excuse to break away. "I remember now. But that's not why you're here."

"No. Your daughter came to see me a few weeks ago," Carter said abruptly. "She told me that my wife, Nora, has been having an affair with your husband."

Gwen briefly glanced in the direction of Abby's room. *What the hell was Abby thinking?* she wondered.

"Do you know anything about that?" Carter asked.

Gwen shook her head. "This is the first I'm hearing about any of it. When did you meet with Abby?"

"Early March."

"You've known this for, what…?" Gwen did the calculation in her head. "Five or six weeks?"

Carter nodded.

Gwen wondered how long Abby had known about this supposed affair. And why the hell was she the last one to find out about it? It was humiliating, and that was unforgivable.

"Have you confronted your wife?"

"No."

"Why not?"

"Because at first—and for a long while—I didn't believe your daughter's story."

"But you do now."

"Do you know Nora?"

"Not really." Gwen shook her head. "I mean, we've met, so I know her well enough to say hello to, but that's about it."

"Nora is the kind of person who always does the right thing. It's deeply important to her. It's like she wants to live in a world of straight lines and squared corners."

"Don't we all." Gwen wondered if he was ever going to get to the point. It was just as she remembered him from the Stewarts' party. *Blah, blah, blah.* She tapped an impatient fingernail against her water glass.

Carter didn't smile at her quip. "No, I don't think so. I think most people tolerate a certain amount of messiness in their lives. Nora's just not built that way."

"Why does Abby think Josh and Nora are having an affair?"

"She said she saw them together. First, kissing in a parked car at the beach, although at that point, she didn't see Nora's face. She just recognized her father and his car."

Gwen absorbed these words with a cool detachment. Whose betrayal was worse, she wondered, a husband kissing another woman, or a daughter who saw it and told a stranger about it rather than coming straight to her mother?

People are so predictably disappointing, she thought.

Carter continued. "Abby began tailing her father around town, and she saw both Nora and Josh enter a hotel. Separately, but when she saw Nora at that time, she believed she was the same woman she'd seen in the car." He gestured vaguely to the back of his head. "They had similar hair. But that could have just been a coincidence."

"But it wasn't."

"No. But, like I said, it just didn't sound like something Nora would do. She's not like that. Deceitful. Dishonest. She's always had a very strong sense of right and wrong."

Gwen was starting to get irritated, both by the lack of evidence being presented of this supposed affair, and by Carter's annoying obsession with how perfect his wife was.

"If you didn't believe Abby, what changed your mind?"

"I guess I needed proof. That's why I haven't said anything to Nora."

"What kind of proof? Did you see them together somewhere?"

"Have you ever looked at your cell phone bill?"

This question seemed like such a complete non sequitur that at first, Gwen wasn't sure she'd heard Carter correctly.

"Of course, I pay all of the household bills. Actually, wait." Gwen frowned. "I take that back. Our cell phone service is run through Josh's office, so his bookkeeper takes care of that bill. Why?"

"The monthly bill they send just says what you owe and when it's due. But, if you go onto your cell provider's website, you can pull up a log of every single phone call and text sent by every person on your plan. Did you know that? I didn't. Not until last night."

"You tracked your wife's phone calls?"

"And texts," Carter confirmed. "There were a *lot* of texts."

His complexion had started to take on a gray tinge. Gwen wondered if his hangover was kicking in. She hoped that if he felt the need to throw up, he'd take himself off to the bathroom. She couldn't deal with vomit on her living room carpet on top of everything else.

"I printed them out for you." He held out the stack of papers he'd brought with him, paper-clipped on one corner. He handed it to her. "I highlighted their texts and phone calls."

Gwen began flipping through the stack of paper. There was one number highlighted over and over again. Gwen recognized it. She knew it as well as her own. Better, even. It was Josh's. "There are hundreds of communications here."

"Thousands," Carter corrected her. "They've been texting and talking multiple times a day for the past six months."

"Is there a record of what they were saying to one another?"

"No, unfortunately. The phone company doesn't keep that information. Or, if they do, they don't make it available to their customers. But Abby was right. From the sheer volume of communication, it's pretty clear something is going on between the two of them."

Gwen stared down at the stack of papers in her hand. She'd stopped paging through them. Josh and Nora Holliday...? Having an affair...? Making out in cars...going to hotels together?

Gwen suddenly wanted, no, needed, to be alone.

"It's time for you to leave," she said, standing abruptly.

Carter stared at her in confusion. "What do you mean? We need to talk about this."

"No, I don't think we do. I mean, if you're right, then I have an issue with my husband. You have one with your wife. I don't think we have anything to say to one another."

"What about revenge? We can't let them get away with this. What they've done to us."

"What?" Gwen frowned, confused not at the concept— she was well acquainted with the benefits of revenge—but at Carter's blunt assumption that she'd share any such plans with him. He was a drunk, not someone she'd ever want as an ally. "I'd like you to leave. Now."

Carter stood suddenly, looking agitated. His face was flushed, and a vein stood out on his forehead. Gwen had to force herself not to lean back, away from him, as she instinctively wanted to do. But that was the thing with bullies. You couldn't give them an inch. Instead, she stood, too, folded her arms and fixed him with her coldest glare.

"I can't believe what I'm hearing. You're going to just let this go?" Carter demanded.

"What I choose to do with this information is none of your business."

Carter shook his head. "You're a cold fucking bitch, aren't you? No wonder your husband cheated on you."

"So why did your wife cheat on you?" Gwen parried. "Maybe because you're a smug asshole? Or, possibly, because you're a drunk?"

Carter fisted one hand and held it up. Gwen wondered for a moment if he was going to hit her. But then he dropped the hand to one side and shook his head slowly.

"This isn't over. Not by a long shot." Carter turned to leave, banging his leg against the coffee table as he did. "Shit!"

Gwen watched while he headed toward the door, stumbling a bit as he went. She trailed behind him, not wanting to get too close. It wasn't until he'd slammed the front door shut behind him, and she'd turned the dead bolt, locking him out, that she exhaled the breath she hadn't realized she'd been holding.

abby

Abby stood at her open bedroom door for the entirety of her mother's conversation with Carter Holliday. She held her phone in one hand, ready to dial 911 if needed. She didn't know if Carter was capable of actual violence, but while he'd been berating her at the front door, she saw something slithering behind his pale blue eyes that chilled her. She hadn't thought it was safe for Gwen to be alone with him, but her mother wouldn't listen to her.

She never had.

Once Abby heard the door slam shut, she hesitated, wondering what to do. It was all out in the open now. Both spouses now knew about the affair. Abby had wondered why it had taken Carter so long to react to her revelation. She should have figured out that he'd want more evidence.

She heard her mother moving around the house, her footsteps

loud and purposeful as she headed toward the kitchen. Abby listened to the clatter of the dishwasher first being opened and then banged closed. She thought Gwen would come to find her at some point, that they'd continue the conversation they'd started before Carter's arrival. But Gwen didn't turn down the hallway toward Abby's room. Abby glanced out, peering toward the kitchen just in time to see her mother striding toward the master bedroom. She closed the door firmly behind her. A few moments later, Abby could hear the sound of dresser drawers being aggressively opened and slammed shut.

Abby didn't know what to do. Should she try to talk to her mother? Warn her father about what he'd be returning home to? Text her brother—who was at school and shouldn't be looking at texts, although no student at Shoreham High followed that particular rule—and let him know that their family was in crisis?

The doorbell rang again, and Abby froze. Was Carter Holliday back? He'd told Gwen this wasn't over. Was he going to yell at her again or insist that Gwen help him with whatever he had planned? He'd used the word *revenge*. Was he going to hurt someone? His wife? Her father?

What have I done...

Abby glanced again at her parents' closed bedroom door, waiting to see if Gwen would emerge. She didn't, so Abby cautiously headed down the hallway, turning left toward the square front foyer. There was a panel of windows to the right of the door, but whoever had rung the bell wasn't in view. Abby was just about to step forward and look out to see who was there, when her mother's voice rang out.

"Don't open it."

Abby started. "I was just going to see who it is."

Gwen gave Abby a look so scornful, it felt almost like a slap. Abby hunched her shoulders forward. It felt like her life was falling apart around her, and she had no idea what to do, how to react.

"Who do you think it is? It's that drunk asshole back to stir up more trouble. Oh, but I forgot. You like stirring up trouble, too, don't you?"

"No," Abby protested. "I just..."

Gwen ignored her, moving past her to look out the windows next to the door.

"Oh, for fuck's safe. What is she doing here?" Gwen muttered.

"Who?"

Her mother unbolted and opened the front door. "What do you want?"

"I just want to talk to you," an unfamiliar, high-pitched voice said.

Abby crept forward, so that she was still behind her mother, but off to one side, so she could see who was at the door. There, on their doorstep, where Carter Holliday had reamed her out less than an hour earlier, stood a woman. She was a brunette with severe bangs and very round eyes. Abby recognized her immediately from the social media research she'd done the night before.

It was Tara Edwards.

"Do you?" Gwen laughed without humor. "Did it ever occur to you that I don't want to speak to you? You certainly picked about the worst possible day for dropping by uninvited."

"Please, Gwen." Tara Edwards wrapped her arms around herself as though she were cold, even though it was hot and sticky outside. She nervously ran one hand up and down her arm. "I just need a minute of your time. I think there's been a horrible misunderstanding, and I want to clear it up."

"What sort of misunderstanding would that be?"

Abby knew this tactic. Gwen had used it on her countless times. It was the sharply barbed question that no answer would satisfy. Seeing Tara Edwards cower in front of her mother, Abby thought that's probably just how she looked when Gwen turned her wrath on her. No one should treat anyone like that, Abby thought. Yet Gwen always got away with it. Her feelings were the only ones that ever mattered. If anyone went against her, dared express a feeling Gwen found inconvenient, she'd find a way to punish them. With a withering look, sharp words and, apparently, whisper campaigns.

Fury began pulsing through Abby. Her mother wasn't just self-centered, she was malignant. Then she realized that what she was feeling wasn't as simple as anger.

It was hatred.

"I've heard that you think that there's something going on between Josh and me. I wanted to come here, in person, to assure you that there's not." Tara had obviously rehearsed the line from the stilted, careful way she said it. "I wouldn't do that, and I'm sure he wouldn't, either. You have to believe me."

"Ah, I see. You came here to dictate to me what I should believe."

"No! I mean… It's just, I heard there's a rumor going around town that we're having an affair. We're *not*. I hated to think that you'd believe that it was true."

Gwen laughed again. "Don't worry, I don't."

Relief flooded Tara's face, and she even closed her eyes for a long beat. "Good. That's good. I've been so worried. I wasn't sure if I should talk to you or let it go, but I thought that it was probably best to just get everything out in the open."

"What I meant is that if my husband were going to have an affair, he would never choose someone like you." Gwen sounded coldly amused. "A little fool who stops by with brownies or who plucks at his sleeve at social events? Do you have any idea how pathetic you are?"

Tara inhaled sharply and took a step back from Gwen. Abby wondered if she might fall right off their porch.

"No," Gwen continued. "Josh has always been attracted to women with more…" She stopped and waved her hand airily, as though trying to think up the right adjectives. "Style, certainly. Substance. Class. If Josh were going to have an affair, I think he would choose someone very different than you."

Tara's mouth opened and closed and opened again. "I didn't… I mean…"

"I'm sure you didn't. Now go away and don't come back. No one here is interested. Not in anything you have to say or anything to do with you at all."

Gwen closed the door in Tara's shocked face, then grimaced when she saw Abby standing there.

"Of course, you're right there, eavesdropping as usual. You've really turned into quite the little sneak, haven't you?"

"Why were you so awful to that woman?" Abby stared at her mother, who didn't seem the least bit ruffled by the ugly exchange she'd just had. "What could she possibly have done to deserve that?"

"Other than chase after your father?"

"But you know that's not the woman Dad is having an affair with."

"So? Not for lack of trying on her part."

"But she was trying to apologize. To make it right. You just destroyed her. Did you see how upset she was?"

Gwen rolled her eyes. "Good God. Why is everyone always so worried about Tara Edwards's feelings?"

She strode past Abby, but this time Abby followed her mother back to the master bedroom. There was a half-packed suitcase open on her parents' four-poster.

"What's going on?"

"Your father is moving out. I'm helping that process along." Gwen moved to the closet she shared with Josh, and began pulling out his clothes and dumping them haphazardly into the suitcase.

"He is? Since when?"

"Since I found out that he's having an affair with Nora Holliday. Information you apparently have been in possession of for quite some time. But for some reason, instead of telling me about it, you went and told Carter Holliday. You know…?" Gwen stopped for a moment and looked thoughtful. "When I was pregnant and found out that you were a girl, everyone told me how wonderful that would be. That having a daughter meant having a lifelong friend." She snorted. "Somehow, I ended up with you. Disloyal to the end. Come to think of it, you're just like your father."

"I didn't know how to tell you." Abby's voice faltered. "I knew going to see Mr. Holliday was a mistake as soon as I did it, but I wasn't thinking clearly. I haven't been myself lately."

Gwen pointed at Abby. "That's where you're wrong. I think this is exactly who you are. It's who you've always been. You're weak and spoiled and selfish. Now, what are you waiting for?"

Abby was so stunned by her mother's casual cruelty, it took her a few beats to absorb the question Gwen had just posited.

"Waiting for?" she repeated dumbly.

"Go pack a bag. Wherever your father goes, you're going with him. If he wants you, that is."

"Wait, *what*? You're kicking me out of the house? You can't do that!"

"Of course I can. You're an adult, and I don't want you living here anymore. It's as simple as that."

Gwen returned to throwing clothes into the suitcase. When it was filled, she zipped it up, moved it to the floor and pulled a second suitcase from the closet. She tossed it on the bed, and began filling that one, too, flinging her husband's things in haphazardly. Almost gleefully. Abby watched her with growing horror. She knew that there would be repercussions for her actions, but it had never occurred to her, not once, that her mother would cast her out of the house. Out of her life. Abby had always known that her mother was different from other mothers, but this woman standing before her who was packing up her father's belongings wasn't just a bit colder or more distant than most.

She was a monster.

Abby began shaking her head, and found that once she'd started, she couldn't stop. "Is there anyone you care about other than yourself?"

Gwen stilled, holding a pile of socks. She tilted her head to one side, as though seriously considering her daughter's question. "No. At this point, I really don't think I do."

"I hate you," Abby said. "I will hate you until the day you die."

"Probably," Gwen agreed. "But at that point, it will be your problem, not mine."

chapter thirty

nora

Nora felt calmer after seeing Josh. Or she did until she got home, walked into the kitchen and spotted the empty vodka bottles she'd lined up on the counter. The sight sickened her.

"Matt, what are you doing to yourself?" she asked out loud, her voice echoing in the empty house.

Nora sat down abruptly at the kitchen table and clasped her hands in front of her. Matt would be home from school soon. While she waited, Nora contemplated how she was going to deal with the mess her life had turned into. No, that was too passive, she decided. The mess she'd created, at least in part. If she'd needed a sign that it was time to sort herself out, a stash of empty liquor bottles in her son's room certainly qualified.

She just wasn't sure what that sorting would entail. Leaving Carter? His drinking had certainly reached a crisis point.

Ending her affair with Josh? Probably, except for the not insignificant problem that she had fallen deeply in love with him, and couldn't bear the thought of not having him in her life in some form. But she also had to face the reality that their relationship was diverting so much of her attention, she'd lost her focus on everything else in her life that mattered to her. While she'd been lost in the mists of infatuation, Matt had apparently developed a drinking problem. Nora had failed him, and that wasn't acceptable.

Right now I need to focus on getting Matt help, she reminded herself. She did wonder, fleetingly, if she should call Carter, and ask him to come home and talk to Matt with her, but she decided against it. He was still barely speaking to her, other than when it was absolutely necessary. Besides, who knew if he was even sober at this point in the day.

Matt walked in at three thirty, after the bus had dropped him off at the corner of their street. He appeared in the kitchen a few beats later, his navy blue backpack still slung over one shoulder.

"Hi," he said, stopping abruptly. "Why are you just sitting there?"

"I'm waiting for you."

"Why?"

Nora nodded in the direction of the line of vodka bottles. Matt followed her gaze.

"Oh, *shit*."

"I think you'd better sit down. We need to talk."

Matt dropped his backpack on one kitchen chair, then collapsed heavily into another, sitting across the rectangular table from his mother. Nora gazed at him, taking in all the details, from his pale, tired face, to his too long hair, to the angry red cluster of acne on his forehead, and realized just how much her inattention was costing him. Why hadn't she taken him to the barber recently? Or made sure that he was washing his face with the right products? But she already knew why. She simply hadn't been paying close enough attention.

"Why were you going through my closet?" Matt asked.

"That doesn't seem like the most important issue at the moment."

"What do you mean?"

"When did you start drinking?"

"What?" Matt stared at her. "Are you crazy?"

Nora shook her head a little, her brows furrowed with confusion. "You have empty liquor bottles hidden in your room."

"I know. But that doesn't mean I was drinking what was inside them."

"If you weren't drinking, what are you doing with them?"

"I was hiding them from you," Matt said.

"Yes, I figured as much. But...why would you be hiding bottles if you weren't...oh." Nora rested her hand against her forehead for a moment as realization flooded through her. "They're your father's, aren't they?"

Matt nodded. "I found the first one when I was in the office, looking for printer paper. It was sort of hidden behind the garbage can, but I figured I could hide it better. Then I started checking in there regularly, and in Dad's car... I kept finding them. I was going to try to sneak them out to the recycling bin on pickup day, but every time I tried, there was someone around."

"But why didn't you just tell me?"

"I thought you'd be upset if you knew Dad had started drinking again."

"I do know," Nora said. "Of course I know. I've known all along."

"Oh. I didn't think you did."

"But the thing I don't understand is, why wouldn't you want me to know? Your father clearly has an issue—I know you all know that—and he obviously needs to get help for it."

"Because when he was drinking before, you'd get into fights." Matt started picking at the cuticles of his nails, a nervous habit he'd acquired in middle school. "I didn't want you to get upset."

"Honey, it's not your job to keep me from getting upset." Nora reached across the table and stilled Matt's hand with her own. "It's okay to be upset by upsetting things. It's normal and healthy."

Matt went silent for a long time. Nora had a feeling something was coming, so she stayed quiet and waited. It was sometimes the only way to go with teenagers. Give them the space and wait for them to talk.

"I saw Dad hit you that night."

Nora flinched. It took her several beats to realize that she had stopped breathing. She had to force herself to inhale deeply.

"I'm so sorry you saw that," she said.

"It's not your fault he hit you."

"I know that. But, still, I hate that you saw it."

"Was it…" Matt stopped and pulled his hands away, leaving Nora's resting on the table. "Has he hit you before?"

"*No.*" Nora tried to make the word sound as definite as possible. "Never before and never since."

"But you stayed married to him."

"Yes. Your dad went into recovery after that, and I thought… well. I guess I thought he needed my support at that point."

"I think you should have divorced him." Matt wasn't looking at her now, he was staring down at the table, as though it held all the answers to life. "I would have, if I were you."

Nora reminded herself to breathe. Parenting was so often the business of keeping everyone on their schedule. Making sure food was on the table. Deadlines were being met. But every once in a while, it involved a conversation that would shape the adult your child was going to one day become.

"Sometimes, it's hard to know what the right thing to do is at the time. Especially when you're in the middle of a difficult situation, and you're trying to make a decision without perfect information. You just have to do the best you can," she said carefully. "But all of that aside, you do know it's not your job to take care of me, right? It's my job to take care of you."

Matt shrugged. It was a gesture he'd made a thousand times before. But today, on this day, he looked so bereft, Nora thought it might break her.

"I don't think it's safe to be around Dad right now," Matt said softly.

Nora looked at her son, her kind, sensitive son, and tried to think of something, anything she could say to make this right for him.

"I won't say don't worry because I always hate it when people say that to me. Worry is another one of those emotions that is normal to have, as long as you don't let it control your life. But I will say this…please trust me that I'll always try to do the right thing. The best thing, for all of us."

Nora meant the words as she said them. She just hoped she possessed the inner strength to make them true.

Long after Matt disappeared to his room, Nora remained at the kitchen table, trying to piece together her conversation with her younger son and all its broader implications. She'd blamed Carter for so many years, but now she saw the part she had played in the downfall of their family. She'd thought she was keeping her children safer, more secure, by trying to hide his drinking and other destructive habits from them. She'd never discussed Carter's alcoholism with them until after he'd gone into recovery and was committed to his sobriety. That way, when she did tell them, she could present it as a problem that had already been solved, so that they wouldn't have to worry about it. But now she saw that by doing so, she'd taught them— or Matt, at least—that hiding things was better than facing up to them.

Nora looked up, startled to hear the mechanical whir of the garage door opening, then glanced at the clock. It was just before five o'clock. This was the earliest Carter had been home in weeks.

When Carter walked in through the back door, he looked agitated. His face was flushed, and he was breathing heavily. He stopped when he saw Nora, and she could see that he was swaying slightly. He was holding a paper bag tucked under one arm that Nora could tell contained a bottle.

"Well, if it isn't my lovely and devoted wife," he said.

"You're drunk." Nora wasn't surprised, but she was defeated. Carter was going to just keep drinking, and there was nothing she could do about it.

"I am indeed. I plan to get drunker yet." Carter pulled a bottle of vodka out of the bag and held it up triumphantly.

"You drove in this condition? Jesus, Carter, you could have killed someone. Or killed yourself. Or been arrested. If you get another DUI, you'll end up in prison."

"You," Carter said, pointing his finger at Nora, "don't get to tell me what to do ever again."

Sometimes when Carter drank, he got goofy. Sometimes, he passed out. Sometimes, he became nasty. Nora watched him apprehensively as he banged the bottle down on the counter, then went to the cupboard to retrieve a glass. He looked at the row of empty vodka bottles Nora had lined up on the counter.

"What the hell is this?"

"They were in Matt's room. He found them in your office and was hiding them."

"Shit." Carter's shoulders sagged, and for a moment, the fight went out of him. "Why would he do that?"

"So that I wouldn't find out that you've started drinking again."

"You?" Mean Carter was back, and he turned on her with

an ugly sneer. "I don't care what you think, about my drinking or anything else for that matter."

Nora remained silent while Carter filled a lowball glass with ice, and after twisting off the top of the vodka bottle, filled it nearly to the rim. It was a bad sign that he was drinking the vodka straight, she thought. There'd been a period—before he admitted to the fact that his drinking had become a problem—when he would try to slow himself down by adding club soda or tonic water to his vodka.

Carter took a large gulp of vodka. "The funny thing about marriage is that you live with someone for years, and you think you know everything about them. But then you find out that you don't really know them at all. That they're a complete stranger to you."

Nora watched her husband carefully. His tone was casual, friendly almost, but there was barbed wire underneath.

"I know the feeling," she said flatly.

"Really? Well, it's nice to know I can still surprise you." Carter toasted her with his now nearly empty glass. "To my beautiful bride, who's always been loyal to a fault."

"I can't go through this with you again." Nora shook her head. "The drinking, the gambling. I can't do it."

"The drinking and the gambling." Carter nodded thoughtfully. "I can see how you'd find those problematic. But, hey, at least I'm not fucking someone else."

Nora went still. "What is that supposed to mean?"

"I had an interesting conversation a few weeks ago. Wait, no, it was a little longer than that. What day did I start drinking again?"

"March fifth."

"See, I knew you'd know. March fifth. That was the day Abby Landon came to see me at my office. Do you know Abby?"

Nora shook her head. Dread was spreading through her like a cold rot.

"She made the appointment under the pretense that she was interested in a summer internship with my firm. But instead, she wanted to tell me something. Do you have any idea what it was?"

Nora shook her head again.

"She told me that you were having an affair with her father."

There it was. Nora's secret was out. It was terrible and yet, strangely, also a relief that at least she wouldn't have to hide it anymore.

"No response? I thought you'd have one. Maybe deny the whole thing? I did at first. I told Abby she didn't know what the hell she was talking about. I asked her to leave my office."

"Then you went out and got drunk, and have pretty much been drunk ever since."

"Well, yes, that's true. I was still in denial about you and… him. But I think I knew deep down that she was telling the truth, even if she couldn't prove it to my satisfaction. So, drink I did." As if to punctuate his point, Carter drained the last of the vodka from his glass, then refilled it from the bottle. "Aren't you going to say anything? Deny it all? Or you could confess. It's supposed to be good for the soul. Assuming, of course, that you do still have a soul."

"It's impossible to talk to you when you're like this." Nora stood. "I'm going to call Paul and have him come get you. I'll pack some things in an overnight bag for you."

"Wait just a minute. You're the one having an affair—I notice you haven't denied it—but you think I'm the one who should leave? Why don't you go?" He was slurring badly.

"I obviously can't leave you alone here with the kids when you're in this state." Nora moved so that the kitchen island was between them. "Matt's here now, and Dylan and Katie will be home soon. I think you should go before any of them see you like this."

"What?" Carter barked a humorless laugh. "You don't trust me alone with my own children?"

"No. I don't."

Carter's face darkened and his eyes hooded. "I have never laid a hand on any of them."

"Yet," Nora said levelly. "You have hit me. I no longer trust you around them. Not when you've been drinking."

"You still haven't denied that you've been having an affair."

Nora looked at Carter and knew she should feel something. Sadness, regret, even fear. But as she gazed upon the face of the man she'd spent over two decades with, she felt empty, as though all of her emotions had been wrung out of her.

"Yes. I've been having an affair with Josh Holliday." Nora was shocked by how calm she sounded. She wondered if this was what shock felt like, but then remembered, no, she'd experienced shock on the night Carter had hit her. On the night when she'd miscarried their baby. This was different.

"I'm not sure how Abby found out about it, but I'm not going to deny it," she continued. "I know it's wrong. But I also know our marriage should have ended a long time ago. I want a divorce."

Carter stared at her, and his breath had grown ragged. Nora wondered if she'd made a terrible mistake telling him the truth, especially now, when he was so intoxicated. He might hit her again. At least this time, if he did, she'd be smart enough to call the police and file a report.

But Carter didn't come at her; he didn't raise his fists or scream threats. Instead, his face crumpled and he began to cry. It was a terrible sound, primal and rasping. Nora didn't know what to do. There was a part of her that wanted to walk the short distance around the kitchen island and comfort this man with whom she'd gone through so much over the years. But then there was the part of her who remembered the sickening pain of his fist hitting her stomach. She didn't move.

"Mom?"

Nora looked up to see Matt in the doorway of the kitchen. He looked from one parent to the other, and then, as if making up his mind, he swiftly moved to Nora's side as if to protect her.

"Dad, I think you should go," Matt said.

Nora wondered if Carter would tell Matt about her affair. She supposed it would come out eventually, but there was a limit to what anyone could process at once. She thought that all three of them had reached that for the day. A sober Carter would have agreed with her. She didn't know what this drunk one would do. But, finally, he nodded in defeat.

"I'll pack a bag," Carter said. "Will you call Paul?"

"Yes," Nora said. "I'll call him right now."

Matt took her hand and squeezed it. Nora was grateful for the comfort, even though she wasn't sure she deserved it. But she was glad that the situation had been defused, at least for the moment. Paul would help, and maybe Carter would sober up long enough for her to be able to talk to him, so they could figure out where they would go from here.

But then Carter looked back, and saw Nora and Matt standing there, hands clasped together, and his expression twisted. He took a stumbling step toward them, and Nora could sense Matt's quick intake of breath, although he didn't move away from her side.

Carter righted himself by grabbing on to the kitchen table. Nora wondered what would happen if he fell again. Last time, he'd cut his head so badly, he'd needed stitches. Maybe this time, it would be worse. Maybe this time, it would be fatal.

And if he did die, would that be the worst thing? a voice whispered inside her head, reminding her of the conversation she'd had earlier that day with Josh.

But no. Of course she didn't want that, especially not in front of their son. Matt would never get over it.

Carter swayed for a moment, but stayed upright. Nora turned to Matt. "Will you do me a favor and pack an overnight bag for your dad? A change of clothes, pajamas, his toothbrush. I don't think he should be going up the stairs right now."

Matt looked unsure, and Nora could tell he didn't want to leave her.

"It will be okay," she reassured him. "Let's just get your father in a chair, and I'll call Paul."

Carter didn't resist as Matt and Nora each took one of his arms and led him over to one of the kitchen chairs. He sat down heavily, then dropped his face in his hands. He was silent now, but from the shaking of his shoulders, Nora thought he might be crying again. Matt was staring at him in horror, and she patted his arm.

"Please pack his bag for me, honey."

Matt nodded and hurried out of the kitchen. Nora grabbed her purse to retrieve her phone. She hoped Paul would be able to come quickly.

"I'll go," Carter said.

She looked up, and saw that he was sitting upright now, staring at her with a cold expression.

"I'll go," he repeated. "But I'm telling you right now, this isn't over. It's not over for any of us."

chapter thirty-one

gwen

Gwen was in the living room, curled up on the leather coach and watching the news, when Josh arrived home from work at six o'clock. She'd placed two suitcases and a plastic storage box containing his shoes, toiletries and other miscellaneous items in the front foyer. She wasn't sure if it was sad or poetic that after he'd lived in this home for twenty-odd years, she'd been able to remove all evidence that he'd ever been there in a single afternoon.

"What's all of this?" Josh laid his keys on the table next to the front door and surveyed the suitcases.

"Your things," Gwen said succinctly. She picked up the remote control and muted the news. "You're moving out. Why don't you come sit down, and we'll have a quick chat before you go."

Josh looked apprehensive, but he walked into the living room and sat on the chair opposite Gwen. It occurred to her that they had picked the exact same spots she and Carter had taken that morning, only this time Gwen was on the couch, and Josh had chosen to put the coffee table between them.

"Where are the kids?"

"Simon is over at Max's house. Abby is in her room."

"What's up with the suitcases?"

"I know everything. Well, maybe not everything, but I know enough." Gwen gestured toward the stack of paper-clipped papers she'd left sitting on the coffee table. It was the printouts Carter had brought with him that morning. The evidence of the affair.

Josh picked up the stack and paged through it. "What is this?"

"The Hollidays' phone records. Carter Holliday brought it over earlier. You know the Hollidays, right? Their kids were your patients. You certainly know Nora. You've been fucking her, after all."

Josh flinched and dropped the phone records back on the table.

"Are you going to deny you're having an affair with Nora Holliday?"

"No," Josh said. "I'm not going to deny it."

"Good. Because that would have been a waste of both of our time. Not that it matters, really, but I am curious. Was it just sex or was it sex and something more? You certainly texted one another quite a bit."

Josh breathed in deeply, steepled his fingers, but kept his gaze steady on Gwen. "I'm in love with her."

Gwen tried to remain impassive. She didn't want to give him the satisfaction of seeing that he could hurt her. Still, his admission cut deeply. A sexual relationship was one thing. Love was quite another. And quite unforgivable. Josh would to have to pay for that transgression at some point.

"Your things are packed. I'd like you to move out immedi-

ately." Gwen was glad she sounded calmer than she felt. Her
rage, which was already pressing hotly in her chest, was exac-
erbated by the expression of relief on her husband's face. She
was kicking him out of the house without warning, and he had
the audacity to look almost *happy* about it?

"Believe it or not, I was planning to tell you tonight that I
want a divorce."

"Fine. You'll get one." Gwen nodded toward the door. "Now
go."

"You don't want to talk about this?"

"What is there to talk about?"

"We should probably have a preliminary conversation about
how we're going to go about starting this process. There're the
kids, for one. Abby's an adult, but Simon will split his time between us, once I figure out where I'm going to live. I would
like to keep this as civil as possible."

Gwen laughed. "I'm sure you would. But you gave up the
right to civility when you decided to have an affair."

"If it helps at all, it wasn't planned."

"What, it just happened to you? Like, whoops, you just accidentally stuck your penis in another woman?"

Josh sighed and rubbed his temples, as though staving off
a headache. "Our marriage has been in a bad place for a long
time."

"And whose fault is that?"

"I think we both share the blame, if you want to call it that."

"Only I didn't have an affair."

"No." Josh looked down at his hands. "You have every right
to be angry about that." He glanced back up at her. "Except,
that I think our marriage had already failed a long time ago.
You told me on Christmas Day that you were done. That you
wanted out."

Gwen wanted to laugh at the sheer absurdity of these justi-
fications.

"This affair of yours…had it started by then? On Christmas, when I told you I was growing increasingly unhappy with our marriage?"

Josh stared at her, without answering. It didn't matter. Gwen knew from the printout Carter had given her that the affair had likely started sometime in October.

"If we had problems, we might have been able to fix them." This was a lie, but Gwen was determined to keep the upper hand. "But you decided to cheat. At that point, you became the bad guy. I want to make sure you're clear about that. This marriage is ending because of you. Because of what you did. And trust me, by the time I'm done, no one—not in this family, not in this town—will be in any doubt about that."

Gwen was picking her words like stones that she could hurl at Josh, seeking the maximum amount of pain she could inflict on him. She wasn't sure yet how she would spin their divorce. She'd be damned if she was going to be put in the role of the abandoned spouse, a discarded first wife, while Josh went on to what…start a new life with Nora Holliday? No. There wasn't a chance in hell she was going to allow that to happen.

Josh stood. "You're clearly upset. We'll talk later, when we've both had a chance to calm down and process all of this."

"I'm perfectly calm. But, yes, you need to leave. By the way, you're taking Abby with you."

"What?" Josh's brow furrowed in confusion.

"She's packed a bag, too. Or I hope she has by now. She's certainly had enough time."

"Why isn't Abby staying here? What does she know about all of this?"

Gwen raised an eyebrow. "Oh, Abby knows everything. She has for a while."

"Shit." Josh shook his head. "What a mess."

"That you created."

"I'm going to check into a hotel for a few nights, at least.

Wouldn't it be better if the kids stay here, for now, while I work out where I'm going to live, at least temporarily?"

"I suppose that would be easier for you, yes. But I don't really care about making your life easier now or ever again. Abby's not staying here because I don't want her here. She can go with you, wherever it is you're going."

"Jesus, Gwen." Josh stared at her in disbelief. "I understand you're angry at me, but why are you taking it out on Abby?"

"Because she blames me, too." Abby appeared in the doorway, an overnight bag slung over her shoulder.

"Oh, good, you're packed," Gwen said. She turned off the television and stood up. "We're done here."

"What's going on?" Josh asked Abby. "Why does she blame you?"

"Because she's every bit as disloyal as you are. A chip off the old block." Gwen walked toward the kitchen, and without looking back, called out to them. "Make sure you lock the door on your way out."

Gwen waited in the kitchen until she heard the front door open and then shut behind them. The house suddenly felt empty and still. It was, Gwen reflected, the first peaceful moment she'd had in months. She went to the refrigerator, took out a bottle of chilled sauvignon blanc and poured herself a glass. It wasn't until she lifted the glass to her lips that she realized her hand was shaking.

Why would that be? Gwen wondered. *What do I have to be upset about? This is what I've wanted. Freedom.* Well, not total freedom. Simon would be home eventually. But of everyone in her family, Simon was the least stressful one to have around. Besides, once Josh found a place to live, maybe Simon would go stay with him, too. That might just be the perfect revenge. It would be hard for Josh to carry on his romantic dalliance with a college-age girl and a teenage boy hanging around. *Let's see how he handles that.*

Gwen sipped her wine, and the alcohol gradually calmed her. She had a lot to do over the next few days. She'd have to find a divorce attorney. She'd heard Marcus Danberry could be a pit bull, the kind of lawyer who would make your ex's life a living hell, which was exactly what Gwen wanted. She'd need to open her own bank account and move as much money into it from their joint account as possible. She'd have to call a locksmith and get all of the locks on the house rekeyed so that Josh and Abby couldn't just let themselves in whenever they felt like it.

No, there's no reason to waste time being upset, Gwen decided. She needed to save her energy for other, more productive pursuits.

chapter thirty-two

abby

Abby and her father drove in silence. She didn't know what he was thinking, but thought it might be similar to the horrifying realization clanging in her head.

I've just been kicked out of my home.

It was the only home Abby had ever known. Her college dorm rooms, and then apartment, didn't count. Not really. While some small part of her was glad that she wasn't dealing with this on her own, she also didn't know what she was supposed to say to her father. Wasn't it his fault that they were here, driving at dusk with no idea where they were going to spend the night? Abby didn't know which parent she was angrier with—her father for his infidelity or her mother for her cruelty.

Finally, her father turned into the parking lot of an extended-stay chain hotel, the kind where all the rooms were suites with kitchenettes. He pulled in to a parking spot and turned off the car.

"I'll go inside and see if they have a room available," he said, still gripping the steering wheel with both hands.

Abby nodded. Her dad didn't ask her to go with him, and she didn't offer. Instead, she waited while he got out of the car and headed into the hotel, looking grave.

Well, what did he expect? she wondered. And yet…it was sad. It was all so terribly sad. Their family was breaking apart, and even though she knew that it wasn't entirely her fault, she also couldn't help but feel she'd played a major role in its destruction.

Abby wondered if Simon knew yet what was going on. If not, she had to warn him about what he'd be returning home to. Their mother had always been easier on Simon, but this was different. Abby had never seen her mother in such a cold, destructive fury. It frightened her.

She tapped out a text to Simon: Are you home yet?

A few seconds later, he texted back: no why.

Abby hesitated. Was this the sort of news you should impart by text? Probably not. She hit the call button instead.

"What's up?" Simon asked, sounding confused. The two siblings never talked on the phone, not even when she was away at school. All communications had always been made via text.

"Something happened. Something bad. I didn't want to text it to you."

"What?" Now Simon sounded scared. "What's going on?"

"Mom and Dad split up."

"You mean, like…they're getting divorced?"

"I think so," Abby said. "Mom kicked Dad out of the house. I don't really know what happens next."

"Damn." Simon exhaled. "I guess I sort of expected something like this to happen."

"I know. Me, too. But it's still kind of shocking."

"Yeah," Simon said. "I guess."

"There's something else."

"Something other than the news that our parents are getting divorced? Did a tornado hit the house?"

Abby smiled, despite herself. Leave it to Simon to make a smart-ass remark in the middle of a crisis.

"Sort of," she said. "It got pretty ugly."

"Oh, sorry." He sounded contrite. "I didn't realize you were there."

"For all of it. And Mom didn't just kick Dad out. She made me leave, too."

"What? Why?"

"It's a long story. Look, I left my car at the house, but I'll get it tomorrow morning, and then I'll pick you up after school. We can talk about it then."

"Okay." Simon was quiet for so long, Abby wondered if he'd hung up. But then he said, "This is weird, isn't it?"

"Totally weird," Abby agreed. "Are you okay?"

"Yeah, I think so. You?"

"Not right now, but I will be."

A few minutes after Abby got off the phone with Simon, her father returned. He tapped on window, and Abby rolled it down.

"I got us a room. It's a two-bedroom suite."

Abby nodded and got out of the car. They went into the hotel, rode the elevator up to the fifth floor and Josh unlocked the door. The hotel suite was sparse and corporate, but it was clean and large enough that they wouldn't be tripping over one another. Abby sat down on the couch and turned on the television. She wasn't really interested in watching anything, but it was better than the awkward silence.

"We should eat something," her dad said. "Do you want to go out or should I order a pizza?"

Abby wasn't at all hungry and the thought of sitting in a restaurant across the table from her father was unbearable. "Pizza, I guess."

Josh nodded. He called in an order for delivery. He sat down on the other end of the couch from Abby. They both pretended to watch the dumb reality show she'd put on, featuring overly made up middle-aged women wearing low-cut dresses who bickered while they drank cocktails. Josh looked at his phone and tapped out a few texts. Abby wondered who he was texting. Simon? Nora Holliday? She didn't really want to know the answer, so she didn't ask. The pizza arrived, and after Josh paid for it, he left briefly to get them each a soda from the vending machine down the hallway.

Is this what life is going to be like from now on? Abby wondered as she picked at her pizza and sipped her soda from the can. Sitting in a depressing hotel suite with her normally gregarious father, who was zoned out and oddly silent? Maybe it really was time for her to go back to school. She'd already been halfway to making that decision, but now it seemed like the only real option she had.

Finally, Josh picked up the remote and muted the television. "How did you find out?"

Abby glanced over at him. He wasn't looking at her but was instead staring at the now silent television picture.

"I walked to the beach one day and saw your car in the parking lot. You were there with…her."

Josh closed his eyes briefly then nodded. "When was that?"

"Before Christmas."

"And you've been carrying this around since then? That must have been incredibly hard for you."

Abby's eyes welled and she nodded. "Mom is really mad at me that I didn't tell her when I found out."

"I know. I'm sorry about that. I think that once she calms down, she'll realize that none of this is your fault." Josh put his barely eaten pizza on the paper towels they were using as napkins. "It's entirely mine."

"Why did you do it?"

"I don't know if I can answer that in a way that will make sense to you."

Abby frowned at this dodge and set down her own greasy slice. The few bites she had eaten were sitting like a lump in her stomach.

"Why don't you try?" she suggested coldly, realizing as she did that she sounded exactly like her mother.

No, she thought. *I will not turn into her. Not now, not ever.*

Her father nodded. "I'll do my best. I think when you're young, your age, life seems very black and white. There's just right and wrong and that's it. But that changes as you get older."

Abby's anger flared. "That's bullshit."

"What?"

"That's complete and total bullshit. There is such a thing as right and wrong. That doesn't just go away because you get older or because you're unhappy. There are some things you just don't do. Like cheating on your wife."

"You asked me to explain why I did what I did. I'm not trying to make excuses." Josh spread his hands helplessly in front of him. "I'm trying to be honest with you. Isn't that what you want me to do?"

Abby bit her lip. Was that what she wanted? She supposed it was, so she nodded and shrugged. She might as well hear him out.

"The thing is, as you get older, you suddenly find yourself in a place where you're no longer looking forward to a future that will change and hopefully for the better. Your life will stay more or less the same forever. If you're not happy in that place you've ended up—fulfilled and loved, and those things we all want from life—it becomes untenable to stay there. Does that make sense?"

Abby considered this. "I guess. I mean, I'm not stupid. I know you and Mom weren't happy together and haven't been for as long as I can remember."

Her father nodded. He looked sad, contrite even, but he also seemed relieved, which had the effect of pissing Abby off even more.

"That doesn't mean what you did was okay. If you were unhappy, you should have left. You should have gotten divorced before you started seeing someone else. That would have been the right thing to do."

"You're right. That's exactly what I should have done."

"Why didn't you, then?"

"There were you and Simon to consider."

Abby snorted. "It's our fault you had an affair? Thanks a lot."

"No, of course not." Josh ran his hands through his hair and grasped his head as though it hurt. "I just mean that when you have kids, which I hope you do someday, it's an immense responsibility. I wanted you to grow up in a home with both parents. Not a broken one, where you and Simon were being shuttled back and forth between the two of us. Besides, Abs, no one goes into marriage thinking they're going to end up getting a divorce. You expect there will be hard times, challenging times, but you also hope that you'll get through those together."

"So why did that change?" Abby shook her head. "Look, I know Mom can be a nightmare. Trust me, I'm her favorite target. But you're the one who chose to marry her."

"I know. I did. I loved your mother."

"Past tense?"

Josh sighed. "I'll always love her in a way. She'll always be the mother of my children."

"Dad, you sound like a character in one of those stupid cable movies, where the parents get divorced but then become best friends who spend the holidays together. And someone usually opens up a cupcake store at some point. That's not the way our family works. That's not the way Mom works."

"Look, I get that you're angry. I know you want answers. But it isn't like there's a clear line of demarcation. It's not like one day I woke up happy and fulfilled in my marriage, the next day I wasn't. Or one moment I loved your mother, the next I didn't. Your mother and I have been married for almost twenty-five years. A lot happens over two and a half decades."

"Okay, well...let me ask you one question."

"Okay." Josh smiled faintly. "I'll brace myself for it."

"Were you planning on having an affair?"

"I don't understand. Do you mean...was I looking to fall in love with someone else?"

Her father's use of the word *love* made Abby feel queasy. "You're in love with her? With that woman?"

"Yes. I am. And no, I wasn't looking for that. I never expected to feel any of those feelings ever again."

"Okay, stop. You're grossing me out." Abby knew she was on the edge of tears again. She'd known about the affair for months, had assumed that it involved sex, as much as she didn't want to think about that part. But the idea that her father had fallen in love with this other woman...that made everything so much worse. She wasn't even sure why. "I just wish I could go back, like six months, and just unknow everything that I now know. Six months ago, I was happy. I was at school, I was still with...well, I was happy. Then all of that changed, and it's pretty much sucked ever since."

"It's definitely been a tough year," her dad agreed.

But Abby noticed that he didn't join in her wish that they could travel back through time, and both choose a different path. He wasn't wishing away his affair or her mother finding about it. This realization made her feel even worse. How was it fair that he had caused all of this pain, all of this heartache, and was now happier than he had been before?

Abby's heart started to pound, her tears were now spilling over and streaking down her cheeks. She opened her mouth, ready to tell her father just what she thought of him—how much he'd disappointed her, how he'd always been someone she'd looked up to and he'd taken that away from her forever. How terrible that was. But then she realized that her dad's focus had shifted away from her. Instead, he was staring at his phone in horror.

"Oh, no," he said. "Gwen…what have you done?"

chapter thirty-three

nora

While Matt packed an overnight bag for Carter, Nora stepped into the living room so she could have privacy while she called Paul Miller. She decided that under the circumstances, she would be completely honest about what was going on, and count on Paul's discretion.

"Nora, how are you?" Paul said. "Is everything all right?"

"No, it's not. Carter found out that I've been having an affair. He's been drinking heavily. I don't think it's safe to have him here around me or the kids. I know this is a horrible imposition, but can you come pick him up and take him to a hotel?"

"Of course, I'll be right over. I'll bring him back to my place. He can sleep my couch."

Nora exhaled a long breath. "You're a lifesaver. Thank you so much."

Nora walked back to the kitchen. Carter was still sitting at the table, his head again resting on his folded arms. He was conscious and mumbling about something, although he'd reached the stage of intoxication where he wasn't making much sense. Nora couldn't see his face, but thought that he might have started crying again.

"You should go to your room," Nora said to Matt when he came downstairs carrying his father's overnight bag. She didn't want him to spend any more time around Carter in his current condition.

But Matt shook his head. "I'm staying with you."

He sounded so resolute, so grown-up. Nora thought she was getting the first glimpse of the man Matt would someday be. The fact that it was happening at such a terrible moment broke her heart.

They all waited in the kitchen for Paul to arrive. It took him only ten minutes to get there after hanging up with Nora, and for that she was especially grateful. Dylan and Katie would be spared the sight of what Matt had to see—his father stumbling out of the house, one arm slung around Paul's neck, Paul's arm around Carter's waist. Carter was the taller of the two men, but Paul was stronger than his stringy frame would suggest. He was able to bear most of Carter's weight as he leaned heavily against him.

"Thank you again," Nora said, walking ahead of them so that she could open the front door. "Thank you so much."

"Anytime," Paul said.

He smiled kindly at her, and Nora did her best to return the smile. But she was thinking, *Not anytime. Never, ever again. This is the end.*

Once the door was closed behind them, Nora went back to the kitchen to find Matt. He was in the middle of making a peanut butter and jelly sandwich. The regularity of this, a teenage boy's bottomless appetite in the midst of all of the conflict and chaos, nearly brought Nora to tears.

"You'll ruin your appetite for supper," Nora said, realizing as soon as she spoke how asinine it was. After everything Matt had been through that day, he should be able to have a sandwich if he wanted one. Besides, she didn't even know what they were going to have for dinner. The day had lurched from drama to trauma, which hadn't left time for meal planning.

"I'm hungry."

"Okay, honey. Whatever you want." Nora hugged Matt, which he tolerated for a few beats longer than he normally would before pulling away and returning to his sandwich making. Nora headed to the living room, needing a moment of quiet and calm to process everything that had happened that day.

Carter had found out about her affair with Josh.

Matt knew that Carter had hit her.

Perhaps, worst of all, she was going to have to sit down with all three of her children and tell them that she and their father were getting divorced. They would have a lot of questions, and Nora was going to have to figure out how to answer them. The whys, the hows, and most important, what would their future lives look like from this moment on. It was exhausting to contemplate. She didn't want to tell them about their father's relapse, but since Matt had already figured it out, she wouldn't be surprised if Dylan and Katie also knew. She *really* didn't want to tell them about the affair, but Carter probably would eventually. Would it be better for them to hear the truth all at once or parcel it out in smaller bites that might be easier for them to take in? Nora had always prided herself on her parenting skills, her instinctive ability to know what was best for her children. Right now, she had no idea what she should do.

It was a lot to figure out, all at once. Nora wasn't surprised that she felt more numb than anything else. It was how her mind and body had always responded to extreme stress. She sat heavily on the couch, tucked her legs up beneath her and began drawing in deep breaths. This was the day her life had changed forever.

I'm going to make it through this, she told herself. It was an echo of what she'd been saying to Maddie for the past year. *When you're a mother, you don't get the luxury of falling apart. You have to stay strong, even in the darkest moments, when you feel like you have failed at everything you've touched.*

Nora's phone dinged. She checked it and saw that she had sixteen unread texts waiting for her. Most of them were from Katie, who never sent just one text when she could send ten in a row, all fired off at a rapid pace. Katie wanted to know who was picking her up from volleyball practice, if she could sleep over at Isabelle's house this weekend, what was for dinner, why wasn't Nora answering her and could she order the new pair of Adidas shoes she was dying for that night, followed by a series of texts that simply said HELLO???

Nora tapped out her responses. Dylan is picking you up, yes, not sure, probably takeout.

Katie's last question, about the shoes, was tricky. Their finances were already beyond strained from Carter's gambling debts. Now they were going to be looking at maintaining two separate households. Nonessential purchases, like expensive new shoes, were going to have to be put on a hold for the time being. We'll see, Nora typed.

Dylan had also texted, saying he was on his way to pick up Katie. Nora sent him a thumbs-up emoji in reply.

There was also a text from Josh. When Nora read it, she inhaled sharply.

Carter told Gwen about us today. She's asked me to move out. Abby and I are staying at the Executive Suites on US 1. Let me know if you can talk at some point.

Nora stared at the text, wondering why she was surprised that it had all come out in a single day. Of course it had. Once she and Josh had knocked down that first domino by sleeping together in Orlando, they'd set off a chain reaction that had ended here. Two marriages irreparably damaged. Two families changed forever.

She desperately wanted to talk to Josh—both to hear his story and to tell him her own—but Matt was just in the other room. Dylan and Katie were on their way home. Even if she went up to her room, she didn't know if they'd have time to get into everything.

She texted back: I'll let you know. Carter just left. For good, I think. I have to tell the kids what's going on.

There was one final text, from a number that didn't have a contact associated with it. Nora tapped on it.

This is Gwen Landon. We need to speak. Please come to the house tomorrow morning at ten o'clock. If you don't know the address, ask your husband. Or mine.

"Don't go," Josh said. "Nothing good will come of it."

Nora had forwarded Gwen's text to him, and he'd called her a few minutes later from the parking lot outside his hotel. Nora had taken her phone upstairs and shut herself in her bedroom, so that she could speak without being overheard. She sat cross-legged on the bed, pressing the phone to her ear.

"Why does she want to see me? Is she going to threaten me to stay away from you or something like that?"

"I can't imagine she'd do that, but to be honest? I've never seen Gwen like this. She was furious. She's never been exactly a warm and fuzzy person, but she usually stays very contained. Today, the mask slipped."

"The mask?"

"Yes. I know that sounds dramatic, but you just have to trust me. You don't want to go anywhere near her. She'll lash out. She'll hurt you in any way she can."

"Okay," Nora said, although she wasn't sure yet if that would be her final decision. Despite the affair, there was still a part of her that firmly believed in always doing the right thing. Her actions had hurt Gwen. If Gwen needed to talk to her, didn't Nora owe that to her? Wouldn't it be cowardly to turn down the request? In fact, didn't Nora *deserve* to be lashed out at, to have hurtful things said to her?

"This has been a crazy day. Have you talked to your kids yet?" Josh asked.

"No, and I'm dreading it. I told Carter that I want a divorce, but I don't know how much to tell them about why. Do I tell them about their father's drinking?" Nora hesitated. "Do I tell them about you?"

"I don't know that I have any good advice for you, but in my experience, everything you try to hide comes out in the end anyway."

"That's what I'm worried about. How's Abby doing?"

"She's shaken. Gwen kicking her out of the house was terribly upsetting for her. She's also upset with me, obviously. She doesn't understand why you and I...well. I don't know if anyone will ever understand that."

"No," Nora said. "I don't know if I fully understand it myself."

"We fell in love. It's that simple."

"Yes." Nora exhaled deeply and pulled her legs up in front of her, wrapping her free arm around her bent knees. "But no one else is going to accept that as being a rational excuse for anything."

"That's the thing about love. It's not rational."

They were both quiet for a moment. He was only a few miles away geographically, Nora knew, but it felt much farther.

"Mom? Dad!" Katie's voice called up the stairway, surprisingly loud. "We're home, and I'm starving!"

Nora's pulse fluttered, and her stomach felt like it had folded in on itself. The moment had come.

"I have to go. The kids just got home," Nora said into her phone.

"What are you going to tell them?"

"I still don't know. I guess I'll start with the basics, then try to answer their questions. I'm sure they'll have a lot."

"I should go, too. I don't want to leave Abby alone for too long." He paused. "Good luck. I love you."

"Thanks. I think I'm going to need all of the luck I can get."

"Let's talk tomorrow."

"Tomorrow," Nora agreed, although she had no idea what tomorrow would bring.

After they hung up, Nora tossed her phone on the bed beside her. She knew she had to get up, go downstairs and face her children. There would be tears and questions, probably recriminations. It was going to be one of the worst moments of her life and theirs, but they'd get through it. They weren't the first family to face the pain of breaking apart. They certainly wouldn't be the last.

And tomorrow…tomorrow, Nora would go see Gwen Landon, and let her have her say.

chapter thirty-four

abby

The next morning Abby woke early. It was still dark outside, so she stayed in bed and watched the sky out the hotel window as it turned first gray, then flamed pink as the sun pushed up over the horizon. It was going to be another beautiful, bright Florida day, the sort of day that used to make Abby want to ditch school and go to the beach. She'd never done that though, and now wondered why. It had always seemed so important for her to be the perfect student and daughter, to stay out of trouble, and yet her life had fallen apart anyway. If she could go back, she'd make so many different decisions. She'd have stopped trying to be so good.

Abby heard the sounds of her father getting up, showering, moving around the hotel suite. She stayed in her room. She didn't want to see him or have another conversation in which he tried to justify his infidelity. So what if he'd been unhappy?

Was anyone ever truly happy? She had been for a while, she supposed, back before Colin had broken her heart. But that was an even scarier thought. If there was one thing she'd learned, it was that your happiness should never hinge on whom you loved. People were inherently untrustworthy.

Her father tapped on her door lightly.

"Abs, are you up?"

"Yes."

"I'm going to work. Do you want me to drop you off at the house on my way, so you can pick up your car?"

"No, I'll get it later."

There was a silence, and Abby knew her father was still standing there, outside her closed door. She wanted to get up—the hotel sheets were scratchy and rumpled, and her body was starting to feel stiff and uncomfortable from having lain there for so long. A few long beats passed, and then she heard her father's footsteps moving away. A moment later, the sound of the heavy hotel door closing shut.

Abby got up to wander into the small living room. The hotel suite looked even more depressing in daylight. The couch was upholstered in an ugly synthetic sage-green fabric. The cupboards in the kitchenette were made out of peeling laminate. It was so different from the pretty house she'd always taken for granted. The plush furniture, the expensive window treatments, the potted orchids in every room. She'd never credited her mother for that, for the pains she'd taken to decorate their family home. Gwen had often dropped that into conversations—how little she was appreciated, how everyone took her for granted. For some reason, that had made Abby even more determined not to compliment her mother on anything. Instead, she'd saved all her parental affection for father. Look how that had turned out. He'd disappointed her more than anyone.

She opened the refrigerator. Her father had stuck the pizza box from the night before inside. Abby opened it and took out a slice of cold pizza. The cheese had congealed, the slices of pepperoni were stiff, but Abby nibbled at it anyway. The day stretched before her, and she had absolutely nothing to do. No school, no job, no detective work. The only thing she had planned was to pick Simon up from school. She was looking forward to seeing her brother. He was the only other person who would understand what she was going through.

I will have to go get my car, she decided. It was still parked at the house, sitting in the driveway next to the pile of paving stones. She probably should have taken her father up on his offer of driving her there, but the thought of sitting in the car next to him for even a short time was unbearable. She'd use the Uber app on her phone to arrange for a ride to the house.

Abby forced herself to finish the slice of pizza. Then she headed to her room to dress and get ready to face the day ahead of her.

It was only later that Abby remembered it was that moment, when she was pulling on her T-shirt and leggings, that she'd had a distinct feeling that something terrible was about to happen.

chapter thirty-five

josh

Josh didn't go to work. Instead, he drove to a nearby diner. The hostess told him to sit anywhere he'd like. He picked one of the booths that lined the wall and studied the laminated menu she'd handed him. When his waitress appeared holding a carafe in one hand, he accepted her offer of coffee and ordered the breakfast special—two eggs, over medium, bacon, hash browns and whole wheat toast.

Josh sipped his coffee while he waited for his food. The diner was nearly full, which surprised him. He rarely ate breakfast out, certainly never on a workday. Most of the people here were older, though. Retirees, probably. Snowbirds who hadn't yet returned to their homes up north. Most of the other diners were couples, he noticed. Gray-haired men wearing short-sleeve button-down shirts that stretched over their rounded bellies sitting with women in tropical print sundresses. Is this where he and Gwen would have ended up if their marriage hadn't broken apart? Eating breakfast out on a Wednesday morning, trying to think of something to talk about after forty-plus years of marriage?

He shuddered at the thought. The idea of spending another moment of his life with Gwen, much less several more decades, horrified him.

Marrying her had been the worst mistake of his life.

When his marriage first began to break down, Josh had done his best to ignore their problems. It was easier to focus on building his practice and the work of parenting two young children. Once the fractures became too large to ignore, he'd convinced himself that Gwen had fooled him. That she had hooked him with her charm and quick wit. She'd hidden her true self during their courtship and early years of marriage. There was probably some truth to that, but Josh knew now that even then there were warning signs he should have picked up on. When they'd first started dating, and Gwen was still working as a paralegal, she'd often complained that the job was beneath her. Instead of recognizing the inherent grandiosity of a narcissist, he'd convinced himself that she was ambitious and driven. And when Gwen's mother died, and her main response was annoyance at having to handle the funeral arrangements and paperwork, he'd told himself that everyone handled grief differently. It was only now, years later, that he could look back with the perfect clarity of hindsight and see how entitled and selfish his wife had always been.

Josh thought back to his conversation with Abby the night before. He knew it had hurt her to hear that he was in love with Nora, and he understood that. Abby was at that age where she thought that everyone should stay in the lane they had chosen, ride it out to the end no matter how miserable they were. But meeting Nora had been a revelation to Josh. He hadn't realized that he still possessed the ability to love like that. He spent his days joking with his patients, while he studied their bites and made decisions about whether they should be wearing bands, and if so, what strength. But the entire time, nearly every moment of every day, Nora was in his thoughts. The graceful arc of her neck. The sexy curve of her hips. The way she tasted when he kissed her.

His feelings for her bordered on obsession.

Nora didn't know this, but whenever possible, he'd find a reason to go out in the evening—offering to buy milk, or pick up takeout since Gwen had gone on her cooking strike—to use the opportunity to drive by Nora's house, hoping to get a glimpse of her through the large front windows that opened to the living room. He didn't always see her. But every once in a while he'd catch sight of her walking through the house, or sitting on the couch reading a book. Those secret glimpses of her made his heart feel like it might shatter.

Then there were the times when he'd see Carter. He'd be equally shocked by the force of the hatred he felt for this man who got to live with Nora and share her life. Who would never appreciate or deserve her.

When his food arrived, Josh ate ravenously, even though the eggs were underdone and the toast was cold. He'd call the office in a bit to have Deirdre cancel his appointments that morning. She wouldn't be happy. Nor would the mothers who'd kept their kids home from school in order to make their midmorning orthodontist appointments. But everyone would just have to deal. He never played hooky from work.

But today was not a normal day.

As Josh ate, he thought about the text Gwen had sent Nora. He hoped Nora would heed his advice and stay away from her. Nothing good would come of the two women meeting; he was sure about that. Besides, he planned to go to the house that morning. He didn't know what sort of emotional state he'd find Gwen in, but there were things they had to talk about. Simon, for one, and what their temporary financial arrangements would be as they started the process of divorcing.

Josh knew he stood to lose a lot of money. He'd never told anyone, not even Nora, but he'd consulted a divorce attorney a few months earlier, not long after the affair began. Gwen would be entitled to half of everything—the house, his retirement account, the value of his practice—as well as alimony and child support for Simon. It would be hundreds of thousands of dollars by the time they were finished. He remembered when his friend Adam was going through his own divorce. One evening when Josh took him out for a consolatory after-work beer, Adam had joked, "Do you know why divorce is so expensive? Because it's *so* worth it."

It hadn't been a particularly funny joke then, and it certainly wasn't now. But he knew Gwen would take every last penny she could. It would be her final revenge.

Except he couldn't even count on that. Josh had told Gwen he'd never again underestimate her capacity for cruelty. But the truth was, he didn't know how far she'd go in her determination to hurt him or, even worse, Nora. And that scared the hell out of him.

Gwen always thought she was the smartest person in the room, the master manipulator. But Josh knew his wife all too well, probably better then she realized. He knew there was something wrong with her, even beyond her rampant narcissism. Something damaged, something twisted.

Something that needed to be stopped.

"Can I get you anything else, hon?" The waitress appeared at his table, again holding the carafe. She smiled warmly at him. "Do you want a top-up on your coffee?"

"Yes, please. And I'll take the check."

The waitress returned with his bill. Josh handed her his debit card without bothering to check the total. He sipped his coffee and waited for her to return with the slip for him to sign. But when the waitress walked back to his table, she was no longer smiling.

"Your card was declined," she said flatly.

Josh frowned. "That's not pos—" Then it hit him. The debit card was for their joint checking account, which, last time he'd looked, had over ten thousand dollars in it.

"Shit," he said.

Gwen must have cleared out the account. But when? He checked his watch. It was only quarter to ten in the morning. He had used that same card to pay for the pizza the night before without any problem. Gwen must have gone to the bank when it first opened. She had access to all their accounts, except for his business account, which Deirdre handled. Thank God for that, at least.

The waitress gave him a hard stare, clearly worried that he was going to stiff her on the check, that she'd be stuck paying for his breakfast. He looked in his wallet, relieved to see that he had cash. He'd gotten so used to paying for everything with his debit card over the years, that he often walked around with only a few dollars. He took out a twenty and handed it to the waitress.

"Keep the change," he said.

She immediately softened. "You should check with your bank. There's probably just a glitch with your account."

"You're right," Josh said. "I should do that."

But when he got in his car and drove out of the diner's parking lot, Josh had no intention of heading to the bank. Instead, he was going to go see his wife to find out what the hell she was doing.

Then he'd put a stop to it.

chapter thirty-six

carter

Carter Holliday woke up to the worst hangover he'd ever experienced in his life, which was truly saying something. He'd had plenty of bad mornings. The pounding headaches, the acidic churning in his stomach, the gnawing worry that he'd done something embarrassing the night before. He remembered a woman at one of the Alcoholics Anonymous meetings he attended saying that she'd decided to stop drinking because she was never proud of anything she did when she was intoxicated. It was a statement that should have been obvious to anyone— and maybe it was to people who weren't drunks—but it had especially resonated with Carter.

He looked around, trying to get a grasp on where he was. He'd fallen asleep on a couch, but it wasn't his couch or his home. His head was resting on an unfamiliar pillow, and someone had draped a blanket over him. Carter's stomach roiled when he sat up abruptly.

The apartment was familiar. His mind struggled to make sense of it, turning over like a sluggish machine, until he was able to recall the memory. He was at Paul's small but extremely tidy condo. Carter heaved himself onto his feet to stagger to the kitchen. He thought he might vomit, so he braced himself against the sink, planning to aim for the garbage disposal if necessary. After a few minutes, the waves of nausea finally subsided. Carter took a glass from the cupboard, filled it with water and drained it in a few gulps.

"How are you feeling?" Paul appeared, freshly showered and dressed for work in a collared shirt and khaki pants. "You had a rough night."

"I'll live," Carter said. "Thank you for letting me stay over."

"Anytime. How much do you remember about what happened?"

Carter thought back. The awful blank spots in his memory had always been the worst part of his drinking. He tried to work backward. Nora had told him she wanted a divorce and asked him to leave... She'd admitted she'd been having an affair... Matt knew he was drinking... He'd confronted Gwen earlier in the day.

Carter pressed a hand to his throbbing head. "Too much."

Paul smiled faintly. "Why don't you get dressed, and we'll go to a meeting?"

It was Paul's answer to everything. He went to meetings every morning before work and most evenings. But Carter couldn't stomach the idea of attending one right now. He didn't want to listen to anyone else's sad story. He certainly didn't want to share his own. His broken marriage to Nora. Her infidelity. That Matt probably hated him. The amount of debt he'd racked up gambling over the past year. Any one of those things was too much on its own to handle sober. Having to deal with them all at once was unbearable.

"If you don't come to a meeting, you're going to end up in a bottle." Paul had always had the eerie ability to know what Carter was thinking. Or maybe drunks were just all the same and it wasn't that hard to guess. "Come on, you don't have to talk. You can just sit in the back row and listen."

"I can't do it today. I didn't show up to work yesterday. I didn't even call in." The receptionist had called his phone a half dozen times. Toward the end of the day, his boss, Sarah Tapper, had called and left a curt voice-mail message on the phone that she wanted to meet with him early the next day to discuss his future with the company. "I don't know if I still have a job, but I can't be late today. Do you mind if I take a shower? Then I'll get out of your hair."

"Go ahead. But I hope you change your mind about the meeting. Or we can plan to go after work. The one at the Presbyterian church always has good cookies."

Carter lifted one corner of his mouth in the closest facsimile of a smile he could manage.

"I'll do my best to make it."

"Where were you yesterday?" Sarah asked.

She was the sort of woman who wasn't beautiful but took such care with her appearance—her shoulder-length brown hair was always shiny and blown smooth, her nails were shaped and painted a shell pink, her clothes were expensive and well fitting—that most would consider her to be quite attractive. Still, Carter had always thought her eyes were too squinty, her jaw too square. Right now, she was sitting behind her big desk staring at him in a cold way that made Carter feel exposed. He had a feeling that she saw too much when she looked at him.

"I had to take a personal day. I'm very sorry I wasn't in touch. There was an emergency with my family."

"What was the emergency?"

Carter hadn't expected her to ask for details; he certainly had no intention of going into any of what had happened the previous day with her.

"It's private."

"It stopped being private when you failed to show up for work, particularly on a day when you had an appointment to show property to potential new clients. The Hazen brothers came in. We had to explain why you weren't here to meet with them."

Shit. Carter had forgotten all about that. He'd set up the meeting weeks ago. It was with a pair of brothers who ran several successful restaurant chains and were expanding into Shoreham. They planned to develop multiple spaces and would have been an excellent account to land. By missing the appointment, Carter had almost certainly lost them as clients.

"What was this emergency that caused us to lose what could have been an extremely profitable relationship?"

Carter desperately tried to think of an excuse that she'd find acceptable. *I'm having marital problems that catapulted me into drinking myself into oblivion all day long* probably wouldn't cut it. He tried to think up a more acceptable lie. It was one benefit of being an addict. Carter had never met one yet who wasn't an excellent liar.

"Yesterday, we found out that one of our sons, Matt, has a substance abuse problem."

Sorry, Matt, Carter thought, and hoped that Sarah wouldn't gossip about it around the dinner table. Her daughters attended a different high school than Dylan and Matt, but it was possible they might have friends in common.

"I'm sorry to hear that." Sarah's voice was still cool. "You still should have called in. Or picked up when we tried to contact you."

"I know. I apologize for that."

Sarah crossed her arms and looked at him. "Were you drinking yesterday?"

"What?"

"There's been talk around the office that's gotten back to me. Stories about you drinking at lunch, possibly also in your office when you have the door closed."

"I never drink at work," Carter lied. "I don't know who would say that, but you know what this business is like. I wouldn't put it past someone to spread malicious rumors about me in order to try to poach my clients."

"I've seen you drunk at work. Last week, when you returned from lunch, you smelled of alcohol. It was coming off you in waves."

"That was different. It was a client lunch. You know how that goes. The client wants to get drinks, you join in to make them more comfortable. We all do it."

"I don't." Sarah uncrossed her arms, picked up a pencil and began tapping the eraser end against her desk. "Why don't you take the rest of the week off to deal with whatever problems you're having. While you're at it, think about how your drinking is affecting your work. We'll meet Monday morning to discuss whether your continued employment here would be mutually advantageous."

"I don't need to take off the rest of the week," Carter protested. "I'm fine, really—"

"Carter, it wasn't a request."

Carter left the office feeling dazed. He had no idea what to do now, where to go or even how he'd get anywhere. His car was back at the house. Paul had given him a ride to the office that morning. He supposed that retrieving his car was the first thing he needed to do. Carter pulled out his phone and ordered an Uber to pick him up and drive him home. Only, it wasn't his home, not anymore. To drive him to the house he co-owned but would never live in again.

The driver chatted for the entirety of the fifteen-minute drive, but Carter's brain was still so foggy that he mostly tuned out the conversation. Once he was dropped off at his house, Carter was glad to see that his car was in the driveway, not in the garage where he normally parked. He remembered now… he'd opened the garage door with plans to pull the car in, but his vision had been so blurred at that point, he'd been seeing double, so he'd decided not to risk hitting one of the kids' bikes. Luckily, he had his keys, which meant he could just take the car and go, not have to knock on his own front door and deal with Nora.

He did not want to see his wife. Not today, maybe not ever again. Not after what she'd done to him.

Carter got in his car, started it and backed out of the driveway. He drove a block down the street, then pulled over to the curb while he tried to think of what to do next. It was nine forty-five in the morning, and he didn't have anywhere to go. Not a job nor a home. He couldn't, shouldn't do what he wanted, which was drive to the nearest liquor store and buy a bottle of vodka. Maybe he should take Paul's advice and find a meeting. There was usually one around somewhere. He could go from meeting to meeting all day long. Maybe that would keep him sober. But what about tomorrow, the day after that?

Carter looked up at his rearview mirror and saw Nora's Nissan backing out of their driveway. She turned onto their street and headed in the opposite direction from where he was parked.

"Where are you off to?" Carter asked out loud. "Meeting the boyfriend?"

He made a U-turn to follow Nora. Carter was careful to keep enough distance between his car and hers so that she wouldn't notice him. She turned once, and then again onto Beach Street, then drove east for ten minutes until she reached an affluent subdivision called the Landing. She made a right turn into the neighborhood.

Carter recognized the subdivision. He'd been there just the day before. It was where the Landon family lived.

"Are you meeting your boyfriend?" he asked out loud again, this time incredulous.

It would be a bold move for Nora to show up at the Landons' house for a rendezvous with Josh in the middle of the morning when anyone could see her. That didn't make sense. What guarantee did she have that Gwen wouldn't be there, or the nosy daughter who'd dropped out of college? Carter continued to follow her. Maybe she was going to a different house, and it was just a coincidence that it was in the same neighborhood. But...no. He watched while Nora pulled over and parked directly across the street from the Landons' house. Carter pulled over, too, down the block so that Nora wouldn't see him.

Nora got out of her car, but then hesitated. She stared at the house for a moment as if contemplating why she was there. Then she closed her car door and headed up the driveway and onto the porch, where she pressed the doorbell.

A Jeep drove by. Carter glanced at it and saw Gwen Landon behind the wheel, obviously returning home. Was Nora there to meet Gwen? Why would she do such a thing?

"What the hell is going on?" Carter muttered.

Whatever it was, he was going to wait to see what happened next.

chapter thirty-seven

nora

No one answered the door. Nora rang the bell again, wondering how long she should wait. Why had Gwen asked her to come over if she wasn't going to be there when Nora arrived? There was one car parked in the driveway—a small white Volkswagen. Did that mean someone was home? Nora resisted the urge to peer through the windows next to the door.

There was the sound of wheels crunching on gravel. Nora pivoted to see Gwen parking a large Jeep in the driveway. She got out and strode confidently toward Nora. Gwen's dark cropped hair shone in the sunlight. The woman was effortlessly chic in a white linen shift and strappy leather sandals.

"Are you early or am I late? I had to run to the bank. I thought I'd have time to get there and back before you arrived."

Nora was taken aback by Gwen's casual tone, her nearly friendly demeanor.

"It's just ten now."

"Then I guess we're both right on time. It's a nice day out. Why don't we go sit in the backyard. Do you want something to drink? Water? Iced tea?"

"No, thank you."

"Are you sure? It's no trouble."

"Yes, I'm sure."

Nora wondered why they were both being so polite. But what was the other option? To scream? Pull one another's hair? Nora certainly didn't want to engage in histrionics.

Gwen turned and walked toward the side gate that led into the backyard; Nora followed her. They passed a neatly stacked pile of paving blocks on the lawn next to the driveway.

"Did Josh tell you we're getting the driveway paved?"

"No." Nora was startled by Gwen's casual mention of Josh, and the acknowledgment that he might have kept Nora up to date on their home renovations. It seemed so odd. Nora was starting to feel like Alice after she'd chased the White Rabbit down the hole.

"Oh, well. I'm still not clear on what the two of you got up to in your time together. Was it just fucking, or did you talk occasionally, too? You certainly texted one another nonstop. Or was that…what do they call it these days? Sexting?"

Nora stopped just as Gwen reached the gate. It suddenly occurred to her that being alone with this woman, who was not a friend and had every reason to hate her, was not wise. Josh had warned her repeatedly about Gwen, telling her that his wife was manipulative and narcissistic. He'd specifically asked Nora not to meet Gwen that morning. Nora knew the encounter wouldn't be pleasant, but she'd assumed it would be safe. What if she'd been wrong about that? What if she'd made a terrible mistake coming here?

Gwen looked back at her, her hand on the gate latch. "What's wrong? Was I not supposed to bring up the fact that you've been fucking my husband?"

"I should go," Nora said.

"Don't be silly, you just got here. We haven't had a chance to talk yet. Do you mind dogs?"

"Dogs?"

"Our Labrador, Izzy, is in the backyard. I'll put her up if you don't like dogs."

"No, I like dogs."

"Do you? I don't like most animals, but Josh and the kids insisted on having a family pet, so I was outvoted. She's sweet enough, I suppose. I'm sure some family will want to adopt her." Gwen opened the gate and grabbed the collar of the large black dog that was waiting by entrance, her long tail wagging happily. "Izzy, get back."

"Adopt her?" Nora realized that she kept repeating Gwen's words, but again, she felt as though she were falling through some sort of alternate reality where nothing was making a whole lot of sense.

"Unless you want her? Maybe you do. Think about it, but quickly, because I plan to drop her off at the animal shelter in the next day or so."

Nora glanced back over her shoulder. A car was approaching, and from a distance it looked like Josh's. Relief washed over Nora. If Josh were there, he'd keep her safe and protected from Gwen's vitriol. But the car didn't stop at the Landon house. Instead, it drove by.

"Are you coming?" Gwen sounded impatient. "If you are, then come in. Izzy's sweet, but she's strong as a bull. I can't hold her forever."

Nora later wondered why she walked into the backyard. What had she been thinking? Everything about the situation felt wrong. But instead of turning and retreating to the safety of her car, Nora passed through the gate. Maybe it was that she felt she deserved whatever ugly words Gwen tossed at her. Or maybe was curious to find out more about the woman Josh had been married to for over two decades.

"I'm sorry, did you say you're dropping your dog off at the animal shelter?" Nora took a few steps down a paved walking path that led around into the backyard. Gwen latched the door behind her, then released the black Lab, who immediately trotted up to Nora, sat and lifted a paw. Nora laughed, despite the oddness of the situation, and shook the dog's paw. "It's nice to meet you, Izzy."

Gwen rolled her eyes. "Simon spent an entire spring break teaching her how to do that. It's the only trick she knows. And yes, her time living here is quickly approaching the end."

"Why?"

"Because I never wanted her. Josh did. And the kids, I suppose. But he's not going to be living here ever again. Abby's permanently gone, too. And Simon...well." Gwen frowned. "I'm not sure what to do about Simon. But that's neither here nor there at the moment." She smiled, almost mischievously. "It's too bad there isn't a shelter for unwanted children. Oh, come on, don't look like that. All mothers have thought the same thing at one time or another," she said as she walked past. "Let's go up to the patio."

Nora was so shocked by Gwen's words, she couldn't speak. She silently followed the other woman down the walkway and around the house into the backyard. There was a patio there with a pergola, and a large pool beyond. The sun rippled on the aqua-blue water. It was a pretty, idyllic setting for what was quickly turning into a bizarre conversation.

"Please take a seat," Gwen said, gesturing to a sectional outdoor couch with overstuffed teal cushions. Nora perched on the edge of the short return.

"It's too bad we're finally getting to know one another under these circumstances," Gwen continued, also sitting. "When we met in the past, I always had the feeling that you and I would probably get on well together. We might even have been friends, in some alternate reality. Now that you're fucking my husband, that's impossible. Obviously."

Nora cleared her throat, desperately hoping that her voice would return.

"I probably deserve every horrible thing you say to me," she finally said. "I completely understand why you're angry. But I shouldn't have come here today. Nothing productive is going to come out of this."

Gwen laughed. Actually, it was more of an incredulous bark than a laugh. "God, you're such a prude. You have no problem fucking my husband, but when I point it out, you want to run away? You came because you know I deserve answers. Your husband told me that you're the most moral person in the world. That you always do the right thing. That you know right from wrong. So how exactly did little Miss Perfect turn into an adulterous whore?"

Nora stared at Gwen for a long moment. She'd always thought that Gwen was one of those atypical beauties, possessing a combination of strong features that added up to something more beautiful. But now, with her eyes narrowed, her mouth stretched into a sneer, Gwen did not look remotely pretty. She looked cruel and slightly unhinged. Nora suddenly knew with an icy certainty that Gwen wanted to harm her. She didn't know how exactly. Would it just be unkind words or did Gwen have more violent intentions?

Nora would never know.

She stood, turned and headed back toward the walkway that led to the gate.

"Where are you going? We haven't even gotten started."

Nora glanced back over her shoulder at Gwen. "I'm leaving."

Gwen's eyebrows arched up. "Before you go, you might want to hear this. I plan to hurt you, and him, in every possible way that I can. By the time I'm done, everyone in this town will know that you, Nora Holliday, fucked my husband. They'll know what a lying whore you are. No decent person will want anything to do with you. Your husband won't. Your kids will beg the judge in your divorce case to let them live with Daddy because Mommy's a slut." Gwen laughed, and it was the most horrible sound Nora had ever heard. "And who, Nora, wants to live with a slut?"

Nora only realized that she'd staggered back when she felt the stab of pain. She'd stumbled off the paved pathway and twisted her ankle.

She's evil, she thought. *She's every bit as bad as Josh ever said. And even then, he never fully articulated how truly awful she is.*

"I'm leaving. Hold your dog," Nora commanded.

"You mean your dog. My husband, my daughter, my son, my dog. They could all be moving in with you tomorrow." Gwen let out another unhinged laugh, and Nora limped quickly toward the gate. "If you live that long. Who knows? Terrible accidents happen all the time."

All Nora could think was, *Please let me get out of here before she hurts me.*

chapter thirty-eight

gwen

Izzy followed Nora to the gate, but for once, didn't try to escape. Instead, she was distracted by finding her tennis ball, which she picked up in her mouth and brought back to Gwen, tail wagging. Izzy dropped the ball at Gwen's feet and barked happily. Gwen stared down at the saliva-soaked ball and shuddered as she picked it up. "This is disgusting. God, I can't wait until I don't have to deal with this shit anymore."

Izzy barked again hopefully. Gwen tossed the ball down the yard; Izzy lumbered off after it. Gwen followed her out into the yard, to the grassy area beside the pool. She wanted to see if any of the orchids she'd repotted and then hung from the lower branches of their trees were blooming. If you tended to them properly—repotting them, fertilizing when necessary— the orchids would come back year after year.

Her meeting with Nora had gone well, Gwen reflected, as she

studied each of the hanging pots in turn. She'd sent her scurrying away terrified, which was exactly what Gwen had wanted. Normally, Gwen wouldn't have given anyone a warning that she was about to dismantle their life, but this was a special case. When Nora lost everything—her children, her home, her precious reputation—Gwen wanted to make sure she had no doubt about who had taken it all away from her. Maybe she would go further than that. What right did Nora have to any sort of a future after what she'd done? As she'd told Nora, people died accidentally every day. How hard could it be to arrange one more?

Izzy found the ball and loped back toward Gwen. She would happily play the chase-a-ball game for hours. However, instead of returning the ball like she normally would have, Izzy dropped it on the grass a few feet from where Gwen stood, then turned and ran back toward the gate, tail still wagging. She barked once.

"Who is it, girl?" Gwen called out, then smiled to herself. It wasn't like Izzy was going to answer back. She was an excellent watchdog. No one ever came and went from the house without her notice. She wasn't much of a protector, though. If an intruder were ever to break in, Izzy would just lick them to death.

The gate swung open. Before Gwen had a chance to warn whoever it was not to let the dog out, Izzy seized the opportunity and bolted through the gate.

"The dog!" Gwen called out, exasperated. Then she saw who it was striding down the walkway toward her. "What the hell are you doing back here? I thought I made it clear that I didn't want to see you again. You're not welcome here. Get out or I'll call the police."

Gwen turned away, refusing to engage any further. Ignoring unwanted visitors was the best way to make them go away. She'd deal with Izzy later. Maybe the dumb dog would get hit by a car while she was running loose and save Gwen a trip to the animal shelter. She turned her attention back to her potted orchids. She thought she saw a spot of dark purple on one of the higher branches. Maybe one of them was blooming.

She was still looking up at the tree, shading her eyes with one hand, when the paving stone hit her on the back of the skull. Gwen pitched forward as the pain registered, searing and white-hot. She'd never experienced anything like it. It was unbearable, crippling. The primal part of her brain was on high alert, yelling at her to move, to get away, to run. But her head…it hurt so much, Gwen couldn't do anything but stagger forward one step. She was still standing there when the paving stone hit the back of Gwen's head again. This time there was more pain, accompanied by a terrible crunching sound.

And then Gwen didn't feel anything at all.

chapter thirty-nine

josh

Josh was circling the neighborhood, rehearsing what he was going to say when he confronted Gwen, when he saw a sight so odd, it took him a few moments to process it. Nora was limping out of the side gate of his house, looking pale and terrified. Nora? At his house? Why would she be here? Then he remembered Gwen's text to Nora the night before, asking her to meet that morning.

"Why didn't you listen to me?" Josh asked out loud before realizing he could actually say it to her. But, no, he was too late. Just as he was stopping and getting out of his car to go to her, Nora had already rushed to her Nissan, which Josh had been too distracted to notice was parked across the street from his house. She started it and peeled off down the street, without ever seeing him.

Josh grabbed his phone to call Nora. She picked up immediately.

"Hello?" Nora's voice was high-pitched with panic.

"I just saw you," he said. He began walking down the street, away from his house. Gwen's Jeep was in the driveway. He didn't want her to spot him and interrupt his conversation. "Leaving my house. I'm out front now."

"Oh, my God. It was… I can't…"

Josh realized that Nora was crying. Not just crying, sobbing so hard, she was incomprehensible.

"Take a deep breath. Tell me what happened."

"She threatened me…my kids…losing everything. And… oh, my God."

"Try to take a deep breath. And I really don't think you should be driving when you're this upset. Is there somewhere safe you can pull over?"

"Hold on. Okay. I just pulled over."

"Where are you?"

"I'm at the Shell gas station on Beach Road."

"Good. Now start from the beginning. What happened?"

"I met with Gwen. I know you said not to, and obviously you were right. I thought I owed it to her to let her have her say."

Josh sighed, rubbed his eyes. "I take it that didn't go well."

"She told me…she told me." Nora drew in a ragged breath. "She said that she'd make sure everyone in town knows that I'm a whore. No one will want anything to do with me. That I'll lose my kids."

"You're not going to lose custody of your kids because you had an affair."

"Dylan and Matt are old enough to decide who they want to live with. Even if Katie isn't, she's a force of nature. What if they all decide they'd rather live with Carter than with me?"

"Carter's an alcoholic. I doubt any one of your kids would choose him over you."

"Gwen said she'd ruin my life. I believed her. She will. She'll ruin both of our lives. Josh... I think she threatened to kill me."

"What do you mean, you think?"

"She said something about an accident happening to me. Do you think she was serious?"

"I don't know. But don't worry. I'm not going to let anything happen to you."

"How are you going to stop her?"

Josh turned back. While he'd been talking to Nora, he'd walked halfway down the block. He turned and stared back at the house that had been his home for over twenty years. And then he started walking toward it.

"I'll do whatever I have to," Josh said. He ended the call and slid his phone into his pocket without waiting to hear Nora's response.

chapter forty

carter

Carter didn't latch the back gate behind him as he stumbled out of the Landons' backyard. Abby Landon was there, trying to catch a large black dog that was running in circles around the front yard.

Oh, my God, she'll see me, he thought, just as Abby looked up and right at him.

"Call 911," he told her. Then he ran to his car. He had to get away from there as fast as he possibly could.

Carter drove wildly, erratically straight to the liquor store. He was still breathing heavily, and sweating so much his shirt was soaked under the armpits. He went inside, grabbed a bottle of vodka off the shelf and brought it to the checkout. The cashier, a young woman with jet-black hair and tattoos on her neck and arms, eyed him warily.

"Are you okay?" she asked.

Carter pushed the bottle toward her as he pulled out his wallet. He realized, with horror, that there was blood smeared on the back of his left hand. "Shit." He glanced up at the cashier. "Do you have a paper towel or something?"

"Sure." She leaned under the counter and pulled out a handful of rough industrial towels. "There's some on your face, too. Did you cut yourself?"

Carter didn't answer her. He paid for the vodka, grabbed the paper towels and headed back to his car. He was tempted to open the bottle right there, but decided it was too visible. Instead, he drove around for a bit until he ended up at a playground at the end of a tree-shaded road. He used to take his kids there when they were little. It was crowded with small children climbing jungle gyms and pumping their legs on the swing set. Carter figured one of the mothers might get suspicious of a childless man sitting alone in his car, watching the children play, so he drove to the far end of the lot and parked in a spot that faced away from the playground. He looked in his rearview mirror and saw the smear of blood on his cheek the cashier had pointed out.

"Shit," he said again.

He opened the bottle of vodka, took a long swig from it, then used the alcohol to dampen one of the paper towels. He scrubbed away the blood first from his face, then his hand and then took another long drink from the bottle. He needed to reach the point of oblivion where he'd unsee the sight of Gwen Landon's prone body...her bloody crushed skull...her exposed brain.

Carter opened his car door, leaned out and retched. He vomited until his stomach was empty. Even then, his body continued to convulse and heave for several more moments. When he thought he was finally finished, he closed the door. Even though it was probably a terrible idea, he took another slug from the bottle of vodka. The alcohol burned as it hit his empty stomach, but at least it stayed down.

He knew he should call 911 or maybe just go straight to the police station to tell them what had happened. But he couldn't seem to make himself do anything, other than sit and glug vodka while his mind gradually went numb.

He heard the short tap of a siren, looked up to see that a police car had pulled up behind his car, blocking him in. The cruiser had its lights on. Carter quickly capped the vodka bottle and tried to push it under the passenger seat. It was a terrible hiding place. The neck of the bottle was sticking out, but maybe if the police didn't look too closely, they wouldn't notice. Then he saw the bloody paper towels that were still wadded-up in his lap. He quickly stuffed those beneath his own seat.

Carter watched in his rearview mirror as a police officer got out of the cruiser and approached the driver side of his car. His right hand rested on his holstered gun. Carter rolled down his car window and saw the officer glance at the ground where he'd just thrown up.

Crap, Carter thought. *I should have moved the car.*

"License and registration, please," the police officer said.

"Right." Carter fumbled with his wallet, and then reached into the glove box for his registration. He handed them to the officer, who took them without comment and returned to his cruiser. Carter knew he was running the information through his computer to see if Carter had any outstanding warrants. A few moments later the officer returned, handing Carter back the license and paperwork.

"What's the problem?" Carter asked.

"We had a complaint that there was a man loitering in the playground parking lot who was vomiting out of his car." The officer glanced again at the puddle of vomit, then into the car. Carter could swear that he then looked directly at the vodka bottle sticking out from under the passenger seat. "Would that happen to have been you?"

Carter should have known better than to pick a playground parking lot. There was no one more vigilant than mothers of small children, always on the lookout for possible danger. He would have been safer sitting outside the liquor store.

"Yes, it was. I wasn't feeling well, so I pulled over and was sick. I was just waiting for my stomach to settle before I drove again."

"Where were you driving to?"

"What?"

"You said you pulled over, but this is a dead-end street. Where were you driving to?"

Carter stared at him, trying to think of an answer through the alcohol-induced haze he was in. "Work," he finally said.

"Where do you work?"

"Um, Pool and Associates. It's a commercial real estate firm."

"That's near here?"

"No, it's not. I was…" Carter stopped, then tried again. "Running errands. I was on my way back to the office."

"Step out of the car, please," the officer said.

"To be honest, I was about to drive to the police station, so I guess it's a good thing you're here." Carter had a feeling he was slurring his words and tried to force himself to speak more clearly. "I have to report a crime."

"Step out of the car."

Carter opened his door, got out, trying—and failing—not to step in his own vomit. The police officer held out a black rectangular object that looked like a small cell phone, except for the plastic straw sticking out of one corner. Carter recognized it with a swoop of dread. It was a Breathalyzer.

"Put the plastic tube into your mouth and blow into the device."

"I wasn't driving," Carter protested. "I was sitting in a parked car."

"Blow into the tube, sir."

"I just saw a murder. I mean, I didn't see it...but someone was just killed. You have to believe me."

"Sir. Are you refusing to blow?"

Carter tried to summon his wits and remember what his criminal defense attorney had told him. *Never blow into a Breathalyzer.* He remembered that part. There were consequences to not blowing, he knew, but better than giving the police evidence they could use against him.

"I'm not blowing," Carter said.

The officer nodded, as though he expected as much. Suddenly Carter found himself being spun around and pushed up against the side of his car.

"Hey!"

"I'm placing you under arrest," the officer said. "You have the right to remain silent. Anything said can and will be used against you—"

"I'd like to talk to my attorney immediately," Carter interrupted him. "And a detective. I told you. Someone's been murdered."

chapter forty-one

abby

Abby sat in the living room of the house she'd grown up in, trying to gulp in a breath through her sobs. Her mother... lying in the backyard...so much blood. So, so much blood. Dead. Her mother *was* dead, right? She had to be, Abby thought, with that much blood. And... Jesus. Abby was sure she had seen fragments of her mother's skull. Another wave of hysteria hit her, and she heard a loud wail erupt. It took her a few beats to realize that the sound was coming from her.

Her father sat beside her, rubbing her back.

Two police officers, one male, one female, had been the first to arrive. When they saw what they were dealing with, they quickly called for backup. Soon, there were police everywhere. Abby had watched them out of the kitchen window, biting her fingernails and wondering why no one was calling an ambulance, before the responding officers had ushered Abby and her father into the living room, which didn't have a view of the backyard. Simon arrived soon after. Someone must have picked him up from school, but Abby had no idea who. She could barely figure out how to keep breathing.

"It's going to be okay," her dad murmured. "Shhh. Everything's going to be okay."

Abby didn't know what the hell he was talking about. How was anything going to be okay ever again? It wasn't. For the rest of her life, there would be a before and an after. Today would mark the line between the two. Abby started panting, trying and failing to swallow enough oxygen. She thought she might pass out and thought that might not be the worst thing. Oblivion would be preferable to this unbearable pain.

"Sir, should I call an ambulance for your daughter?" one of the officers asked.

"I don't know. Abby, can you take in a deep breath for me?" her dad asked.

Abby tried, but she choked on the air. Another sob ripped out of her.

"The detectives are going to want to take statements from all of you." The male officer was young, not that much older than she was, Abby thought. He looked almost as freaked out as she felt. Maybe it was the first dead body he'd seen. It was hers. The female officer was calmer, more circumspect.

"I saw it," Abby gasped. "I saw everything."

"Abby, wait," her father said, sounding anxious. "Hold on. Try to take a deep breath."

"But I have to tell them," Abby said, her voice rising.

"Right now, you need to focus on calming down."

The young officer looked anxiously from Abby to his partner. "If she wants to make a statement, we should probably have the detectives come inside."

"She's in no condition to talk to anyone right now," Josh said.

At the same time, Abby said, "I am. I'm ready to tell you everything."

★ ★ ★

When the Uber driver had dropped her off at her house, Abby had been confused to see her father standing halfway down the block, his phone pressed to his ear.

Why is he here? she'd wondered. *He's supposed to be at work.*

Suddenly Izzy was there, capering around the front yard. Abby had immediately started to chase after her, even though all she wanted to do was to get in her car and drive away before her parents saw her. She didn't want to talk to either one of them.

"Izzy, come on," Abby had pleaded. "Stop running away from me."

Then another person, someone she hadn't expected to see, had exited through their side gate. A person who looked dazed, and…was that *blood*?

What the hell is going on? Abby had wondered.

Abby now looked at the young, shell-shocked police officer standing in front of her.

"I saw what happened. I mean… I didn't see…well, you know. But I saw who was here. At the house."

"Abby," her father cautioned.

"Dad, stop. I know what I saw. I know who did it."

The officer spoke into a walkie-talkie. "Please send Detectives Monroe and Reddick inside. One of the family members is ready to make a statement."

chapter forty-two

tara

I still had Gwen's blood all over me when the police came to arrest me.

I probably should have showered. But by the time I got home, I was too tired to do anything other than curl up on the couch with my cat—Eddy, a gray tabby—and wait for whatever was going to happen next. I wasn't even particularly upset. I just felt drained, the way I used to after final exams in college. I'd been prepared to do what I had to, but executing my plan had exhausted me. I wasn't sure why. It wasn't like I regretted it.

Gwen needed to die. She was evil.

As long as she lived, she'd continue to keep Josh and me apart. That was completely unacceptable.

Josh and I fell in love at first sight.

It happened when I brought Mason and Jared in for their initial consultation with Josh before they had their braces put on.

When Josh introduced himself to me, he took my hand in his to shake it…and something just clicked into place. I knew that he was the person I was meant to spend the rest of my life with. I thought I'd felt that before, with…well, that doesn't matter. But this time, it was different. I knew Josh felt it, too. That moment was magical, like something out of a movie. He was handsome, dashing, funny… He was everything I'd ever wanted.

Every time I brought the boys back for an appointment, Josh would always make a point of talking to me. Even though it was mostly just chatting about the boys' progress with their bite corrections, he always made sure to ask me personal questions, too. Where I'd grown up, when we'd moved to Shoreham. Sure, it might have seemed like innocuous chitchat, but after all, his dental assistants were always nearby. We had to be careful. I knew what he really meant. He was letting me know that he thought about me as much as I thought about him. Every time our eyes met, I could feel the connection between us growing stronger, more electric.

We were meant to be together.

I tried signaling him back—making him the brownies he'd raved about, buying his kids Christmas presents so that he'd know I'd be a good stepmother to them. I even went to his house one day when no one was home and let their dog out of the yard. I was hoping it would run away and be one less tether tying him to his marriage. I could sense how desperately Josh wanted to get away.

But every time I tried to get close to Josh, Gwen blocked me. She made it clear that she would keep us apart, no matter how much he and I loved one another.

I thought Josh might finally tell me he was leaving Gwen for me on the night of the Heart Ball. It was nearly Valentine's Day, so the timing would have been so romantic. I made sure I was around him as much as possible that night, to give him the opportunity. I could tell that he wanted to talk to me privately—he even went outside shortly after we first spoke, I'm sure hoping that I'd follow him. I tried to, but Kynan intercepted me before I could, looping me into his conversation. Poor Kynan. He's never had very good interpersonal skills and making small talk at parties is painful for him.

When I was growing up, I never had many friends, much less a serious boyfriend. Every time a boy showed interest in me—and there were a few that did—they'd quickly back off and fade away. I never knew why, never knew if I was doing something wrong. But I tried not to worry about it. I knew that I was destined for a great love, the kind that shakes you to the core, that changes you forever. I craved it so badly, that I accepted Kynan's proposal after we'd only been dating for two months. I wanted to believe that he was that great love, that our whirlwind courtship was proof of it.

I'd just graduated from Georgia State University, and was living in Atlanta and temping while I applied for real jobs when I met Kynan at a wine bar after work one day. I was there alone, nursing a glass of pinot grigio, and Kynan was sitting on the stool next to me. I don't know how he worked up the courage to talk to me, much less ask me out, but somehow he did. I thought his crippling shyness was adorable, and evidence that he was so in love with me, it rendered him speechless. It was only later I realized that he simply didn't have anything to say. But by then we were married, and I'm pretty sure we conceived the twins on our wedding night. By the time I figured out that I had not married the great love of my life I'd been waiting for, I was a stay-at-home mom with two babies and no real work experience.

Still, I never gave up hope. I knew in my heart that one day the right man, the one I was meant to spend the rest of my life with, would show up. And then, finally, he did.

Josh. My one true love.

I do wonder how Kynan will cope when I finally do leave

him to be with Josh. I plan to be fair with him when it comes to the boys, to let him see them as often as he wants. It's not his fault that our marriage didn't work. He can't help that he's not the person I was meant to spend the rest of my life with. He isn't my destiny.

Gwen is different. *Was* different, I reminded myself. She's in the past tense now. Well, good. She would never have left Josh and me in peace, once he and I were finally able to be together. She would have always been there, hovering nearby like an evil witch in a fairy tale, seeking her revenge on us.

I couldn't let that happen.

I thought that killing someone would be hard. But, in the end, it was far easier than I'd ever imagined. Still, I hadn't been prepared for the sound of it, the sickening, crunching sound the paving stone made as it crushed open her skull. It sounded like a coconut falling out of a tree and splitting on the pavement. The amount of blood surprised me, too… There was suddenly so much blood, more than I'd thought possible. It sprayed at me, splattering my clothes, trickling down my face and into my eyes, blurring my vision. I'm not even sure how I got home. I barely remember leaving the Landons' house. I have no memory of the drive back. But I must have…unless I just imagined the whole thing.

But no, there's the blood. Gwen's blood. Eddy is licking it off my hand, his tongue rough against my skin.

Maybe I should clean myself up, I thought. But then there was a loud bang, which I later learned was the sound of the police kicking in my front door.

eleven weeks later

chapter forty-three

nora

Josh's car pulled up beside Nora's just after dawn on the Fourth of July. They were back at their old haunt, the parking lot at the beach. Because of the holiday, it would be crowded later. For now, theirs were the only two cars there.

Nora unlocked her passenger door so Josh could get in.

"Hi," he said.

"Hi."

They stared at one another for a long moment. It was the first time Nora had seen Josh since the day before Gwen was killed. He leaned forward to kiss her, but Nora pulled back and looked around.

"No one's here," Josh said. "I wasn't followed."

"Are you sure?"

"Yes. The reporters have stopped camping out in front of the house all day, every day. They'll probably be back when Tara's case goes to trial. If it goes to trial."

Gwen's murder had sparked significant interest from the news media. First locally, then snowballing to national prominence. The murder had been discussed at length on multiple cable news channels. Nora had heard a rumor that there was a reporter in town from a crime show that was looking to do a feature on it. She supposed she could understand the interest. A suburban woman had been bludgeoned to death by another woman who was so obsessed with the dead woman's husband, she'd fantasized an entire relationship between the two of them.

The fact that the husband had been having an extramarital affair—with someone else—just added texture to the already titillating story.

Nora had hoped that their affair would be kept out of it. But that had been impossible. Carter was the one who discovered Gwen's body, who had kneeled by her side and felt for her pulse. Josh told Nora about it a few days after the murder, when they had finally had a chance to speak on the phone.

"Abby saw Tara leave the backyard, covered in blood." Josh had sounded drained and distant as he told her. "Abby asked her if she was okay, but Tara didn't respond. Abby said it was like she was in a trance. Then Carter appeared. I have no idea why."

"I don't know, either. He and I haven't spoken. I suppose he must have followed me to your house."

"He's the one who found Gwen. Her…body." Josh had hesitated, drawing in an audible breath. "He saw Tara, too, saw her leaving covered in blood. He went into the backyard to see if anyone was hurt. Then he came running out, yelled at Abby to call 911, got in his car and took off. The police detectives asked her why he was there. She told him about our affair. How it had all come out the day before."

Any chance that the affair would stay secret or confined to their two families was lost in that moment. They'd never know who leaked that aspect of the story to the press, but someone had. For weeks, reporters had camped out in front of both their houses. Nora and Josh were followed wherever they went. It's why they hadn't had a chance to see one another before today. Which was, Nora thought, probably for the best.

A lot of damage had been done.

Josh was back living at home, doing his best to cope with Abby and Simon as they processed their grief. Nora didn't know if Josh grieved Gwen, too, but suspected he probably did to some extent. Twenty-five years was a long time to spend with someone not to be affected by their death, especially when it came about in such a violent, sudden way.

Nora had her own issues to deal with. Carter had been charged with a DUI and would almost certainly be going to jail for some period of time. His attorney was hopeful that he could arrange for Carter to serve his time on the weekends but wasn't making any promises. In the days after Gwen's death and his arrest, Carter had been fired from his job. He decided to check himself into a live-in rehab facility to sober up. Nora had visited him there a few times. On one of those occasions, they'd agreed to move forward with a divorce. They were putting the house on the market immediately. She couldn't afford to maintain it on her own, and Carter would need his half of the proceeds from the sale to pay for his rehab and gambling debts.

Then there were her kids. Dylan seemed fine, or maybe he was just distracted by his imminent departure to college. But Matt was still withdrawn. Katie was very, very angry at her. She blamed Nora entirely for the disintegration of their family. Nora knew she had a lot of work ahead to help both of her younger children to heal.

Nora had tried calling Maddie a few times. She could have used a friend during that awful time. But Maddie never answered or called her back. Nora finally gave up. Losing Maddie's friendship was one more terrible unintended consequence of the choices she'd made.

"I've missed you," Josh now said. He took her hand in his, and Nora felt her anxiety and trouble ebb away as it always did when she was near him, when he was touching her.

"I've missed you, too. But..."

"You don't think you can do this anymore." Josh looked resigned, but also incredibly sad. Nora understood. She felt the same way.

"I don't see how we could ever get past this," she said quietly. "Too much has happened. There's been too much damage. Even if we moved away..."

Josh looked up, hope shining on his face. "I thought the same thing. We could move somewhere else. Somewhere no one knows us. I'd have to sell my practice, establish a new one, but that's doable. You can work from anywhere, right?"

"But what about our kids?" Nora smiled unhappily. "I don't think they'd ever accept us being together. Do you?"

"Simon and Matt will be off to college in three years. Katie a year after that."

"Four years is a long way away. Who knows what will happen between now and then?"

They were both quiet for a moment.

"Then this is a goodbye," Josh said. "If that's what you want, I understand. I'll respect your decision."

No, Nora wanted to say. *This isn't what I want. None of this is what I wanted.*

"I think it's a goodbye for now," she said carefully. "I think it has to be."

Josh nodded and ran one arm over his eyes, wiping away the tears that were glittering there.

"I'll always love you," he said.

"I love you, too."

They sat for a while longer, their hands clasped, although

neither one of them spoke. Finally, Josh nodded once, put his hand on the door latch and prepared to go. Then suddenly, he stopped and turned to Nora.

"No."

"No?" Nora looked at him in confusion. "What do you mean?"

"No, this can't be it. I can't have finally found you to lose you now."

"I don't think we have a choice."

"There's always a choice. I'm going to call you." Josh put his hand against her cheek. "Not right away…but sometime in the future. I'll be in touch. This isn't the end."

Before Nora could reply, Josh was gone.

chapter forty-four

abby

On the morning of the Fourth of July, Abby knew her father was going to meet Nora Holliday. She figured it out as soon as she heard him get up early, shower and head out of the house while he believed that she and Simon were both still asleep.

Abby was awake. She hadn't slept much since the day her mother was murdered.

The weeks that had passed since Gwen's death had been difficult. Why was it when someone died, that no matter how awful a person they'd been, everyone pretended they were some sort of paragon? Initially people kept showing up at the Landons' front door, bearing casseroles and cakes that none of the family felt like eating, announcing tearfully what a wonderful person Gwen had been. That she'd been taken too soon. It was all such a tragedy.

It was all such bullshit, Abby thought. If the situations were reversed, she couldn't picture her mother shedding a single tear over any of these people. Were they all clueless as to what kind of a person Gwen had really been?

At least that was one good thing when the news crews started camping outside their house—it had completely stopped the well-wishers from dropping by. No one wanted to get shouted at by reporters asking how they knew Gwen, or if they'd ever met Tara Edwards, or if they thought Josh's affair had been a factor in his wife's murder. But the media's constant presence had first dwindled and then disappeared. Once they were finally gone, Abby figured her father would take the first opportunity to see Nora Holliday.

That's why she'd put GPS trackers on both his and Nora's cars.

She'd ordered the trackers online. Installing one on her dad's car had been easy enough. She'd simply slipped into the garage one night after he and Simon had both gone to bed, and followed the instructions she'd read online on how to secure it on the undercarriage of his vehicle, where it wouldn't be detectable. Getting to Nora's car had been more challenging. The media rarely followed Abby when she left the house, but they'd swarmed Nora for weeks. Abby had finally tracked down Katie Holliday's travel volleyball schedule online, and waited in the middle school parking lot one Saturday afternoon when Katie had a game. Nora pulled in five minutes before it was due to begin. Abby had watched as Katie stepped out of the car, and stalked into the school gymnasium without waiting for her mother. Nora climbed out more slowly and trailed behind her daughter, glancing over her shoulder to see if anyone was following her. Abby waited a few minutes to make sure there weren't any reporters lurking around, and once she was satisfied she wouldn't be caught, she slid out of her own car and hurried across the parking lot to where Nora had parked her Nissan. She had the second tracker installed in under a minute.

Now, she opened her laptop, turned it on and pulled up the GPS tracking software. Both her father's and Nora's cars were on the move, two dots on a digital map heading in the same direction. Straight to the beach parking lot, where both of the dots came to abrupt stops.

"Right where I first saw you together," Abby said out loud. "How sweet."

She watched and waited, and as she did, she wondered what she should do with the information that Nora and her father were meeting. Obviously, neither one had learned the lesson that there were consequences to making bad choices. Gwen wouldn't have stood for it, and whatever complicated feelings Abby had about her mother, there was one subject they were— or had been—in perfect agreement on.

There were times when revenge was justified.

Even if she wasn't the one who had bludgeoned Gwen with the paving stone, Nora Holliday had certainly caused irreparable harm to the Landon family. Her affair with Abby's father had set in motion all the events that led up to Gwen's death. So didn't Nora bear some of the responsibility for what had happened? Shouldn't she face repercussions for what she'd done?

Abby thought so. And this time, she wouldn't lose her nerve, the way she had when Lana and Colin betrayed her. Abby wasn't sure what Nora's punishment should be. She tried to imagine what her mother would have wanted. Certainly, to see Nora humiliated, alienated from friends and family. But she had a feeling somehow that Gwen would have gone a step further.

For a transgression this large, wouldn't Gwen have wanted Nora dead?

Abby thought about this for a while as she watched the dots on her computer screen start to move again, signaling that her dad and Nora Holliday were both driving away from the beach parking lot in their respective cars. She wasn't sure what she was going to do about Nora yet, but Abby wasn't heading back to FSU to start the fall semester until mid-August.

She had plenty of time to figure out a plan before then.

★ ★ ★ ★ ★